SEVEN
DAYS
OF
YOU

SEVEN DAYS OF YOU

Cecilia Vinesse

POPPY

Little, Brown and Company

NEW YORK   BOSTON

Poppy

Hachette Book Group
1290 Avenue of the Americas, New York, NY 10104
Visit us at lb-teens.com

Poppy is an imprint of Little, Brown and Company.
The Poppy name and logo are trademarks of Hachette Book Group, Inc.

The publisher is not responsible for websites (or their content) that are not owned by the publisher.

First Edition: March 2017

Library of Congress Cataloging-in-Publication Data
Names: Vinesse, Cecilia, author.
Title: Seven days of you / by Cecilia Vinesse.
Description: First edition. | New York ; Boston : Little, Brown and Company, 2017. | Summary: "Seventeen-year-old Sophia has seven days left in Tokyo before she moves back to the United States, and she unexpectedly finds herself drawn to Jamie, a boy with whom she shares a heartbreaking history. Can their one short week of Tokyo adventures end in anything but good-bye?" —Provided by publisher.
Identifiers: LCCN 2015039542| ISBN 9780316391115 (hc) | ISBN 9780316391160 (library edition ebook)
Subjects: | CYAC: Americans—Japan—Fiction. | Love—Fiction. | Tokyo (Japan)—Fiction. | Japan—Fiction.
Classification: LCC PZ7.1.V57 Se 2017 | DDC [Fic]—dc23
LC record available at http://lccn.loc.gov/2015039542

10 9 8 7 6 5 4 3 2 1

LSC-H

Printed in the United States of America

FOR RACHEL, MY FIXED STAR, MY GUIDE HOME

07 : 00 : 00 : 00
DAYS   HOURS   MINS   SECS

AT THE BEGINNING OF THE SUMMER, I tried to get on top of the whole moving-continents thing by reminding myself I still had time. Days and hours and seconds all piled on top of one another, stretching out in front of me as expansive as a galaxy. And the stuff I couldn't deal with— packing my room and saying good-bye to my friends and leaving Tokyo—all that hovered at some indistinct point in the indistinct future.

So I ignored it. Every morning, I'd meet Mika and David in Shibuya, and we'd spend our days eating in ramen shops or browsing tiny boutiques that smelled like incense. Or, when it rained, we'd run down umbrella-crowded streets and watch anime I couldn't understand on Mika's couch. Some nights, we'd dance in strobe-lit clubs and go to karaoke at four in the morning. Then, the next day, we'd sit at train-station donut shops for hours, drinking milky coffee and watching the sea of commuters come and go and come and go again.

Once, I stayed home and tried dragging boxes up the

stairs, but it stressed me out so much, I had to leave. I walked around Yoyogi-Uehara until the sight of the same cramped streets made me dizzy. Until I had to stop and fold myself into an alcove between buildings, trying to memorize the *kanji* on street signs. Trying to count my breaths.

And then it was August fourteenth. And I only had one week left, and it was hot, and I wasn't even close to being packed. But the thing was, I should have known how to do this. I'd spent my whole life ping-ponging across the globe, moving to new cities, leaving people and places drifting in my wake.

Still, I couldn't shake the feeling that *this* good-bye—to Tokyo, to the first friends I'd ever had, to the only life that felt like it even remotely belonged to me—was the kind that would swallow me whole. That would collapse around me like a star imploding.

And the only thing I knew how to do was to hold on as tightly as possible and count every single second until I reached the last one. The one I dreaded most.

Sudden, violent, final.

The end.

CHAPTER 1

SUNDAY

———

06 : 19 : 04 : 25
DAYS HOURS MINS SECS

I WAS LYING ON THE LIVING-ROOM floor reading *Death by Black Hole: And Other Cosmic Quandaries* when our air-conditioning made a sputtering sound and died. Swampy heat spread through the room as I held my hand over the box by the window. Nothing. Not even a gasp of cold air. I pressed a couple of buttons and hoped for the best. Still nothing.

"Mom," I said. She was sitting in the doorway to the kitchen, wrapping metal pots in sheets of newspaper. "Not to freak you out or anything, but the air-conditioning just broke."

She dropped some newspaper shreds on the ground, and our cat—Dorothea Brooke—came over to sniff them. "It's been doing that. Just press the big orange button and hold it."

"I did. But I think it's serious this time. I think I felt its spirit passing."

Mom unhooked a panel from the back of the air-conditioning unit and poked around. "Damn. The landlord said this system might go soon. It's so old, they'll have to replace it for the next tenant."

August was always hot in Tokyo, but this summer was approaching unbearable. A grand total of five minutes without air-conditioning and all my bodily fluids were evaporating from my skin. Mom and I opened some windows, plugged in a bunch of fans, and stood in front of the open refrigerator.

"We should call a repairman," I said, "or it's possible we'll die here."

Mom shook her head, going into full-on Professor Wachowski mode. Even though we're both short, she looks a lot more intimidating than I do, with her square jaw and serious eyes. She looks like the type of person who won't lose an argument, who can't take a joke.

I look like my dad.

"No," Mom said. "I'm not dealing with this the week before we leave. The movers are coming on Friday." She turned and leaned into the fridge door. "Why don't you go out? See your friends. Come back tonight when it's cooled down."

I twisted my watch around my wrist. "Nah, that's okay."

"You don't want to?" she asked. "Did something happen with Mika and David?"

"Of course not," I said. "I just don't feel like going out. I feel like staying home, and helping, and being the good daughter."

God, I sounded suspicious, even to myself.

But Mom didn't notice. She held out a few one-hundred-yen coins. "In that case, go to the *konbini* and buy some of those towels you put in the freezer and wrap around your neck."

I contemplated the money in her hand, but the heat made it swim across my vision. Going outside meant walking into the boiling air. It meant walking down the little streets I knew so well, past humming vending machines and stray cats stretched out in apartment-building entrances. Every time I did that, I was reminded of all the little things I loved about this city and how they were about to slip away forever. And today, of all days, I really didn't need that reminder.

"Or," I said, trying to sound upbeat, "I could pack."

———

Packing was, of course, a terrible idea.

Even the thought of it was oppressive. Like if I stood in my room too long, the walls would start tightening around me, trash-compacting me in. I stood in the doorway and focused on how familiar it all was. Our house was small and semi-dilapidated, and my room was predictably small to match, with only a twin bed, a desk pushed against the window, and a few red bookshelves running along the walls. But the problem wasn't the size—it was the *stuff*. The physics books I'd bought and the ones Dad had sent me cluttering up the shelves, patterned headbands and tangled necklaces hanging from tacks in the wall, towers of unfolded laundry built precariously all over the floor. Even the ceiling was crowded, crisscrossed with string after string of star-shaped twinkly lights.

There was a WET PAIN! sign (it was supposed to say WET PAINT!) propped against my closet that Mika had stolen from outside her apartment building, a Rutgers University flag pinned above my bed, Totoro stuffed toys on my pillow, and boxes and boxes of platinum-blond hair dye everywhere. (Those, I needed to get rid of. I'd stopped dyeing my hair blond since the last touch-up had turned it an attractive shade of Fanta orange.) It was so much—*too* much—to have to deal with. And I might have stayed there for hours, paralyzed in the doorway, if Alison hadn't come up behind me.

"Packed already?"

I spun around. My older sister had on the same clothes she'd been wearing all weekend—black T-shirt, black leggings—and she was holding an empty coffee mug.

I crossed my arms and tried to block her view of the room. "It's getting there."

"Clearly."

"And what have you been doing?" I asked. "Sulking? Scowling? *Both at the same time?*"

She narrowed her eyes but didn't say anything. Alison was in Tokyo for the summer after her first year at Sarah Lawrence. She'd spent the past three months staying up all night and drinking coffee and barely leaving her bedroom during sunlight hours. The unspoken reason for this was that she'd broken up with her girlfriend at the end of last year. Something no one was allowed to mention.

"You have so much crap," Alison said, stepping over a pile of thrift-store dresses and sitting on my unmade bed. She balanced the coffee mug between her knees. "I think you might be a hoarder."

"I'm not a hoarder," I said. "This is not hoarding."

She arched an eyebrow. "Lest you forget, little sister, I've been by your side for many a move. I've witnessed the hoarder's struggle."

It was true. My sister *had* been by my side for most of our moves, avoiding her packing just as much as I'd been avoiding mine. This year, though, she only had the one suitcase she'd brought with her from the States—no doubt full of sad, sad poetry books and sad, sad scarves.

"You're one to talk," I said. "You threw approximately nine thousand tantrums when you were packing last summer."

"I was going to college." Alison shrugged. "I knew it would suck."

"And look at you now," I said. "You're a walking endorsement for the college experience."

The corners of her lips moved like she was deciding whether to laugh or not. But she decided not to. (Of course she decided not to.)

I climbed onto my desk, pushing aside an oversize paperback called *Unlocking the MIT Application!* and a stuffed koala with a small Australian flag clasped between its paws.

Through the window behind me, I could see directly into someone else's living room. Our house wasn't just small—it was surrounded on three sides by apartment buildings. Like a way less interesting version of *Rear Window*.

Alison reached over and grabbed the pile of photos and postcards sitting on my nightstand. "Hey!" I said. "Enough with the stuff-touching."

But she was already flipping through them, examining each picture one at a time. "Christ," she said. "I can't believe you kept these."

"Of course I kept them," I said, grabbing my watch. "Dad sent them to me. He sent the same ones to you, in case that important fact slipped your mind."

She held up a photo of the Eiffel Tower, Dad standing in front of it and looking pretty touristy for someone who actually lived in Paris. "A letter a year does not a father make."

"You're so unfair," I said. "He sends tons of e-mails. Like, twice a week."

"Oh my God!" She waved another photo at me, this one of a woman sitting on a wood-framed couch holding twin babies on her lap. "The Wife and Kids? Really? *Please* don't tell me you still daydream about going to live with them."

"Aren't you late for sitting in your room all day?" I asked.

"Seriously," she said. "You're one creepy step away from Photoshopping yourself in here."

I kept the face of my watch covered with my hand, hoping she wouldn't start on that as well.

She didn't. She moved on to another picture: me and Alison in green and yellow raincoats, standing on a balcony messy with cracked clay flowerpots. In the picture, I am clutching a *kokeshi*—a wooden Japanese doll—and Alison is pointing at the camera. My dad stands next to her, pulling a goofy face.

"God," she muttered. "That shitty old apartment."

"It wasn't shitty. It was—palatial." Maybe. We'd moved from that apartment when I was five, after my parents split, so honestly, I barely remembered it. Although I did still like the idea of it. Of one country and one place and one family living there. Of home.

Alison threw the pictures back on the nightstand and stood up, all her dark hair spilling over her shoulders.

"Whatever," she said. "I don't have the energy to argue with you right now. You have fun with all your"—she gestured around the room—"*stuff.*"

And then she was gone, and I was hurling a pen at my bed, angry because this just confirmed everything she thought. She was the Adult; I was still the Little Kid.

Dorothea Brooke padded into the room and curled up on a pile of clean laundry in a big gray heap.

"Fine," I said. "Ignore me. Pretend I'm not even here."

Her ears didn't so much as twitch.

I reached up to yank open the window, letting the sounds of Tokyo waft in: a train squealing into Yoyogi-Uehara

Station, children shouting as they ran through alleyways, cicadas croaking a tired song like something from a rusted music box.

Since our house was surrounded by apartment buildings, I had to crane my neck to look above them at this bright blue strip of sky. There was an object about the size of a fingernail moving through the clouds, leaving a streak of white in its wake that grew longer and then broke apart.

I watched the plane until there was no trace of it left. Then I held up my hand to blot out the sliver of sky where it had been—but wasn't anymore.

CHAPTER 2

SUNDAY

———

06 : 18 : 34 : 27
DAYS HOURS MINS SECS

I WAS BORN IN JAPAN, but I'm not Japanese.

Technically, I'm French and I'm Polish. (Well, my dad is French and my mom is Polish, but Mom moved to New Jersey when she was a baby, so I guess she's basically American?) Alison said we were American by default, but I've lived in Japan more combined years than I've lived in the States, and I spend at least a month a year in Paris, so...I'm not sure.

I was five the first time I left Tokyo, when Mom, Alison, and I moved to New Jersey so Mom could teach at Rutgers. Then, when I was thirteen, Mom got a research grant that brought us back to Tokyo for four years. Now I was seventeen, and the research grant was up, and we were New Jersey–bound. Yet again.

Sometimes, this whole good-bye thing wasn't so bad. Like, I'd had no problem leaving the giant public school I'd gone to in New Jersey or the few math and science geeks I'd occasionally sat with at lunch. And the things I actually did miss—my favorite brand of hot sauce and cheap pairs of jeans—I had my grandparents send me for my birthday.

But other times, it was awful. It was moving from Tokyo when I was a little kid and knowing my dad would be far away. It was going somewhere new and knowing that, eventually, I'd have to leave it behind. Like I was constantly floating in the second before a dream ends, waiting for the world to evaporate. Waiting for everything that seemed real to suddenly be gone.

That's what this good-bye would be like.

I knew it.

With Alison safely back in her batcave of misery, I cranked my laptop to life, put on a mix of thrashy punk songs David had made for me, and decided to go to the konbini for my mom. I shoved my wallet into my pink Musée d'Orsay tote and, since my clothes were getting sweatier by the second, picked a new outfit. A sleeveless Laura Ashley dress I'd bought at a secondhand store in Paris and a pair of bright blue sandals. I fastened my hair into two braids on top of my head, holding them in place with a couple of daisy pins. I loved this—poring through my mismatching dresses and headbands and blouses, finding stuff I'd forgotten about, combining things in a way I never had before.

Like a cracked-out preschool teacher, Mika would say.

I headed down to the kitchen and saw…Mika. Sitting on a countertop, eating from a box of koala-bear-shaped cookies.

"There you are!" she said mid-chew. Her bright blue hair was gelled into spikes, and she was wearing baggy men's jeans and a ripped T-shirt held together with a couple of safety pins. "Why didn't you answer your phone? Did you know it's really fucking hot in here?" She shook the box at me. "It's okay if I eat these, right?"

I didn't get the chance to answer, because David strode in from the living room.

"Sofa!" he said. "We were going to come find you, but then Mika started eating herself into a coma and I was going through your books. You own a lot of excellent books. This one, for example, is a personal favorite." He tossed my sister's volume of Emily Dickinson poems into the air and caught it.

"Oh my gosh!" Mika pressed her hand to her chest and fluttered her eyelashes. "Your opinion on books is, like, so fascinating!"

"Watch it," he said, flipping through the pages. "You might think Ms. Dickinson is all about weird grammar and death, but there's some seriously sexy stuff in here. Hold on. I'll read you one."

Mika flipped him off, and he playfully ruffled her spikes. And I kept standing there, trying to breathe evenly, trying not to stare at his red, smirking mouth or his dark, styled hair.

It always took a minute to acclimate to David's presence. Not just because he was gorgeous—although let the record show that he really was gorgeous. Tall with lanky muscles and deliberately tousled hair and stupidly perfect clothes. He was also the son of the Australian ambassador, which meant he had an Australian freaking accent. I wished Mika hadn't stopped him from reading that poem.

"Anyway," David said, putting the book down, "you need to get a move on, Sofa. We're going out."

My attention snapped back. "I can't. I have to pack."

"Screw that," Mika said dismissively. "You can pack after my birthday."

"Your birthday's on Friday," I said. "That's when the movers are coming."

"No!" She tossed a koala in my direction, and it landed on the floor. "Don't you ruin my birthday and your going-away party by talking about movers. Boo and hiss."

"It's not a party," I said. "You just want to go clubbing in Roppongi."

"Duh," she snorted. "Roppongi is the party." The stud in her right eyebrow glinted in the light coming through the window. She'd gotten the piercing only a few weeks earlier, when she was visiting her grandma in California. She said she'd done it for the pure pleasure of seeing her parents' faces when she landed back at Narita Airport.

"Does my mom know you're here?" I asked, feeling exactly as childish as I sounded.

David cracked up. "Who do you think let us in? She had to leave, though. Something about dry cleaning." He draped an arm around my shoulder. "Now, seriously, Sofa.

Shoes on. Can't you see Mika's on the verge of a nervous breakdown?"

"Here's a thought." Mika slammed the koalas down on the counter. "Shut up."

David pulled me closer. "Don't get snippy with me. You've been peeing yourself with excitement all afternoon. All because Baby James is coming home."

"Rules!" Mika sent another koala sailing toward David's mussed hair. He caught it and popped it into his mouth, then turned to me with both eyebrows raised.

I laughed. That was his Inside Joke face. The face he made when we'd watch episodes of *Flight of the Conchords* in computer science instead of doing work. When he'd make up stupid songs about my hair and sing them in the lunch line. Or when we'd sit next to each other at school assemblies and he'd slip me one of his iPod earbuds. It never ceased to amaze me that David—funny, charismatic, outgoing David—wanted to spend so much time with *me*.

"Rules?" David swallowed. "What rules?"

"We went over this," Mika said.

David grinned. "Did we?"

"Don't be an ass," Mika said. "No making fun of Jamie tonight. No strutting around and pissing on your territory, okay? Tonight is not going to be Middle School: The Sequel."

David walked over to Mika and picked up one of her hands, holding it in both of his. "Miks. You don't have to worry about me. Baby James is one of us. We're here to welcome him back into the fold. Aren't we, Sofa?"

My mouth dried up.

"Christ." Mika tugged her hand away and dusted it off on her shirt.

David frowned.

"I can't go tonight!" I said, taking a step back, my shoulder bumping into the doorframe. "I have to pack."

Mika and David exchanged looks.

"Pack later," Mika said.

"My mom will be pissed if I leave," I said. "Besides, he's your friend. You can all hang out together, without me."

Mika seemed wary. I waited for the inevitable grilling to continue—*Why don't you want to see Jamie? Why do you need to pack right now? Why are you incapable of maintaining eye contact?*—but then Mika's phone rang. As soon as she answered it, her whole face lit up.

"Jamie!" she squealed.

David gasped dramatically, and Mika kicked his leg, knocking over the box of kitchen stuff Mom had been packing earlier. "Damn it!" she said. "Sorry, Sophia! No, sorry, Jamie. I'm at Sophia's, and I just knocked some shit over." She laughed. "I'm crazy pumped you're here!"

David made a gagging face and glanced at me for approval. I smiled, but it was halfhearted at best. There was a roaring in my ears. I wanted to open the fridge and crawl inside. I wanted to push my hands against the sides of my head until I couldn't hear the tinny version of Jamie's voice coming out of Mika's phone.

Jamie Foster-Collins.

Mika's best friend, who'd been shipped off to boarding school in North Carolina three years ago while the rest of his family stayed in Tokyo. Who I hadn't contacted since then, who I hadn't even contemplated contacting. Mika's best friend. And my nothing at all.

"That is so fucking great!" Mika said. "We'll meet you there." She hung up the phone, still grinning. "He got to his apartment basically five minutes ago, but he's heading to Shibs now."

"Right, Sofa," David said. "We're leaving. The all-powerful Mika hath commanded it."

"I can't go," I said. "It's impossible for me to leave this house."

"Of course it's possible," David said. "Here, I'll show you. First, you walk to the door." He looped his arm through mine and began leading me slowly toward the back door.

I laughed and David smiled, just the corners of his lips curling up. We were standing close enough that I could smell him—the new-shirt smell of him, the dark, sweet smell of him. He looked so thrilled about making me laugh, like it was something he worked hard for. Like it was something he cared about.

"*God, he practically performs for you,*" Mika had once

said. *"Whenever he makes some stupid-ass joke, I swear, he does it to impress you."*

"Fine," I said. "I'll go."

David nudged my temple with his nose. "Of course you will."

CHAPTER 3
SUNDAY

———

06 : 17 : 46 : 07
DAYS HOURS MINS SECS

BUT AS SOON AS THE TRAIN LURCHED away from Yoyogi-Uehara Station and toward Shibuya, I started to panic.

What on earth was I doing? Why had I allowed myself to be sealed inside a metal container inching closer and closer to Jamie Foster-Collins? I didn't want to see him. As it so happens, I never wanted to see him again *for the rest of my life.*

At the beginning of May, when Mika had told me Jamie was coming back to Tokyo, I'd felt practically upbeat about moving to New Jersey. Until I found out he was flying in from North Carolina exactly one week before I left the country for good, and then I'd just been pissed. Couldn't he wait a week? Did he have to ruin my life? And, on top of that, did he have to steal all my leaving thunder with his stupid arriving thunder?

The train picked up speed. Outside the window, the late afternoon sun drooped heavily toward the skyline. There was a map by the door, showing all the Tokyo train lines looping around one another like a tangle of blood vessels. Flyers hanging from the ceiling flapped in the air-conditioned breeze. (At least there was freaking air-conditioning on this thing.)

We changed trains. Eventually, a reassuring electronic voice came over the loudspeaker and said, "*Tsugi wa, Shibuya. Shibuya desu.*"

Next stop, Shibuya Station.

The train slowed, a familiar jingle playing as the door finally opened. We got off behind a group of women wearing *yukata* and walking slowly toward the ticket barriers. Their tightly bound robes were dark blue with undulating patterns on them like moving water. They had jeweled *kanzashi* pinned in their hair and wooden *geta* on their feet.

"Come the frick on," David muttered to their backs. "Do you think it's possible to move slower than that? Or would you stand still if you tried?"

"Shut the hell up," Mika said.

"What?" David asked, lifting his hands in faux surrender. "I'm not being an asshole. I'm asking an important question. About physics."

"You are kind of being an asshole," I said. "And also, you should shut up. They might speak English."

"Doubt it," David said, slinging his arm over my shoulder. The sleeve of his T-shirt brushed the back of my head, which, despite the heat and my perpetual sense of unease, was not unpleasant.

"Would you assume I didn't speak English if you saw me on the street?" Mika asked.

"Of course not, Americano," David said. "You're way too obnoxious to actually be Japanese."

Mika punched him on the arm four times. "Stop! Being! Culturally! Insensitive!"

David swerved us away from her and laughed, but I didn't join in. The impending arrival of Jamie Foster-Collins had removed my ability to laugh. Which was a problem. I needed to calm down. I needed to focus my energy on being cool.... *Oh, hello, Jamie. I almost didn't see your big, smug face hovering right there in front of me.*

Maybe not like that.

I reminded myself of Newton's first law. I was not going to let external forces slow me down. I was *not* going to let Jamie get to me. After all, it had been a long time since I'd seen him. Three years and two months. Over two months, in fact. I was older, and my friends were awesome, and I'd gotten the best grades in my AP Physics class last year.

Oh, hello, Jamie. Did I mention that I got the best grades in my AP Physics class?

God, I really was pathetic. Of course I wouldn't have friends when I started at a new school next week. Of course I would never have friends again. This was it. My final week of friendship, and I wasn't going to get to enjoy it, because Jamie was here and I couldn't avoid him anymore.

We exited the station and ended up in the plaza that stretched toward Shibuya Crossing. The unabashed madness of the place forced me back into the present. My senses went into overdrive as I took in the crazy scramble crossing with currents of people rushing over it, the circle of buildings stacked with billboards and television screens blasting movie trailers and advertisements and music videos all at the same time. It was a whirlpool of energy. A thunderstorm of sounds colliding and humming. It was my favorite place in Tokyo.

And soon I would be gone—and it would dim to nothing.

———

We waited for Jamie by Hachiko, this statue of a dog that sits between Shibuya Station and the famous crossing. It was where my friends and I always met when we hung out in Shibs. Honestly, it was where nearly every young person in Tokyo met when they hung out there. Crowds from the station would flock toward it, almost like it was calling them home.

The depressing but true story about Hachiko is that he was once a real dog who sat outside Shibuya Station every day waiting for his master to come home from work, even after his master died. And then, one day, the dog died, too.

Like I said—depressing. But there was something about that story I liked. When I was a kid, I'd make Dad tell it to me as we walked past the statue on our way to the Tower Records bookstore. (I'd e-mail him later to ask if he remembered that.) And I still liked how the statue stared longingly into the crowd, constantly waiting for someone to appear. Which was exactly how I felt about Jamie—minus the longing.

David dug a cigarette from his back pocket, so Mika grabbed my forearm and dragged me away. Her eyes were darting around. Searching, searching, searching. There were so many people. All of them searching. All of them waiting. A guy wearing enormous green headphones, a girl with a clump of brightly colored charms hanging off her cell phone, another huddle of girls waving wildly at someone across the plaza.

It made me queasy.

"You look so miserable," Mika said. "Come on. You and Jamie used to be friends."

I shrugged, practicing my nonchalance. "He was always better friends with you."

She snapped her gum. Mika and I didn't talk about Jamie, even though I knew she Skyped him a lot. And, thankfully, she still had no clue what had happened between us.

Mika and Jamie had been friends since their Play-Doh-eating days, and she'd (probably) do anything for him. As evidenced by the fact that, on top of her usual screw-you black eyeliner, she was wearing...silver eye shadow. Mika was the first friend I'd made at the Tokyo International Academy, back when I was thirteen and a lowly newbie. She was a Lifer, someone who'd been there since preschool, but for some reason, she wanted to hang out with me. By now, we'd spent so much time together I knew practically everything about her. Like the fact that she was a secret Harry Potter nerd and that she was addicted to C.C. Lemon soda and that she never—*ever*—wore eye shadow. Especially not the sparkly kind.

Her gaze caught on something across the plaza, and she pointed. "Hey! Look who it is."

My chest started to constrict.

Oh God.

Oh *God*.

What was I going to do? I couldn't be nonchalant. Nonchalant wasn't even an option anymore. Neither was talking. Or breathing, apparently.

But it wasn't Jamie.

It was Caroline, bedecked in a denim miniskirt and tank top, blond ponytail swinging behind her as she picked her way through the huddle of girls. David strode forward and started kissing her face and cheeks and neck. She squealed and kissed him back.

"Avert your eyes," Mika said flatly. "I'm already scarred."

The knot in my chest relaxed, then tightened in a different but familiar way. I let my arms fall by my sides and flexed my fingers until I felt the blood moving again. At least I'd found a conversational diversion. "Well. There goes David for the night."

"Whatever," Mika said. "If it distracts him from being a dick to Jamie, I'm all for it. Keep making out with your girlfriend, D."

"Ugh, no, don't."

"Oh, sorry," Mika said. "I forgot she was your arch nemesis."

I felt myself blush. "Please. She is one girlfriend among many. We're his real friends."

"But he doesn't make out with us." Mika leaned against the statue's base. "Thank God."

I glanced in their direction. David's arms were suctioned around Caroline's waist, and Caroline's hands were crammed into his hair. They might have been performing a complicated face-fusion procedure. "What the hell does he see in her, anyway?"

Mika pulled distractedly at the spikes on the top of her head. "I don't know, dude. You're the one who's all BFF with her."

"I am not," I huffed, already hating how this night was going. "She's just nice to me because I'm nerdy and unthreatening."

"Whatevs," she said, eyes lost in the crowd.

"Anyway," I said, "she can't be completely superficial. David wouldn't like her if she was."

"Uh, have you met David?" Mika snapped her gum and looked disapproving.

"Maybe things would be different," I said, "if—you know—if I told him I *liked* him."

Mika pushed herself off the statue and grabbed both my wrists. "Please don't take this the wrong way, but don't do that. You are out of your fucking mind."

"I don't think so."

"I think so," Mika said. "In fact, I know so. You do not want to tell David you like him. He will lord it over you for the rest of your life."

I glanced back at David and whispered, "He won't get the chance. I'm moving."

Mika's face was so full of concern, it was making me uncomfortable. I examined a bit of chipped nail polish on my thumb. "I've known him for six years, Sophia," she said. "When shit gets serious, he turns into an insensitive A-hole."

"Oh, and I *don't* know him?"

Mika sighed and shook her head. She was always doing that, reminding me how romantically ignorant I was.

And in a lot of ways, I knew she was right. I'd never so much as kissed anyone, and I'd definitely never had a boyfriend. Not in Japan and not in New Jersey, where the only boy I'd ever had a crush on ran the Anime Appreciation Club and said "Sorry, Sarah" the one time I bumped into him in the hallway.

Still, I knew there was something between David and me. I *felt* it—even if Mika couldn't.

"God! Where is Jamie?" Mika pulled my wrist up so she could see the time.

My airway constricted again. All the dark thoughts I'd been pushing down for the past three years floated to the surface. Jamie and his big, sad eyes and all the horrible things I'd said to him. I thought about it, and it felt like pressing a bruise. Like pressing and pressing and pressing it.

"I'll be right back," I said, wrenching my hand away from Mika. "Okay?"

"Be right back?" Mika repeated. "What do you mean? Where are you going?"

"I...I need to make a phone call."

"You need to *make a phone call*? Are you secretly forty years old? Are you here on business?"

I yelled over my shoulder, since I was already walking away, "From the station! I need to call my mom from the station!"

Mika shouted back, "You're not saying things a sane person would say!"

"I'll be right back!"

No way in hell was I going back. I pushed my way through the closely packed groups of people coming and going, carrying shopping bags, fanning themselves with portable fans. It was early evening, and the sky was a hazy orange and purple. The neon lights were just starting to come to life.

The farther I walked, the better I felt. This was the perfect time to leave. Right before the night went from sour to unsalvageable, right before I had to see Jamie again. Jamie in real life. In real time. I'd go home and send Mika a text telling her I didn't feel well. It would be better this way. Better for everyone.

By the time I started down the stairs into Shibuya Station, I felt pretty good. Less like the entire city was about to crash down on my head. Less like karma had a cruel sense of humor and was out to get me.

And then I ran right into Jamie Foster-Collins.

I'm running through the cemetery. Cutting across lawns, weaving around gravestones. Everything is gray and muted, and the air feels like static.

It's going to rain.

Great. I'm gonna go home looking like a bedraggled cat. On my birthday. And the last day of middle school, the last day of my first year at the Tokyo International Academy . . .

"Sophia?"

The sound of Jamie's voice breaks my stride. I stumble and grab the top of the nearest gravestone.

I can't face him. The thought of it stretches me thin, like I could snap apart at any second. But he's standing next to me now. "Hey. Um, are you okay?" he asks. "You just ran off campus, and—well—you forgot this. It's your birthday present, remember? And a good-bye present, I guess." His eyebrows bunch together and he holds out his palm. In the center, there's a small button with a picture of Totoro on it.

But I don't take it. I'm still clutching my phone, the edges of it imprinting on my palm.

Jamie's hand drops by his side. There are red splotches on his neck, and he looks so small and young. His shirt is a size too big, and the belt on his jeans is pulled too tight. "You don't want it?" he asks.

I swallow, and it takes me a second to find my voice. "Did you mean to send this to me?"

"Send what?"

I hold out my phone for him to read. His eyes swipe over the screen, and his face crumples.

I had been standing by my locker with David when my phone buzzed. A text from Jamie.

Ladies and gents, it's the Sophia Throws Herself at David Show. Airing all day, every day. Come on down and enjoy the desperation!

And now I can't think straight. I should cry, but I'm too confused to cry. I should scream at him, but I can't, because I still can't believe he did this. Jamie is sweet and goofy and kind. Jamie would never be cruel to anyone.

Jamie would never be cruel to me.

"Shit," he whispers. "I—I meant to send that to Mika."

Pain rips me up from the inside. "So this is what you do? You pretend to be my friend, and then you say this kind of stuff behind my back?"

The splotches on his neck intensify, but he sounds so cold when he says, "I just don't get it."

"What does that mean?"

"I don't get why you like him so much. Why you try so hard to make him like you."

My head swims. I stagger backward, holding the phone to my chest. "Get away from me, Jamie. Get away from me right now."

He kicks at the ground, and a few clods of dirt explode into the air. "I am getting away, remember? I'm going to the States, and then I'll be in boarding school, and you weren't even going to say good-bye, were you? Because you were too busy flirting with David."

"You know what?" I shout. "I'm glad you're leaving! At least now you'll stop following me around like a sad, pathetic puppy dog all the time!"

His expression hardens. "You mean the way you do to David?"

"Oh my God, what is wrong with you?" I shove him. My cheeks are warm and wet, and I know I sound totally crazy, but I want to hurt him as much as he's hurt me. "Do you think I'm completely oblivious? I know you like me, Jamie. I know you've LIKED me all year. But nothing was ever going to happen. You're a loser. A twitchy little loser who hides behind Mika because you can't make friends for yourself—"

My last breath is a sob, and it seems to wake him up from a spell. His wide-open eyes fill with sadness, but he doesn't apologize. It's starting to rain, and he tugs at his curly hair. His stupid, curly hair that always sticks out.

I pull something from my messenger bag. A collage of pictures of us I downloaded from my phone and edited together. In the middle, I wrote, "I'LL MISS YOUR NERDY WAYZ. COME HOME SOON." I ball it up and drop it at his feet, and I think maybe he's crying or maybe he just can't look at me anymore.

I turn around and run away without looking back. Without even saying good-bye.

CHAPTER 4

SUNDAY

———

06 : 17 : 22 : 24
DAYS HOURS MINS SECS

JAMIE WAS RIGHT BELOW ME ON THE STAIRS. There were people moving around us, into the station, out of the station. But we were standing still.

"Hey," he said. His *hey* sounded different. Warmer somehow and slower.

"Hi," I said. "I was looking for you."

"You were?" He quirked up an eyebrow and smiled. Same overlapping front teeth, same green-gold eyes. But he was taller now. Not David tall, but taller. And he had broader shoulders and thicker arms. His hair had grown just past his ears, and it was less curly. Although I couldn't say that for sure. He was wearing a knit maroon hat that covered most of his head.

A *hat*. In this heat.

"We're blocking the way," I said, and turned around before he had a chance to respond.

———

"It's cosmic destiny!" David said when we were standing in line for a karaoke room. The karaoke place was busy for a Sunday night. Workers in red shirts moved briskly from the bar to the nearby elevator bank, balancing trays of drinks on their shoulders. Loud J-pop played from speakers built into the walls.

"It wasn't cosmic anything," I said. "That doesn't even make sense."

"Thousands of people walk through that station every day!" David said. "What are the chances you'd find Baby James for us?"

"There aren't that many people with blond hair," Caroline said, smiling generously at Jamie. "We stick out."

"Or orange hair." David tapped the braids on the top of my head. "Don't forget the orange-haired people."

I was ignoring Jamie. At least I was trying to, but I kept failing spectacularly. Ignoring him was like trying to ignore a solar eclipse. And besides, no one else was ignoring him. They were all cooing over him and lavishing him with attention like it was his freaking birthday or something.

"Are you excited about being a senior?" Caroline asked him. She had her arm linked through mine and kept squeezing it encouragingly whenever I said things. I was cordial and didn't try to strangle her in return.

"He's not going to be a senior," Mika said.

David pointed at Jamie with a cigarette. "Baby James here is in the year below. A mere junior."

"Yeah. Thanks for clearing that up." Mika shot an annoyed look at David, who gave her a broad smile in return.

The line moved forward.

"So." Jamie nodded his head. "Karaoke. I've really missed this."

"Yeah?" Caroline said. "I only moved here last year. My friends in Tennessee think it's weird that I go to karaoke all the time. They think it must be super embarrassing."

"I like that," he said. "The embarrassing part. I tried to bring karaoke to the dorms of Lake Forest Academy, but I wasn't successful. My most recent roommate was really against it. Very low threshold for public humiliation. Or for music. Or for me, if we're being brutally honest about the situation..."

He was rambling like a crazy person. Which actually made me feel a whole lot better. He might have been taller and broader and theoretically more attractive, but at least he wasn't *cool* now. He was still awkward, nerdtastic Jamie. Ridiculous hipster hat or no ridiculous hipster hat.

"I can't fucking believe you're back." Mika punched his shoulder.

Jamie beamed. "Well, I am."

David rubbed one of Caroline's hands between his. "You're back. Sofa's leaving. The world giveth, and the world taketh away."

"Totally sad!" Caroline said.

"*Sofa?*" Jamie said, acknowledging my existence for the first time since the station.

33

I took a sudden interest in the front of the line. Two TV screens behind the counter played the exact same music video of girls in frilly dresses dancing in a hot-pink room. "It's my nickname," I said.

"A lot has changed since you left, James," David said.

Mika sighed and rolled her eyes.

Jamie was still studying me. "Mika told me you were moving at the end of the week. Where are you heading?"

"To New Jersey," I said, pulling away from Caroline under the pretense of fixing one of my daisy pins. "Well, back to New Jersey. My mom teaches at Rutgers. We only came here because she got a four-year sabbatical with Tokyo University."

"Yeah," Jamie said. "I remember."

"Oh." I circled my watch with the forefinger and thumb of my other hand.

"Right! Jamie!" Mika said. "Things you need to know. Number one, it's my birthday this week, and Sophia's leaving on Sunday, so we're all going out on Friday night, and we're going to party so hard. Number two, I'm really happy you're back, oh my God. Number three, you are singing 'Giroppon' tonight, and I won't hear another word about it."

Jamie grinned. He seemed so infectiously, perfectly happy, it almost made me smile. But I didn't. "That," Jamie said, "is *definitely* happening."

"'Giroppon'?" Caroline asked. "Isn't that a cartoon fish?"

Jamie and Mika glanced at each other, then burst out laughing.

34

Caroline crinkled up her nose. "I don't get it."

"You're not the only one," I muttered, too quiet for anyone to hear.

But I wasn't quiet enough, because David laughed and nudged me with his elbow. I felt this incredible swell of gratitude for the fact that he existed.

———

We took an elevator to the fourth floor, to a narrow, winding corridor lined with karaoke room after karaoke room.

"Whoa!" David said. "They gave us a huge-ass room!" He ran over to one of the three faux-leather couches that lined the walls and jumped on it.

We were in room 47, which was, admittedly, pretty big. I'd been in some karaoke rooms that wouldn't have passed for walk-in closets. Room 47 had all the standard karaoke-room accessories: a black table in the middle with drinks menus scattered on top, a TV screen mounted on one wall, and a basket that held two controllers and microphones.

David grabbed a controller and started pushing buttons. "Where are all the frigging English songs?"

"You have to press the kanji for foreign songs," Mika said, walking in behind me. "Just like you had to the last ten thousand times we were here."

"What's the point remembering things other people will remember for you?" He shook the controller and gave Mika puppy-dog eyes. "Help me, Miks. How the hell am I supposed to know which button to press?"

"It's that one." Jamie pointed at the controller screen.

David raised an eyebrow at him. "Well, well. James can read kanji now."

"A little," Jamie said, clutching the back of his head with one hand, suddenly shy.

I was still standing by the door. Caroline had already curled up next to David on one couch, so I couldn't sit with him. Jamie took the one across from them, so no way was I sitting there. But if Mika sat with Jamie, I'd be all on my own. On the third couch.

Since Mika was the only one of us who spoke fluent Japanese, she picked up the phone by the door and ordered drinks from the bar. My own Japanese was terrible. Mom blamed the T-Cad. She said I used to speak a lot more when I was a kid. I said I didn't really *need* the language. The T-Cad was an English-speaking school, and anyway, I could always point at things.

Or get Mika to talk. She asked for a round of beers and a melon soda for me, then sat down next to Jamie.

So. Third couch it was.

"Okay!" David said. "I picked a song!"

"Surprise, surprise," Mika deadpanned.

As David started to sing, the lights in the room dimmed, the TV blared to life, and all these neon images lit up the walls. They were dolphins and mermen and starfish. I guess it was supposed to make us feel like we were under the sea, but it just made everyone look insane. Our teeth got whiter, and our skin glowed like we were radioactive. Still, it did make me a little less self-conscious. It's hard to be socially awkward when you're surrounded by a bunch of fluorescent mermen.

My friends were getting drunk.

Really, *really* drunk.

It didn't matter that we were all underage. Horrifically underage, as a matter of fact. The drinking age was twenty, and Mika, the oldest one of us, was just about to turn eighteen. But that didn't matter. We could all buy booze wherever and whenever we wanted. No fake IDs required.

This, as Mika had explained to me four years ago, was just how things ran. Expat kids got away with drinking and spending all night in bars because Tokyo was a safe city with reliable trains and a lax carding policy for foreigners. Mika thought our parents had no idea what was going on, but I figured they were just willfully ignorant of the debauchery. It was probably easier than locking us in our rooms and flushing our train passes down the toilet. Although, to be honest, I told my mom everything—willful ignorance was not her strong suit.

Mika kept going to the phone to order drinks. Beer, whiskey sours, something called a ginger-hi that I think had ginger ale in it. She ordered melon sodas for me because I was the semi-responsible one who never drank. ("*Because* someone's got to talk to the police if the police need talking to," Mika had once slurred, her arms around my neck. Which had made me feel exactly like the Boring Friend.)

"Mika and James should sing a duet," David said. He'd just finished an Iggy Pop song and was swinging the microphone over his head.

"Yeah, great idea." Mika smirked at Jamie, who smirked right back at her. The smirkers.

"Does anyone want to sing Katy Perry with me?" Caroline asked.

"Seriously!" David said. There was no music playing, and he was talking a lot louder than necessary. "Look at you two! Just like old times. Except Baby James is all grown up now."

"Yeah, thanks, man." Jamie stared determinedly at one of the controllers.

"For Christ's sake," Mika said. "Rules!"

Jamie glanced up at her, confused.

David held the microphone up to his face and sang scratchily, "Baby J. and Mika, sitting in a treeeeeeee—"

"Hey! Sophia." Mika tossed the other microphone my way. "You're up."

The title of the next song appeared on the screen in English and *katakana*: "Last Nite" by the Strokes. I gave Mika a quizzical look—*what is David talking about?*—but she just shrugged it off. I sang jumping up and down on the couch, rocking my head until my braids fell out. When I was done, David whistled and applauded. I opened my eyes and—Jamie was staring at me. Smiling at me, actually, with his mouth closed. What right did he have to stare at me? And smile? *And stare at me?*

I sat down and pressed my hands against the hot surface of the couch. My phone buzzed in my bag. A text from David:

THAT FUCKING HAT!!

I laughed and then covered my mouth. Thank God someone was on my wavelength. I texted back:

careful!! or mika will challenge you to a duel...

His response came a few seconds later:

Pah!! Mika always forgets her dueling pistols. PS, Why is Lonely Sofa on the lonely sofa?!

A content, dreamy feeling flooded through me. I started to type back when someone plopped down next to me. I jumped in surprise.

Caroline.

"That was great!" she said.

"Uh-huh." I shoved my phone back in my bag, covering the screen with my hand. "Thanks."

Nirvana started playing, Mika screaming along in a way that didn't exactly resemble a tune. I picked up my melon soda from the table. Caroline fanned herself with a menu and whispered, "Oh my God! That Jamie guy is cute. Did he used to be that cute?"

"No," I said. "Definitely not."

Caroline checked him out, like she was weighing up his pros and cons. "Well, he's cute now. In a geeky way, but I think it's charming. He does seem kind of nervous, though."

"Trust me. He used to seem way more nervous than that." Also fidgety. He was always tugging at his hair or shuffling his feet or drumming his fingers against something.

"It's probably because he's so in love with Mika," Caroline said.

I spat a watery ice cube back into my glass. "What? He's not in love with Mika."

"Look at him!" she said. "Look at *them*! They're all over each other."

I looked. "They're just sitting."

Caroline shook her head, and her ponytail smacked my face. She smelled like an abundance of raspberry body lotion. "Sophia, I know you're super smart and all, but you have no idea how to read *signals*."

There was a signal I would have really liked to give Caroline, but didn't.

"Who needs more drinks?" Mika asked.

"I'm okay," Jamie said, sipping his beer.

Caroline made a show of yawning and leaned across me so she could talk to Jamie. "I'm so tired. Hey. Aren't you tired, Jamie? You've been on a plane all day!"

Jamie sat back against the couch and put one hand behind his head. Everything about him seemed easier than it used to. There was even a lazy southern twang to his vowels that definitely hadn't been there before. "I'm all right. If I go home now, I'll have to unpack. Besides, you only move to Tokyo for the second time once, right?"

Caroline pouted. "Mika said your parents made you go to that school in the States. Why'd you come back?"

"Hello!" Mika said. "Did anyone hear me? Drink orders, please."

Mika called for the drinks. She asked for *takoyaki* as well, and my stomach growled when they arrived; I hadn't even realized how hungry I was.

As I broke apart my tiny ball of fried dough with octopus in the middle (more delicious than it sounds), Caroline leaned over me again. "Anyway," she said to Jamie, "I bet your parents are super thrilled you're back."

He shrugged, and I noticed his gaze flicker down. "Yeah," he said. "Super thrilled."

———

An hour or so later, room 47 was hot.

Way hotter than my house. Hot enough to reach critical mass. I twisted my sweaty hair into a knot on the top of my head, and Mika took off her T-shirt, revealing a white tank top underneath. The air in the room had gone thick and boozy. Caroline was quietly singing some schmaltzy, romantic song, and David kept making ridiculous moon eyes at her, kissing her forehead and the side of her neck as she sang. Then came the moment I'd been dreading. The moment when Caroline and David began to completely and unapologetically make out.

"Aaaaaaghhhh! Nooooooo!" Mika groaned. "Get a room!"

"Technically this is a room," Jamie said. He reached across the table and dragged over the basket of takoyaki David had been eating from.

Caroline straddled David's lap, and he ran his hands up and down her back, grasping at the fabric of her shirt. My stomach wadded itself into a tight ball, and the inside of my head ballooned with pressure. Critical mass achieved.

"Making out at karaoke is so raunchy," Mika said, pulling a disgusted face.

"So you've never done it?" Jamie teased. He tossed a takoyaki into the air and caught it with his mouth.

Mika hit him on the arm, hard this time. "God. You know way too much about me."

On the screen, a woman was standing on a bridge, staring forlornly at some boats. The video had nothing to do with the song playing, a synthetic melody pulsing through the room that no one was singing to. This was awful. To my right, the boy I liked was slobbering all over a girl I definitely didn't like. To my left, Jamie and Mika were talking and giggling and flirting.

Majorly flirting.

Maybe Caroline was right. Maybe they liked each other.

Maybe they'd made out in a karaoke room before—or would do so in the near future.

I held on to the seat and felt dizzy. Like gravity was threatening to loosen its grip on me and send me hurtling out of orbit.

"I'm going to the bathroom," I said, pushing myself off the couch. I was so desperate to get out of there that I tripped over Jamie's feet on my way to the door. He reached out to grasp my arm, and the heat of his hand made me even woozier. It was like time traveling back to three years ago and the last time I'd been close enough to touch him. Except now, when he looked at me, his face was blank. I'd expected to see something—hatred maybe—but what if even that was gone? What if I'd become nothing? Just the girl who tripped over his feet while he was talking to Mika.

I tugged my arm away and stumbled outside. The sounds from the surrounding karaoke rooms were muffled as I made my way down the compressed hallways, past rooms and rooms of other people in the middle of other songs. In the middle of other nights.

I didn't go to the bathroom. I stopped at a window, pressed my forehead to the cool glass, and gazed down. It was like tipping into a sea of people and night and all these neon signs growing brighter and brighter.

All I wanted was to go home.

CHAPTER 5
MONDAY

———

06 : 11 : 21 : 45
DAYS   HOURS   MINS   SECS

MIKA AND JAMIE LIVED in the same apartment building. They had for basically their entire lives. Mika was born in Tokyo, but Jamie had moved there from North Carolina when he was only two years old. I'd seen pictures of them when they were really little kids, wearing yukata at Children's Day festivals, dressed up like Power Rangers on Halloween.

After karaoke, we stood in the crush of people in Shibuya Station. I was waiting to watch Mika and Jamie skip home merrily together.

"Well, kids. This is where we part." David saluted us. Caroline had her arm around his waist. Her hair fell in disheveled waves in front of her face, and she looked half-asleep. She was probably going to stay over at his place. (*"The ambassador never finds out because my apartment is huge, and he's never home, and also he's an idiot,"* he'd explained to me once.)

It was after midnight, and it seemed like everyone in Shibuya was streaming into the station, trying to catch the last trains. People running and shouting, some of them eating konbini sandwiches, most of them drunk. Electronic boards above us blinked a red warning sign: four minutes till the final trains started leaving the station. If we missed them, we'd be screwed. We'd have to walk or take a cab or stay out all night until the first train came at five AM. David and Caroline disappeared down a set of stairs, and Jamie went to a bank of machines to buy a ticket for himself.

"I guess I should go to my platform." I fished through my tote for my Suica card.

Mika squinted at me. "I'm soooooo drunk. Im'ma barf."

"Really? You seem all right. You're just loopy."

"Oh yeah. Im'ma barf and Im'ma pass out. I can feel it. I had, like, six beers and three of those ginger whiskey thingys. And I know they're karaoke drinks, and I know they're watered down, but it's simple math." She smiled a vacant smile. "Too many drinkys make me sicky."

"Okay," I said. "So you're drunk."

"Sophia?" She clung to my arm.

"Uh-huh."

She lost her balance and collapsed against my chest. I immediately grabbed her around the shoulders and pulled her upright. Jamie appeared beside me and tried to help. "It's fine," I said tersely. "We're fine."

"Come on," he said. "We'll take her home."

"She can't go home like this. What if her parents see her?"

"It's okay," he said, his tone obnoxiously reassuring. "Her parents are away for a couple of nights."

"How did you know that?" I snapped. "I didn't know that."

"It's true," Mika mumbled. "Anniversary trip. The bastards."

I glared at Jamie. "Can't you take her home by yourself?"

"I could," he said, "but she probably wants you to come with her."

"And what makes you think that?"

"Well." He swallowed, and I watched his throat muscles contract. "You're her best friend."

"Oh," I said. "Right."

It was so bright in the station after the shadowy karaoke room. There were dark bruises under Jamie's eyes, and we were sweaty and our clothes were wrinkled. I could smell stale cigarette smoke and thin, sweet beer. Mika's head rolled against my shoulder. She opened her eyes and smiled up at me. A huge, beautiful Mika smile. Mika didn't genuinely smile all that often, but when she did, it made you want to do anything for her.

"I'm soooooo happy," she cooed. "It's the two of you. My two favorite people. Don't ever leave each other. Promise me. Promise Mika."

Jamie and I were holding her between us. He shrugged and I sighed.

We were officially going home together.

————

Mika and Jamie's apartment building was near the Imperial Palace, as in the actual palace where the actual emperor of Japan lives. Obviously he didn't go walking around the neighborhood or anything, but Mika said when she was a kid, she and Jamie used to ask the doorman why he never came to visit.

Standing in their lobby, waiting for the elevator to come, I really did feel like I was in some kind of royal residence. Like this was the palace itself. The lobby had a fountain, and a lot of potted ferns, and an enormous window overlooking an enclosed garden space. The floor was marble, and the walls were lacquered with wood panels so dark and glossy, they were almost reflective.

Jamie seemed uncomfortable. He kept adjusting his ridiculous hat and asking Mika how she felt.

"My internal organs want out," she said matter-of-factly. And then, "Do I have my keys?"

"I have them." I pulled her keys out of my tote and caught Jamie examining the side of it, where there was a picture of the Degas sculpture *Small Dancer Aged 14*. My dad had given me the bag for my fourteenth birthday.

"When did you take her keys?" Jamie asked.

"I didn't take them," I said. "She gave them to me earlier. She always gives me her stuff."

"I lose *everything*," Mika said. She drew out the word *everything*. She had reached her Exaggerated Drunk phase.

We got on the elevator, and Mika decided to sit down. Jamie and I pulled her up when we reached the eleventh floor. Jamie lived on the twelfth.

"Okay," I said to Jamie. "Good night."

"*Noooo*," Mika moaned, opening her eyes in horror. "Jamie *can't* go. He has to come *with us*. He *has* to."

"I'll help you take her in," Jamie said. He sounded so tentative and considerate, it was seriously grating my nerves.

I glared at Mika, but she just widened her eyes at me. Like a confused owl.

Even though I knew Mika's parents weren't home, I still had the urge to be as quiet as possible when we pushed open the door to 11A. The glow from the surrounding buildings poured in through the windows, illuminating the meticulously clean *genkan*. Mika bumped into a bulky umbrella stand with polished wooden handles sticking out of it. I cringed. Those umbrellas were probably expensive.

Jamie and I took off our shoes and picked out two pairs of slippers from a stack by the door. Mika kept her shoes on.

Beyond the genkan, her apartment opened up into a spacious living room with sleek black leather couches and a glass coffee table. There were glass-topped pedestals arranged by the windows displaying antique vases and a Buddha statue. We hauled sleepy Mika through the living room, past a framed white scroll covered in long, vertical lines of painted black kanji.

The last time I'd come over for dinner, Mika's dad had explained to me that it was Japanese calligraphy. Mika sat next to him slurping her shiitake mushroom pasta as loudly as possible while I nodded vigorously with my hands squeezed together in my lap, hoping my brightly colored hair didn't offend her parents as much as I knew Mika's did.

We took Mika into her room and lowered her onto the bed. She crawled under her covers, kicking her scruffy black clogs to the floor.

"Are you going to put pajamas on?" I asked.

"Why?" Mika asked into her pillow. "I have to wear new clothes tomorrow. Why change now if I have to change again later? Pointless."

So she'd moved on to Philosophical Drunk.

Mika's room was less chaotic than mine. The desk was neat with a huge flat-screen computer on it. A pastel pink-and-yellow plaid comforter lay over the bed with matching throw pillows clustered at the headboard. There was a vase of flowers on her dresser that Mika's mom arranged in her weekly ikebana class at the American Club, and the whole room smelled of lavender and lemon.

Of course, there were little Mika touches as well. A chunky serial-killer novel on her nightstand, a pair of running shorts draped over her desk chair, and all the '90s stuff: a Daria doll on her dresser, a poster of *The Craft* hanging on her wall, and DVDs of all seven seasons of *Buffy the Vampire Slayer* stacked by the foot of her bed.

I dug through Mika's pajama drawer until I found the red ones with an *M* monogrammed on the pocket, the ones Mika had always refused to wear. I glanced at the doorway. Jamie was still standing there. The confident veneer he'd had all night was definitely wearing off. He was chewing his lip.

"I think you can go now," I said.

"Aren't you going to call your mom and tell her you're staying over?" he asked.

"I texted her." I folded my arms. "Did you call yours?"

He shook his head. "I've been at boarding school for three years. They don't care what I do."

"Whatever." I shoved past him and went into the kitchen to fill three glasses with tap water.

"Here." I gave one to Jamie. "You've been drinking."

"Only a beer," he said. He took the water, though, and leaned against the refrigerator. He was smiling but with only half his mouth. I thought about the way he used to smile at me. With his teeth showing. With his whole face.

"Hey," he said. "You want a mint?" He reached into his pocket and took out a slim, credit-card-sized box of tiny Japanese mints. "This is going to sound dumb, but I really missed these. Mika bought me some as a welcome-back present. Take one." He held out the box and rattled it a little, but I didn't move a muscle. He fidgeted with the tab on the box's side.

In the light coming through the window, I noticed the

slight bump on Jamie's nose. He'd broken it when he was a kid, falling face-first off a slide, and it had never set properly. The memory of him telling me this made me physically recoil. I was being assaulted by things I'd spent a long time trying to forget.

"I really can't get over this," he said.

"What?"

"Tokyo. Karaoke. All of this." His eyes met mine, and I winced again, knocking my elbow against the counter behind me. "You know, I kept wanting come back and visit, but my parents always flew to North Carolina for Christmas and summer. Being here doesn't feel real yet."

I shrugged. "It is real."

"Yeah," he said. "I guess you're right." His hat had shifted, and I could see more of his hair now, the messy, unraveled curls. I stared down at my feet—my toenails were painted a bright purple.

"So," he said after a moment. "David, huh?"

Every defense mechanism inside me switched on. Hearing Jamie say David's name made me feel like we were still standing in that deserted cemetery, rain spitting down on us, that text message glowing in my hand. "What about David?" I asked.

"Nothing in particular," he said, sounding lighter. Confident Jamie was back. "He's the same, I guess. Good ol' passive-aggressive David."

"You don't talk to David anymore. You have no idea what he's—"

He interrupted me. "Caroline seems cool, though."

"Caroline?"

"Yeah. I mean, she seems like his type."

"And what type is that?" I asked through nearly gritted teeth.

He shrugged again. "I don't know. She's—outgoing. She's pretty."

I gripped the glass in my hand.

His words spilled out, like he was trying to say them before he lost his nerve. "Which I guess means the you-and-David thing never worked out."

My cheeks were burning. He was doing this again. We were picking up exactly where we'd left off. I squeezed the glass hard enough to make my hand hurt. "Even if it did," I said quietly, "you're the last person I would tell."

Jamie didn't back down. "So that means it didn't."

"Shut up!" I snapped, embarrassment ripping through me. "I don't want to talk to you. I don't even want to *see* you, Jamie. Not you or your ridiculous hat or anything. You should have stayed in the States another fucking week."

Jamie looked up at me. His eyes were exactly the same, as green, as gold, as telling as they used to be. Meeting his gaze was like holding my hand over an open flame. I hated him. I officially hated him. For coming back, for making me feel this way, for turning me into *this* person.

"You need to leave," I said. "Now."

Something that might have been guilt flickered across

his face, but was quickly replaced with a cool, blank expression. "Sure," he said. "I'll go."

He walked to the kitchen door. And then turned right back around. He washed out his water glass in the sink and put it on the drying rack. I stood awkwardly to the side, waiting for him to get out. My throat felt so tight, I could hardly believe there was air moving through it.

And then he was gone.

When I heard the front door click shut, I ran to lock it. I even stood there for a minute, staring out the peephole, just to make sure he wasn't coming back. The paranoia passed, and I went into Mika's colossal bathroom to change and brush my teeth with the spare toothbrush I kept there. I placed Mika's glass of water on her nightstand before crawling into bed.

When I flicked off the light, the glow-in-the-dark stars on her ceiling burned slowly to green. Mika must have put on music because Alanis Morissette *Unplugged* was playing from her computer.

"Mika?" I whispered.

"Hmmm."

"Are you awake?"

"Mmmhmm."

"Are you actually awake?"

"Hm."

"I really don't want this to end," I said. "I really, really don't want everything to change."

Mika snored. She'd reached the final stage: Dead-Asleep Drunk.

I rolled onto my stomach and parted the curtains behind the bed. There were blinking lights everywhere—on the antennae on top of buildings, on an airplane passing across the sky, on the streets below in moving headlights. So many lights floating in front of me, a universe of infinite stars.

I really, really, really don't want this to end.

The music stopped as I closed the curtains and lay down. In the quiet darkness, I thought about stars. The ones that aren't stars at all, but memories of ones that burned out millions of years ago. I thought about the stars that had already collapsed and turned into black holes, places where even light can't escape. Places where, from a distance, time seems to stop.

I held my wrist above my head and clicked the button on the side of my watch. The screen turned a bright blue— 1:07 AM. I clicked the button again and the display changed to a countdown: 06:10:42:10, 06:10:42:09, 06:10:42:08...

I lay awake for hours, wishing I could grab the seconds and hold them between my fingers—but only watching as they fell away, and disappeared forever.

———

"It's awesome!" I say to Dad.

"It's pink," Alison says. She's ten years old and wearing her new Pokémon pajamas. "Mom does not let us wear pink."

"It's not pink." I run my hands over the embroidered flowers on the wristband of my new watch. "It's purple."

"It's purple and the flowers are pink," Dad chimes in. "And it's not just a watch." He smiles and raises both his eyebrows. When Dad makes that face, he looks like a zany science teacher, which is exactly what he is. "Behold!" Dad takes the watch from me. "You press this button on the side two times and— ta-da! You have a countdown!"

"I love it!" I scrunch up my nose. "What's it for?"

Dad jumps up and goes into his bedroom, which is also his study.

It's never quiet in Dad's apartment, not even when no one is talking. The Birds is playing on the TV, and there are church bells going off across the street and motorcycles vrooming below. Pigeons flutter by the window like Christmas doves.

When Dad comes back, he's holding a calendar full of pictures of Japan. He flips through them, and I see cherry blossoms and shrines covered in snow and koi-fish kites, their colorful tails wriggling in the wind. Dad hands me the calendar. "The next time you two come to France, it will be May sixteenth. This watch tells you how many days and hours and minutes and seconds are left until May sixteenth. See? Not just a watch!"

"So it's a time machine," I say.

Alison makes a "gah" noise and rolls her eyes—Mom calls that her signature move.

Dad laughs. "Yes. It is. You just have to wait until it beeps and all the numbers are zeroes."

"What happens then?" I ask.

Dad rubs his chin. "You can start another one. For next Christmas maybe. For anything you want."

His phone starts to ring, so he jumps up again to answer it.

Alison leans toward me and hisses, "You better not let Mom see you wearing that. It is so not gender neutral, and she will totally kill you."

"Shut up," I say, cradling the watch against my chest. "I love it, and I'm going to wear it every day until forever."

CHAPTER 6

MONDAY

———

06:05:00:00

DAYS HOURS MINS SECS

WHEN MY PHONE ALARM WENT OFF, I lay in bed for a minute and waited for memories of last night to suck me into a vortex of embarrassment and self-pity.

But I felt okay.

Maybe because Mika's apartment was so bright and sunlit in the morning, so unlike the ethereal cavern it had been a few hours earlier. The kitchen was flooded with daylight, and I could see construction going on in the building across the street, orange cranes moving around like robots from *Neon Genesis Evangelion*. I texted my mom to let her know I was up, toasted two thick slices of *shoku-pan*, and ate them at the table by the window.

Mika's parents didn't care if I ate their food. They liked it, I think. They liked having me over for dinner, anyway, because they were always telling Mika to invite me. Mika's dad made amazing food: hot soba noodles with an egg cracked on top, hand-rolled sushi stuffed with salmon, tiny strawberry-and-cream cakes for dessert. After dinner,

Mika and I would watch TV, and her mom would bring out tortilla chips and homemade guacamole with lots of chopped-up tomatoes and chili peppers in it.

"They really like you," Mika would say drily. "You're the daughter they never had."

I couldn't say it to Mika, but I really liked her parents, too. I liked how smart they were. Mika's mom wrote a column about being an American expat for the *Japan Times*. Her dad was the vice president of a big Asian airline and was constantly jetting off to places like Thailand and China and India. Every time he saw me, he'd lend me a brand-new science book or ask me how my physics class was going. He kind of reminded me of my dad, actually.

It was early, and Mika had slept through both my alarm and hers. According to the schedule tacked to the corkboard above her desk, she was supposed to go on a four-mile run that morning.

"Eff no," Mika said when I tried to wake her up. "Do you want me to vomit and then die?"

She didn't look great. Spiky hair flattened against her head, and a weird white crust crystallized at the corners of her mouth. Seeing Mika like that was enough to keep me sober for life.

"Can I borrow some clothes?" I asked. "My stuff smells like an ashtray full of beer."

"Dude, yeah. Take whatever."

I grabbed a dress from the bottom of her closet, a grungy

plaid one that could have been stolen from the set of *My So-Called Life*.

There was no time to wash my hair, so I put it in a high ponytail and crammed all my old clothes into my tote. It occurred to me that this might be the last time I ever did this—get ready at Mika's, borrow her stuff. Her apartment felt like a real home, and I was jealous that she got to stay here, in one place. And I was *really* jealous that Jamie could just come downstairs whenever he felt like it and hang out in her room....

I grabbed the Suica card from the bottom of my tote. I had to leave before eight to get to the T-Cad by nine for the last day of my summer job. It sounded quiet outside Mika's front door, but I looked through the peephole before I opened it. And I sprinted all the way to the train station. Just in case.

————

The T-Cad was what everyone called the Tokyo International Academy.

It's an hour outside Tokyo's city center, in a suburban neighborhood full of little houses and little shops and a train station with only one platform. But the defining feature of the T-Cad neighborhood is definitely the cemetery. To get from the station to the school, I made my way through a cemetery so large and complicated there were maps posted at the entrances.

I could feel heat creeping into the morning air, but I walked slowly because it was the last time I'd be here, wandering down concrete paths that wound between dark green lawns, past graves made of rough gray stones arranged to resemble small houses or temples. There were more flowers lying in front of the graves than usual, I guess because of Obon, the Buddhist festival of the dead. The flowers made the air smell like sweet floral tea. Walking there alone, I could almost trick myself into believing the rest of Tokyo didn't exist.

"Sophia!"

Well, except for the fact that Caroline was racing up behind me, shouting.

"Hey! Sophia!" She ground her bike to a halt and put both feet down to steady herself. "I knew it was you! Your hair is, like, *very* recognizable."

"Hi," I said.

Caroline lived nearby and worked as a lifeguard at the T-Cad swimming pool, which was open for students during the summer. I sometimes ran into her on the way to work.

"Wow!" she said. "You look exhausted."

"Do I?"

"Oh my God, yeah!"

Caroline didn't look exhausted. Which was completely illogical. "What time did you even get up?" I asked.

She pursed her lips, thinking. "Like five-ish? I guess? I went home first so I could shower and get my bike."

"Jesus," I said. "How are you awake?"

"Konbini coffee!" Caroline pushed her sunglasses into her hair and smiled a terrifying cheerleader smile.

"Uh-huh." I started walking and she walked with me, wheeling her perfectly functioning bike beside her. I kicked a stone along the path and silently fumed. I did not want to spend my morning with Caroline Cooper. She was so—*blond*. And swishy. And she totally wasn't David's type, no matter what Jamie said. David made jokes about hating school, but he was smart. I'd seen him sitting at train stations, hunched over paperback copies of Kurt Vonnegut stories and *On the Road*. He needed someone who appreciated that side of him. Someone who got his jokes.

"What do you tell your parents when you stay over there?" I asked.

"Oh!" Caroline glanced at me self-consciously. "I tell them I'm staying with you."

"Seriously?" I asked. Christ! Who did this girl she think she was? Had she forgotten that we were not—by any stretch of the imagination—*friends*? She'd moved to Tokyo a year ago, and we hadn't so much as been to each other's houses.

"They think you're totally great," she said, as if *that* was what I'd be worried about.

"Well, I'll be gone next week," I said tightly. "So I guess you can't use that excuse anymore."

"I know." Caroline sighed. "Totally sucks."

Yes—for me. Because I am the one who is MOVING CONTINENTS.

We turned right at an intersection of the cemetery's paths, and Caroline grabbed my arm. "Oh my God!" she squealed, startling a black bird out of a nearby tree. "You'll never guess what David told me last night." She didn't even pause for breath. "About *the movie*?"

"What movie?" I adjusted my bag on my shoulder, pulling loose of her grasp.

"*A Century Divided*! He told me Jamie was in *A Century Divided*!"

I fidgeted with my watch, unstrapping and restrapping the Velcro band. "Oh?"

Caroline leaned down to me. "Did you know about this?"

I shrugged.

"Oh my God! What is with you and David? You both act like it's no big deal. Your minds should be blown! We know someone who was in *A Century Divided*! *A Century* freaking *Divided*! It's only on all the lists of Best Movies Ever."

I shrugged again. Caroline was turning me into a highly proficient shrugger. "He was only in it for, like, a minute."

"But it's the most emotional minute of the whole movie! I've seen it at least ten times, and that minute always makes me cry. Always."

I yanked open a gate, and we walked out of the cemetery. Across the street, I could see the T-Cad's massive building peeking out from behind a metal fence, and a blue uniformed guard sitting in his windowed booth.

"That was another reason I went home early," Caroline said. "I had to tell my parents about it. And my sisters. They totally freaked! Do you think it would be weird if I asked Jamie for an autograph? Oh! Do you think he went to the Oscars? The next time I see him, I'm going to make him tell me everything."

"Good luck with that." I checked my watch even though I knew exactly what time it was.

———

Caroline and I showed our ID cards and went through the main gate. The T-Cad always made me think of a secret government organization. It was a compound of buildings, like a military base, secured by a metal fence topped with sharp-eyed security cameras and a guard booth manned twenty-four hours a day.

Caroline had to park her bike, so I was spared further dissection of Jamie's former acting career as I walked through the parking lot. The T-Cad is made up of three schools—elementary, middle, and high—all built around a central courtyard. As I approached the entrance to the high school, I saw the school's motto emblazoned over the door: TRAINING GLOBAL CITIZENS TO ENCOUNTER THE WORLD!

"*It's vaguely threatening, isn't it?*" Jamie had said to me once. "*It's like, 'You will be trained, and then you will encounter the world, and you will DESTROY IT!'*"

I shook off the memory and opened a door into a waiting

room full of blue couches and coffee tables scattered with college brochures. At the back of the room, another door led to a hallway of school counselors' offices. I worked in the waiting room, at a computer next to a shelf of SAT-prep books, updating the school website for a few hours a week—changing over semester calendars, uploading pictures of sports games and class trips to Mount Fuji.

It was easy, and the counselors were all really nice to me. Probably because I wasn't one of the T-Cad rich kids. (We were easy to tell apart. The rich kids had important parents and good haircuts and expensive backpacks. The rest of us wore fake Converse and bought most of our clothes at discount stores.)

I logged in to my computer and got to work on a job-evaluation form.

But I couldn't concentrate. My thoughts dragged me back to Mika's kitchen last night, to the light splashed across Jamie's face as he'd talked about David. Pain bloomed in my chest, the vortex of embarrassment finally sucking me in. It was like I was fourteen again and staring at that awful text for the first time. And even though I'd told him to fuck off, confusion gnawed at me just the way it had back then. *(Why did he say that? Didn't we used to be friends?)* The hurt was fresh and brutal. A scar slashed open.

After he'd gone to boarding school, I'd spent a cloud of painful days obsessively checking my e-mail, hoping he'd write to explain everything. To tell me it had all been a big, comical misunderstanding. But he never wrote. And I tried to tell myself it was for the best. That I didn't actually care about what he'd have to say.

That I'd *never* care.

Caroline texted to say her day was already boring, and I texted back a smiley-face emoji. I started an e-mail to Dad but quit because I wasn't sure when he'd get it. (He was on vacation in the south of France with Sylvie and the babies. Whenever he was away, though, I missed hearing about life in Paris—about sitting at my favorite patisserie prepping for his high school physics class or going to Hitchcock movie marathons at the theater near his house.) A new kid came into the waiting room for a school tour and sat on one of the couches, talking on his smartphone in a language I couldn't understand. Possibly something Scandinavian? Although he must have spoken English as well. T-Cadders were a mixed bunch, but we all had to speak English in class.

The new kid turned to the side, and his profile almost reminded me of Jamie's...

God. I'd only been working for fifteen minutes, but I already needed air. I went to buy a can of iced coffee from one of the many vending machines in the courtyard. The heat was a blanket weighed down with the croaking of cicadas. I clicked on my countdown and stared at it, imagining each second was something I could grab and flick away. Something I had control over.

When I came back inside, Jamie was in the waiting room, leaning heavily against one of the walls.

I backed into the hallway.

"Sophia?" he said, pushing himself off the wall to walk toward me.

This couldn't be happening. I looked around for some kind of explanation. I even looked at the Scandinavian kid, but he was just playing on his phone.

"What are you doing here?" Jamie asked, his posture rigid. He was looking at me like he wanted me to disappear.

Well, of course he wanted me to disappear. Last night had proven beyond all reasonable doubt that the two of us should never be in the same room together, ever again.

"I could ask you the exact same question," I said.

He shoved his hands into his pockets, then pulled them out and flexed his fingers. I noticed how tired he looked. There were deep grooves under his eyes, and he was wearing a scruffy T-shirt, faded jeans, and black-framed glasses instead of contacts. Plus, the pretentious hat was gone.

Thank God. Or maybe not thank God, because he looked so much smaller and so much less confident without it. It made me want to ask him if everything was okay. It made me want to reach out to him. But as soon as I felt that, my stomach twisted in rebellion. I wanted to sit down. I wanted to close my eyes and make him disappear, too.

"Do you have to see a counselor?" he asked. Still annoyed.

"Of course not," I said. Also annoyed. "I work here."

The annoyance on his face turned to confusion. "You do?"

A skinny, tan woman started walking down the hall

toward us, cork wedge sandals smacking angrily against the ground. Jamie turned away from me just as she stepped between us.

"Good," she said. "You found the office."

"Yup," he said, all low and mumbly. He didn't sound like Jamie anymore.

"Well," she said, "have you talked to anyone? Have you done anything?"

"Mom..."

She pinched the bridge of her nose between her forefinger and thumb. Her nails were painted beige; they almost matched the color of her leather bag. "Answer the question. I want to be here for as little time as possible."

"I talked to Sophia." Jamie pointed at me. "She works here."

Great. Now his mom was staring at me. I'd seen her around, of course, even after Jamie moved. Sometimes she came to Mika's apartment to talk to Mika's mom. Or, when Mika dragged me to the American Club, I'd notice her coming out of conference rooms with a group of women gathered around her like skinny, well-dressed bodyguards.

"Well," she said, "who are you?"

"Uh. I work here."

His mom sighed. "And?"

"And—I update the website every week."

Out of the corner of my eye, I saw Jamie smile. A little.

His mom took her cell phone out of her bag and tapped the screen. "This is ridiculous. Someone was supposed to meet us outside at nine fifteen."

The can of iced coffee was starting to sweat in my hand. I shifted it to the other. "You're probably looking for Mr. Frederic. He's the admissions counselor, in room four."

"No." She dropped the phone in her bag. "We're here to see Ms. Suzuki."

Ms. Suzuki? I felt my eyes widen.

The only reason anyone saw the head counselor was if they were in the kind of trouble I could only dream of. Couldn't even dream of! I'm the type of person who recoils at the *subconscious imagining* of trouble. But how could Jamie be in trouble? He wasn't even a student yet.

"*Mom*," Jamie said quietly.

"Oh, stop it," she said. "You're not allowed to be precious about this. Especially not after showing up at one in the morning without telling us where you were. I swear to God, Jamie, you..."

"Ms. Suzuki's in room two," I blurted.

"What?" She blinked at me. "Oh. Good. Thank you." She walked right through the waiting room, breaking all sorts of waiting-room protocol, and leaving Jamie and me to face each other.

What's going on? I mouthed at him.

He cringed and glanced over his shoulder. *Later,* he mouthed back.

God. Why did I ask that?

Ms. Suzuki opened her door. "Oh, Mrs. Foster? Did you find the office all right?"

"Jamie," his mom called. "Come on."

His back stiffened, and the look in his eyes changed, becoming closed off and insular. And then he was turning away from me. Again.

CHAPTER 7
MONDAY

———

06 : 01 : 01 : 30
DAYS HOURS MINS SECS

IT HAD BEEN AN HOUR.

An hour and *twenty-three minutes*.

Enough time to down my iced coffee. Enough time to listen to Mr. Frederic talk to the Scandinavian kid who, in typical T-Cad fashion, was the son of a Norwegian diplomat.

I kept my headphones on but not plugged in. I couldn't hear what Ms. Suzuki was saying, but I did a crack job of obsessing over it. I obsessed over why Jamie had come back to Tokyo in the first place. Mika said it was because his parents thought he'd be happier here.

Yeah. Right. After seeing him with his mom, I definitely didn't think that was the case. Maybe Jamie had done something at boarding school that meant he had to leave. Maybe he'd cheated on a test or been caught with a girl in his room. Or maybe he was in legal trouble. Maybe he'd stolen a car or robbed a gas station for cigarettes and booze and condoms.

Maybe he'd killed a man.

I checked to see if Mika was online. If she was, I could ask what Jamie had said about boarding school or about his parents or—no. I couldn't do that. She'd have serious questions if I showed a sudden, reinvigorated interest in Jamie. I'd lain low the whole summer after he left, and when I came back to the T-Cad at the beginning of freshman year, I was convinced he'd have told her everything and that she'd come up to me in the cafeteria and punch me.

But she didn't. And I realized he hadn't said a word. Still, she must have known *something* had happened. Whenever she brought him up, I got so distant and twitchy that, eventually, she dropped it altogether. Jamie had turned into this strange, vacuous space between us. The He-Who-Must-Not-Be-Named of our friendship.

God, why couldn't I stop fixating on this? I wished Jamie had never come back to Tokyo or followed me into Mika's kitchen or stood in front of me in this waiting room looking lost and uncertain. Like someone familiar. Like someone who used to be my friend.

At 10:49, Ms. Suzuki's door finally opened. I hunched over my computer and squinted at it. (The only thing on there was my screen saver. A picture of a cat.)

"Hey," Jamie said.

He was standing over me, looking worse than he had an hour and twenty-four minutes ago. His skin was pale, and he'd pushed some of his hair off his forehead so that

71

it stuck straight up. "Ms. Suzuki said there was a water cooler out here?" He said it like it was a question.

I jerked my head back. Since my headphones weren't attached to my computer, the cord just fell to the floor. The door to Ms. Suzuki's office was open, and I could hear her asking Jamie's mom about North Carolina beaches.

"Yeah, it's right..." I started to point over my shoulder. "I'll just show you."

The water cooler was on the other side of the SAT bookshelf. The bookshelf itself almost blocked our view of Ms. Suzuki's office. Jamie stood behind me as I filled a plastic cup with water. When I turned around, I was standing so close to him I could see a faint bleach mark on the chest of his T-shirt.

"Did you get in trouble this morning?" I whispered. "For staying out so late?"

"Yeah, I guess you could say that." He glanced over his shoulder. "But it wasn't a big deal. It was just because I left the house without telling my parents where I was going. And without having a cell phone."

"Jamie," I said. "You're an idiot."

He shrugged. "I know. But hey, sorry about my mom."

"You're sorry about *your mom*?"

He exhaled slowly. He seemed irritated, but I wasn't sure if it was with me or with himself. "I'm just sorry. That was a general apology for—all kinds of things."

My cheeks warmed up. I couldn't have a serious conversation with him about last night. Not when I could hear his mom's voice—her strong southern accent—wafting into the room. Not when I was in my *place of business*. "Forget it, Jamie," I whispered.

He pressed his lips together and furrowed his brow. I could see the few freckles on his neck, right above the collar of his T-shirt. Jamie had fair skin spotted all over with freckles and moles, the type of skin the sun could probably burn right off. It was always turning red, where his backpack rubbed his neck, where he scratched the back of his hand. Whenever he blushed.

The first time I'd noticed this was back in eighth grade, when I was eating lunch with him and Mika and David. Mika had just laughed at one of his jokes, and his face went red up to his hairline. I thought it was really annoying. Everything about Jamie annoyed me back then. He was squeaky and small and desperate. Desperately desperate. He told too many jokes; he tried too hard to make other people like him. I found it all so infuriating that for the first few months I hung out with them, I could barely handle his presence.

Until, one day, he talked to me.

"You've got such a cool name," he said. "It's like Sophie Hatter, in *Howl's Moving Castle*."

"My name is Sophia," I huffed. "And what's *Howl's Moving Castle*?"

"Sophia. Of course." He blushed. "And it's a Ghibli movie."

"I don't watch those."

"Why not?"

"Uh, they're *cartoons*. That's why not."

The next day, he brought his copy of *Howl's Moving Castle* to my locker after school. I mumbled a thanks and shoved it in my backpack, and I might not have watched it at all if I hadn't finished my homework early that night. (I finished my homework early a lot.) I watched it twice, until Alison said I was hogging the TV, and then I watched it two more times on my laptop, curled up on my bed till three in the morning.

"It was so weird," I said to Jamie at lunch the next day.

"Weird in a bad way?" he asked.

"No," I said, thinking it over. "Weird in a…crazy way. I liked it when Howl turned into a bird and when Sophie got so angry she turned young again."

"I know, right? Sophie is awesome. She's such a badass."

Jamie brought me all his Ghibli DVDs, one after the other. *Spirited Away* and *Princess Mononoke* and *My Neighbor Totoro*. I'd thought they were kids' movies, but they weren't. They were the closest thing to magic I'd ever experienced. More beautiful than real life. More beautiful than anything.

We'd talk about them at lunch, sitting in the courtyard next to Mika and David, who got bored and started ignoring us.

"I think I might have seen *Totoro* when I was a kid," I said. "But yes, I loved it. I loved the cat bus."

"We should find a cat bus," Jamie said, pointing at me. "My whole life, I have wanted to find a cat bus."

I rolled my eyes. "Obviously we should do that. I mean, God, it's a freaking cat bus."

He laughed and his ears turned pink, the color of strawberries in cream.

He has skin like a mood ring, I'd think. *Or a modern-art painting.*

Looking at Jamie's neck, I remembered the way he used to make me feel. It was stupid, but there it was, a familiar dull ache in my chest and stomach. I remembered waking up in the morning, already excited to talk to him. I remembered the wrench of disappointment whenever he stayed home from school. I remembered running late to lunch and seeing him scanning the crowd, trying to find me.

It was such a disorienting feeling, I almost had to sit down. I almost forgot how much I currently hated him.

He took the water from me. "Thanks," he said, relaxing the set of his shoulders a little.

I pulled at the heavy sleeves of my dress and gripped them in my palms. "You're welcome."

He started to walk away but then came back and leaned down to my ear, his breath warm and minty against my cheek, making the tidal wave of memories grow stronger and stronger as he quickly whispered, "I got kicked out, that's why I'm back, don't tell Mika."

CHAPTER 8
MONDAY

——————

06 : 00 : 46 : 55
DAYS HOURS MINS SECS

"WHAT UP?" MIKA SAID when she answered the phone.

"Hey," I said. "Nothing. Bored. What are you doing?"

"Running eight miles."

"Really?"

She laughed. "Fuck no. I'm microwaving cookies."

There was no one else in the bathroom, so I pressed myself into the space between the hand dryer and the sink. My skin felt crawly and alive, like I'd just chugged a liter of soda.

"So?" Mika said. "You want to come over tonight? We can watch *One Piece*. Eat some cookies or something."

"Yeah," I said slowly. "Maybe. Are you going to invite David?"

"Why? Are you trying for a last-minute make-out session before you abandon us forever? You can't make out in my apartment, you know. I don't want to be haunted by the visuals."

"Mika. Gross."

"It's not gross. You want to make out with him, right?"

Heat rushed over my face, and I was glad Mika couldn't see me. "I like David. I would not be opposed to kissing him, if it came to that."

"Wow!" she said. "That there was some sexy talk. Bust that out on David, and he won't be able to resist."

"Shut up. I back up my statements with data."

"Stop it! You're turning me on!"

"Anyway," I said, talking over her, "it's probably sexier than anything Caroline could say. Like, *wow!* You are so much *cuter* than all the guys in Tennessee *combined!*"

"You got that right, baby," she said in her mock David accent. "I am one hot Aussie. I am—the Thunda from Down Unda."

"Oh God." I giggled so loud it bounced off the bathroom walls. "You are *disturbed*."

————

David did come over to Mika's, and they decided we should go to Shibs. It was dark out, but the air was still cloying with heat. David and Mika kept walking ahead of me, which was irritating. We went to an arcade and they played video games, which was even more irritating. They were all built for two players.

"I keep kicking your ass," Mika said matter-of-factly.

"Damn it, Tamagawa!" David said. "Do you even know which score is yours?"

"I saw Jamie today," I said, and instantly regretted it. The idea of talking about Jamie made me fizzy and anxious. But his name had come out so easily, like I couldn't physically keep it inside.

David and Mika didn't notice my awkwardness, though. They were playing the *taiko* drum game, each of them smacking wooden drumsticks against wide-barreled drums, trying to match their beat to the one scrolling across the screen.

"Baby James!" David said. "And where is Baby James this evening? Didn't he want to hit on Mika again?"

"Fuck off," Mika said.

"Oh, come on," David said. "I just don't get why you like the guy so much. He's so boring. He's like..." David slouched and pouted and rubbed the back of his head.

A nervous laugh escaped my mouth, and Mika scowled at the screen. "Ugh, guys. Concentrating now."

"Hey." David pointed at Mika with his drumstick and then at me. "Anyone else think it's odd that James just moved back here? All of a sudden?"

"Maybe?" I said and scratched my collarbone. I could have told them what I knew. I could have told them and given up my new duty as Jamie's official secret keeper.

Mika sighed through her teeth. "Thanks for throwing the game, jackass."

"Bloody suspicious," David said, "if I do say so myself." He smiled at me, but I couldn't bring myself to smile back.

"It's not suspicious," Mika said. "He hated that snobby-ass school. He's been begging his parents to let him come back for years. And, trust me, if you knew them, you'd get why it took so damned long to wear them down."

"So... what's up with his parents?" I asked, trying to sound casual.

But not casual enough, I guess, because Mika frowned at me. "Why do you care?"

"I don't *care*. It's just a question."

She watched me for a second longer, then shrugged. "His parents are—I don't know. They're uptight. His dad's always away on business, and his mom wants to move back to the States, but his dad won't ask for a transfer. I swear, they make my family look normal."

Your family is normal, I wanted to say. But didn't. I stared at the opposite end of the aisle, where there were *purikura* booths and a guy feeding money to a claw machine full of *Sailor Moon* dolls.

David clapped me on the back. "That must have been nice for Sofa. Seeing James." He rubbed circles between my shoulder blades. "Sofa can't wait to spend some quality time with James."

I recoiled. "Don't be weird."

"You were acting pretty fucking weird last night," Mika said, the blue spikes framing her face like an angry tiara. "You didn't talk to him at all. What? Are you too good for him now or something?"

"I talked to him. He just—he's different. Which you obviously noticed."

David guffawed. "Well spotted."

Mika's face was frozen in irritation, the colors on the screen glimmering in her eyebrow stud. "Whatever," she said. "Clearly you're not Team Jamie anymore. That doesn't mean you have to go all *sullen bitch* whenever he walks into the room."

"I don't go all *sullen bitch*," I said, in a distinctly sullen and bitchy way. They ignored me and went back to their game. But in the *chirps* and *pings* and *ploings* of their machine, I heard it. I couldn't stop hearing it.

I got kicked out, that's why I'm back, don't tell Mika.

———

Mom was still at work when I got home, but she texted to say I should order pizza. I hated speaking Japanese on the phone. I couldn't even gesture—I was completely powerless. I had to ask for toppings that were almost the exact same word in English as they were in Japanese. (*Cheezu.* Oh! And *hamu* please. I mean, *hamu onegaishimasu.*)

Alison was in the living room, sitting on the floor going through a box of Mom's old CDs. She'd put on *Scarlet's Walk* by Tori Amos, the one Mom used to play when we were little kids. Back when her hair was longer and she'd burn dinner almost every night. It was right after my dad left.

I sat down in front of my sister. There was a fan going, but it barely shuffled the lethargic air around. I picked up a pile of Bubble Wrap and started popping it.

"Don't do that," Alison said.

I popped one in defiance. "I think Dad's calling tonight."

"Sure he is."

"He's calling from Provence," I said. "It's the big vacation month in France, remember?"

She picked out a Cranberries CD and flipped it open so violently the cover flew out. "And I care because? It's not like I live there."

I shrugged. We didn't talk about it much anymore, but four years ago, I almost *had* lived there—almost moved in with Dad and Sylvie in Paris. It didn't work out because Sylvie got pregnant with the twins and Mom and Dad thought it would be hard on me, living with newborn babies.

And even though I was glad I'd come to Tokyo and met Mika and David, a part of me still wished I'd ended up in Paris. In a place I could have stayed.

But I didn't want to get into all that with Alison—not when I was about to start on something way worse. "Question," I said, rubbing a bubble between my fingers. "If your girlfriend sent you an e-mail right now and said she wanted to talk, what would you do?"

Alison's head snapped up. She sucked her lips into a thin, pale line. My sister wasn't one for forgiving, or forgetting. If she knew what Jamie had done, she would have told me cutting him off was the smartest move I could make. She would have told me that no one—*no one*—deserved a shot at hurting me twice. The room filled with Tori's piano, with the noise of traffic moving to and from the station, with the Japanese commentary over a sports game playing in someone's apartment.

"Fuck that," Alison said finally.

"Right," I said, and popped two more bubbles.

CHAPTER 9
TUESDAY

——

05 : 03 : 44 : 18
DAYS HOURS MINS SECS

THE DOOR TO JAMIE'S APARTMENT looked a lot like
the door to Mika's. Except it said 12A instead of 11A,
and there was a straw welcome mat out front with MY HOME
IS MILES FROM HERE written on it in a fancy curling script.

I slid my index finger into the space between my watch-
band and wrist. It was so early. He wouldn't be awake. Or
if he was awake, he'd be doing things. Normal morning
things like showering and eating breakfast. I had no idea
what I was doing here.

All I knew was what I'd decided last night after I'd talked
to my sister. After I'd tried (and failed) to fall asleep in my
stuffy room, the windows open, the warm air ballooning
with the sounds of the city. I'd stayed up thinking about
the week slipping away, imagining it as a fraying rope I was
desperately clinging on to. In a few days, I'd be gone and
then I'd never have the chance to ask Jamie why he'd sent
me that text. Or why he'd never told Mika about our fight.
Or why he trusted me not to tell her about boarding school.

I needed to talk to him. But first I had to knock on this door.

The door flung open, and Hannah careened into me. I stumbled back.

"What the hell?" Jamie's sister staggered back, too. She was carrying a red duffel bag that thunked against the doorframe.

"Hey," I said. Oh *crap*. I hadn't expected this. "Is—uh—is Jamie home?"

She narrowed her eyes. "He's home. Because he's sleeping."

"Of course," I said, backing up a little. "That makes sense."

Hannah popped her gum. She was four years younger than I was and athletic and kind of scary. She was always skipping school to go shopping in Kichijoji. Mika and I had seen her once, hopping the fence at the back of the football field. She was the type of person who'd get thrown out of boarding school.

Not Jamie.

"Hey, Hannah. Who are you talking to?" As soon as he came to the door, the floor seemed to spin beneath me. Jamie was the exact opposite of asleep. His hair was damp, and he was wearing a navy-blue T-shirt and jeans worn to white at the knees. When he saw me, his eyebrows shot up.

"Hey!" he said.

"Hey," I said, steadying myself against a wall. I felt like I might disintegrate. Like confronting him was an idea that only made sense at two in the morning, when I was hot and sleep deprived and delirious.

Hannah snapped her gum again. "I'm going to the American Club. I've got dance rehearsal, and Mom's setting up her boring lunch thing. She took Alex, too. You coming?"

He turned to her and my resolve collapsed even further, a weight towing down through my stomach.

"Later," he said. "I need to get dressed."

"You are dressed," she said.

"I need to put on shoes."

"*Shoes?*"

"Yeah." He gave her a pointed look. "Both of them."

"Okay." She rolled her eyes and pulled a pair of large purple headphones over her ears. "Don't take forever. Mom says you have to be there before ten." She shoved past me and walked toward the elevators.

Jamie held on to both sides of the doorframe and pushed himself forward. "Do you want to come in?"

"I can't," I said, my shoulder still pressed against the wall.

He laughed. "Are you a vampire? I already said you could come in. So we're cool."

"*No*. That's not—" I gestured behind me, at the elevators. "I thought you had to leave."

He waved his hand dismissively. "Nah. Not for another minute, at least. Come in."

He stepped back. And this was it. The moment where I

followed him or turned around. I could go forth into the apartment and confront him exactly the way I'd planned, or I could run away. Like a crazy person.

I walked into the genkan and stepped out of my shoes. It was weird because I could hear the same construction noises I'd heard in Mika's apartment the day before. She might have been below my feet at that very moment. Maybe *right* below them, lacing up her sneakers and getting ready for a run.

I slid my finger back under my watch.

"You've never been here before," Jamie said.

"No." I let go of my watch. "We always hung out at Mika's."

Jamie crossed his arms, and his expression turned cold. "My parents get sort of weird about guests."

"Okay," I said. "Does that mean I should leave?"

He shook his head and his eyes softened. "It doesn't mean that."

And then we fell into an awkward silence. I tried again to conjure up the things I'd planned on saying—*Why did you send that text? Why did you tell me about boarding school? Why are you talking to me, period?!*—but he was being so nice. *Disturbingly* nice. All I could choke out was "Okay."

"Come on." He tilted his head toward the hallway. "I'll give you the tour."

I followed him, furious at myself for chickening out. And, honestly, a little unnerved by the state of his apartment. It was just so—American. Every room was practically a display case of potpourri bowls and dance trophies and reclining leather armchairs. It was like, if you looked out the window, you might not even see Tokyo.

We stopped by his room, and I stood in the hallway while he rooted through two open suitcases. This was more like Jamie. There was a loft bed covered by a crumpled green comforter and a small framed picture of Japanese calligraphy hanging above the pillow. The walls were lined with built-in shelves crammed with Harry Potter and *The Lord of the Rings* and Japanese grammar and kanji workbooks, which reminded me of my own collection of astronomy and physics tomes—stacked on top of one another, spines cracked and worn.

My gaze settled on a framed movie poster hanging on the wall beneath his bed. The image was familiar: a woman's face superimposed over a sweeping mountainscape, messy hair blowing across her face and one hand clutched to her chest. Across the top, in gargantuan gold font, it read, A CENTURY DIVIDED.

"That's a—big poster," I said.

Jamie shrugged and yanked on a pair of black sneakers with red laces. "My mom put it there while I was gone. You should see the one in my grandparents' house." He made a face. "Actually, no, you shouldn't."

I stepped closer to the room. It smelled like tea and allspice.

"Ready?" Jamie grabbed a blue hat from one of the suitcases and pulled it over his half-dried hair.

"For what exactly?" I asked. Ugh. What was I *doing*? I wasn't supposed to be making small talk.

Jamie bit his bottom lip, like he thought I was being cute. "The American Club, unfortunately. Mom has important presidential duties with her International Women's Group. I have to help for post-expulsion-groveling reasons."

"Right," I said.

"You could come?"

I pointed at myself. "Not a member."

"Ah," Jamie said. He looked embarrassed, which made me embarrassed, too. Everyone was a member of the American Club except us lower echelons of the T-Cad community. Also, my mom once said she'd rather amputate her own foot than belong to a club where all you do is eat hamburgers and take yoga classes with smug, wealthy expats.

"It's as pointless as pointless gets," Jamie said. "All I have to do is fold napkins."

"I see."

"But..." He pulled at a loose thread in his hat. "We could walk together?"

I assumed we'd stop at the train station since that was the best way to get to the American Club, but we kept going—mostly in silence—until we reached Kitanomaru-koen, the park that surrounds the Imperial Palace. I'd been there tons of times with Mika. It's vast and treed and veined with moats. It's where the *sakura* bloom in April, where people come to walk under petals that float through the air like origami rain.

Each step I took beat out another syllable of the question I wanted to ask.

Why?

Why?

WHY?

"Check out this moat," Jamie said, veering toward a metal railing at the side of the path. I sidestepped a group of joggers to catch up with him. There were pastel-blue rowboats bobbing in the water below, but I didn't want to talk about boats. My heart was pounding so fast, it hurt. I was bracing myself for a leap, for a free fall.

"*Why?*" I blurted.

"Why?" he asked. "Well, it's a moat—"

"No." I squeezed my eyes shut and tried to suppress the dizziness washing over me. "Why did you send that text? Is that—is that what you and Mika used to say about me?"

"No. Oh God, *no*." He stepped toward me but stopped himself before he got too close. He looked panicked, the way he had three years ago when I'd told him I didn't care about him. "Mika never said anything like that. I was just mad. Mad that I was leaving and that my parents were sending me to that stupid school and that you were standing there, laughing it up with David. I was so—mad." He gripped the back of his neck. "I know that's not an excuse."

"Of course it's not," I said, my voice coming out high and shrill. "What you said—I trusted you, Jamie. We were friends. But you called me desperate. And I used to worry that I *was* desperate. That I didn't deserve people like

Mika and David and that everyone could see that. And then you sent that text, and it was like you *could* see that. Even now—even just talking about it—it makes me feel all—" I shook my hands out as if that conveyed something.

"It's all my fault," Jamie said. "I've thought about that so many times."

I pushed my hair behind my ears and concentrated on the water. "You have?"

He threaded his hands together and glanced down at them. He was wearing a thin leather band on one wrist I'd never noticed before. "I should have sent you an e-mail or something. I wanted to, but I didn't think you'd write back."

"You're right," I said. "I wouldn't have."

He shrugged and shifted his gaze back to the moat. A couple more joggers ran past, music playing through their headphones. We were in the park, but the city wasn't far away. The roads around us were heavy with traffic, and the paths were swarming with tourists.

"Look." I sighed and surprised myself when I said, "You're not the only one who screwed up that day, all right?"

He leaned against the railing. "No shit."

"It was—" I started. "Well, it was the worst day ever, if you want me to be honest."

He turned to face me, his eyes warm but cautious. I didn't know what we should do. Where we could possibly go from here.

What do I say to him now?

"Okay..." He tipped his head toward me and my breath went sharp. "Are you hungry?"

"What?"

"I'm hungry." He nudged me with his elbow and bounced on his heels. "Starving, actually. We should find a konbini."

I exhaled. My veins were still thrumming, but there was something different, some minute change in the atmosphere I couldn't quite place.

Maybe this was a truce?

Or maybe I was nuts.

"Sure," I said. "Why not?"

"Excellent," Jamie said. "But we have to do it fast."

And then he started to run.

———

The morning sun reflected in the skyscrapers that circled us, and a rainbow-patterned kite flashed above, glittering like fish scales. There was a miraculous breeze, maybe because I was running.

"I'm not Mika!" I shouted. "I don't run!"

He grabbed my hand and pulled me along. We guessed streets to turn down until we found a konbini. "Success!" Jamie said, tightening his grip to stop me from skidding forward.

"Is it like you remember?" I asked and tried to see the konbini the way I would have if I'd been gone for the last

91

three years—small and fluorescent and stacked with every snack and drink and plastic bento box one could begin to imagine.

"Everything and more." Jamie pointed to the fridges at the back of the store. "Behold! Caffeine!"

The fridges brimmed with sodas and green teas with kanji and pictures of flowers on the labels. But most importantly, they had coffee. Milky coffee and black coffee in bottles and cans and cartons with straws attached to their sides. Some of them weren't in fridges at all; they sat in a separate section under warm yellow lights.

"Heated coffee in a can." Jamie's face lit up. "I forgot about these!"

"Well, it's called a *convenience* store for a reason," I said.

"Because it's konbini-ent?"

"Good one." I reached out to press the palms of my hands against the cold fridge. Palm prints appeared briefly and then faded.

Jamie wandered around the store, picking out food: a bag of seaweed potato chips, chocolate-covered almonds, Tomato Pretz sticks. I watched as he examined different bags of *senbei* and wondered if any of this seemed new to him. When I'd moved back to Tokyo, some things had seemed like shadowed memories brought to life. Snippets from dreams.

I realized I was staring at him and pretended to read a label I couldn't understand on a bag of lychee gummies. Some things about Jamie seemed new, too. (Or maybe they weren't?) Like the fact that he was sort of funny. Or the easy way he laughed, his eyes and nose crinkling up so much, it was practically bunny-like. He was broad on top and tucked-in at the sides and not exactly *un*attractive.

Or, at least, some people probably thought so.

"Done?" he asked.

I dropped the gummies. "What do you mean?"

He was standing in front of me, holding enough food to feed a family of rabid bears. "I mean, what do you want to eat?"

I actually felt my eyes bulge. "You're getting all that for yourself?"

"No, of course not. But this is my first week back, and your last week, so what we have to do is eat everything." He grinned. His regular grin this time, enormous and goofy. "Everything in Japan."

I rolled my eyes and grabbed a Meiji strawberry chocolate bar from the nearest shelf.

———

"Holy crap!" Jamie said. We were sitting on a stretch of grass in the park, downing our iced coffees and tearing our way through chocolate bars and potato chips. "I really missed this. I missed all the junk foods of Japan!"

I breathed in the metallic city air. "What else did you miss?"

He didn't say anything for a minute, and I fidgeted with

the foil on the corner of my chocolate bar. Bah. Terrible question.

He leaned back on his elbows and stretched out his legs, crossing one ankle over the other. "I missed my brother and sister. Alex is only eight, so I'm pretty sure he doesn't remember living with me. And I missed walking around the city. Everyone at Lake Forest drives, and nobody understands the wonder of karaoke, and a lot of people are under the impression that Tokyo is the capital of China."

"Is that why you wanted to come back?" I asked.

His eyes were teasing. "Because they thought Tokyo was the capital of China?"

"I just—" I shook my head. "I don't get how your parents could send you away. You clearly didn't want to go."

He sat up. "They sent me because of my grandfather. He gives a lot of money to Lake Forest, so it was all about 'keeping up the family name.' They care about that. Looking good on paper." He paused and mulled something over. "And they thought it would be good for me, I guess."

"Was it?"

He leaned forward, his elbows on his knees. "Why are we still talking about me? Sophia Wachowski"—he held an imaginary microphone up to my face—"what are *you* going to miss about Tokyo?"

"The lower crime rate," I said.

He laughed.

I pulled a few blades of grass from the ground and rubbed them between my fingers. "I don't know. I'll miss the T-Cad, I guess. And I can't imagine anything without Mika and David." I searched for more to say. "And I'll miss the sounds. You know, like the sound of the trains from my house and the sound of cicadas in summer. I considered recording some, which is stupid, I know. And I'll miss Ramune ice cream from the konbini. And those boxes of cakes wrapped in that fancy paper you can buy at department stores. I love those. And—" I crushed the grass in my hands. "Whatever. None of this matters."

"Of course it does," Jamie said, smiling.

I shrugged.

For some reason, I was thinking about my family's first apartment in Tokyo. About the Thai restaurant across the street with red lanterns hanging in the windows and the corner of the living room where Dad used to sit and read me *Winnie-the-Pooh*. About the day before we moved out, when Mom had leaned down next to me to ask what I'd miss about Tokyo.

The answer had been so obvious.

It had been home.

Jamie shifted toward me. I thought he was going to say something, and I really didn't want him to, because I really didn't want to cry in front of him. But he just handed me a Pretz stick. We ate in silence for a moment or so. The traffic on the nearby road sounded like a river, like water crashing over rocks and tumbling by.

"Hey," Jamie said after a moment. "Did you mean what

you said the other night? About my hat? Do you really not like it?"

I swallowed my mouthful of Pretz. "God no. It's awful."

His lips twitched. And then we were doubled over with laughter, falling toward each other like a book closing shut.

CHAPTER 10
TUESDAY

---

04 : 23 : 06 : 19
DAYS HOURS MINS SECS

"DON'T ASK ME," MIKA SAID on the phone. "It's David's stupid plan. That dude has some screwed-up ideas about how to spend an evening."

"Why does he want to go to the T-Cad?" I was sitting on my desk, staring out the open window, listening to the trains whooshing in and out of the station. Dorothea Brooke was stretched out beside me, luxuriously chewing the tail off a toy mouse. "Is this a joke?"

"Who knows? He's a fucking psychopath. He also said you should wear all black and that we're meeting at the T-Cad train station at eight. In other news, where the hell have you been all day?"

"What do you mean?"

"I've been calling you for the last ten hundred hours."

"You have? I didn't hear my cell."

"Did you get my texts at least?"

"Um. I didn't open them."

"They said 'help!' and 'save me!' and 'this is urgent!'"

"Sorry. I was gonna open them later."

"You're useless, you know that? Mom's back in town, and she's been terrorizing me all morning."

"How is she terrorizing you?"

"Have you finished your summer reading? Have you been keeping up with your preseason training? How many miles did you run yesterday? Have you checked to make sure you're still registered for your AP classes?"

"Yikes."

"What she doesn't understand is I am exhausted."

"Why? Did you and David go drinking last night?"

"Jesus, no. I'm not an alcoholic."

"I thought you two were hanging out after I went home."

"We barely did anything. Anyway, boring. Have you been home all day?"

"What do you think?" There were no trains going at that moment, and the city seemed loud and quiet at the same time, like it was holding its breath, like it was hovering at the top of a roller coaster, waiting for the perfect moment to fall. If I told Mika the truth about being with Jamie, she might think it was weird. Or she might think it meant nothing at all. I let out a breath. "I've been packing."

———

At 8:07, the only other person at the T-Cad train station was the guy in the booth behind the barriers.

I stood by myself at the top of the steps that led down to

the darkened street. All the small shops were closed except for the always-reliable konbini, which glowed like a fluorescent blue-and-white beacon.

This was probably part of David's ridiculous plan. Dress me up like a cat burglar and send me to the T-Cad alone to—to what? David lived for ridiculous plans like this. Usually, it was one of the things I liked most about him. Usually, it made me feel like life was electric and unpredictable.

Tonight, it did not.

I sat on the steps and checked my phone. Mom was texting me updates on her packing and asking—*again*—if I was okay. She'd seemed worried when I told her I was going out tonight. ("I've barely seen you since Sunday," she'd said as I'd scarfed a peanut butter sandwich over the sink before I left. "Mom," I'd said between bites. "In a week, I'll see you all the time because I won't even have friends anymore.")

In retrospect, that probably hadn't made her worry less.

I closed my phone and tried as hard as I could not to think about Jamie.

But that was impossible. It was like trying not to get a song stuck in your head. A song you (reluctantly) like. A song you (kind of, sort of) want to hear again. I still didn't know why he'd been at the T-Cad, and I didn't know why he'd been kicked out of boarding school, but I was starting to get a picture of him *at* boarding school. Studying Japanese instead of doing schoolwork, not going home on weekends. I could almost see him, could almost fill in the last three years.

I rubbed my eyes with the heels of my hands. This feeling—this kind of, sort of liking feeling—was massively inconvenient. Inkonbinient, even.

I got up and wandered down the street, taking in all the closed-up stores. The only noises I could hear were the buzzing of the konbini and the croaking of cicadas. And also... Caroline?

"You didn't show up," she said.

I stopped and looked around.

"I forgot," David said. "Christ, it happens. People forget things."

It took me a few seconds to find them because they were huddled in an alleyway between two stores. David had his hands on Caroline's shoulders.

"I waited for you till midnight!" Caroline hissed. "I called your phone, like, ten times! You seriously expect me to believe you *forgot*?" She pushed past him and stumbled into the street, stopping short as soon as she saw me. "Sophia?"

"Hey," I said. Oh God. Her face was pale and blotchy. She'd clearly been crying.

"Sofa!" David said, turning around.

Before I could say anything back, the door to the konbini slid open and Jamie and Mika toppled into the street. Mika's mouth was open wide with laughter, and she was clinging to Jamie's arm. She was wearing her Wonder Woman T-shirt, and her hair was gelled into a small blue fauxhawk. Jamie held a plastic bag and gazed down at her adoringly.

I felt my chest expand and then tighten. Oh crap. I was going to implode.

"Sofa!" David said again. His eyes gleamed as he strode toward me, a streamlined figure all in black. Tight black T-shirt, black pants, black pointy shoes that glinted in the light. His clothes made him impossibly tall. They made his eyes intensely blue. When he got to me, he wrapped an arm around me and kissed the top of my head. Then he squeezed my shoulder and kissed the top of my head again. "Sofa! You're here!"

Caroline stayed back, combing her hair in front of her face.

Were she and David breaking up?

"Check out the goth twins," Mika said when she reached us. Jamie wasn't wearing a hat anymore, but he had the same navy-blue T-shirt on. His cheeks and nose were pink, like maybe they'd been sunburned.

My head filled with static. I didn't know what to say to him. I didn't know if I should say anything. We'd been in the same vicinity for approximately twelve seconds, and he hadn't said one word to me.

Mika reached up to ruffle Jamie's hair. "Dude, how did you hide all this under that hat?! It looked a lot smaller on Skype."

Jamie ducked away from her, but he was grinning. "Yeah, well. It's not quite as impressive as that Smurf Mohawk."

David sighed. "Break it up, you two." He rolled his eyes conspiratorially at me, and I exhaled loudly in agreement. Despite everything else, I still liked being on his team.

"So," I said. "Any desire to tell me what's going on?"

He pulled me into a tight hug that felt lanky and secure. I caught another glimpse of Caroline, standing away from us, outside the light of a streetlamp. She seemed crumpled and heartbroken, but she lifted her hand to wave at me.

David's voice whispered in my ear, "Not a cat's chance in hell, little Sofa."

———

It was dark out, but not *dark*-dark. Purplish clouds curled across the sky, glowing from light pollution. Tokyo never blacked out, not even at night. Not even by the T-Cad, where the buildings didn't touch the sky.

We waded through the muggy air of the cemetery, David leading the way and Mika and Jamie just behind. They were still being jokey and playful with each other.

And they were ignoring me.

Mika was probably still pissed about how I'd treated Jamie his first night back. And Jamie—he was being cool and aloof again, exactly the way he'd been at karaoke. Once, he glanced over his shoulder at me, like he was thinking about saying something.

But I pretended not to notice.

Which was fairly easy because Caroline was walking next to me, emitting a series of sniffling noises.

The harsh truth was that David broke up with everyone. He didn't always do the actual breaking up, but he always did the thing that caused the breaking up. He got distant, he got flirtatious, he got desperate for the relationship to end. And then it would.

But even though I'd spent the last year daydreaming about this moment—the moment when David realized Caroline was not his type—I felt a little bad for her. I had a compact mirror in my tote that I shoved wordlessly into her hand. She clutched it gratefully and linked her arm tightly with mine.

We trudged out of the cemetery and into the park that wrapped around the back of the T-Cad, away from the gate and the ever-present guard, along the line of the school fence.

"This is it?" Mika said when David stopped us. "*This* is the plan?"

"This is it," David said, opening his arms like a circus ringmaster.

We were standing where the fence touched the back of the football field.

David hoisted his long body up and clung to the mesh of the fence like Spider-Man. "We're taking Sofa inside the T-Cad so she can say a proper good-bye."

Mika groaned. "Dude. The school is closed. This is so lame."

"Careful with the 'dudes,' nineties girl," David said cheerfully. "You might wake up and realize you're in the wrong century. Anyway, it's not lame. It's symbolic."

"It's *illegal*," I interjected. "Or semi-illegal, at least. We're breaking and entering."

David gave me a wicked grin. "Don't worry. This is the blind spot. No security cameras, remember?" He detached one hand from the fence and pointed up.

He was right. Everyone at the T-Cad knew about the blind spot. Everyone had taken advantage of it at least once.

Except me, of course.

"Besides!" David said. "We are students trying to get into school. Someone hand us some friggin' medals!" He swung over the fence and landed on the ground in an elegant crouch. When he stood up, he fist-pumped the air. "Hell yeah! Ten-point-oh! The judges are unanimous!"

"So lame," Mika said, but she sounded more on board with the whole thing. She grabbed the konbini bag from Jamie, tied it, and hurled it over the fence. Then she made her own way over. It was like watching two acrobats. It was like watching two people who had definitely done this before.

Caroline pouted, her bottom lip actually sticking out. "I don't want to climb a fence."

Jamie pushed his hands through his hair. "Right. I'll go next. Spot me if I fall."

"You should just leave," I said quietly.

"What?"

I was trying to catch his eye, but he wasn't paying attention to me. Not really. He was watching the football field, where Mika and David were running around.

The air grew so thick, I struggled to breathe.

Jamie was watching Mika. She was his best friend, and he'd missed her, and now they had a whole year together, stretching out in front of them. It was going to be exactly the way it used to be. Mika and Jamie texting and laughing and keeping secrets. Mika and Jamie in their own little world. I felt myself starting to fade.

"If you get caught, you'll get kicked out of the T-Cad," I said.

He scowled, like he wanted me to shut up.

I kept talking. "And if you get caught, Mika will definitely know why you're back. I won't be able to protect your secret anymore."

Jamie appraised me carefully, like he wasn't sure who he was looking at.

Caroline held out her hands, palms up. "It's going to rain. This is *so* not fun anymore."

Jamie held my gaze, then turned to hook his fingers through the diamond-shaped pattern of the fence. In the dark, he was nothing but a silhouette. He could have been anyone at all.

CHAPTER 11
TUESDAY

———

04 : 13 : 19 : 53
DAYS   HOURS   MINS   SECS

"JAMIE COULD SPELL *ORANGUTAN* when he was five!" Mika took a swig from a can of grapefruit Chu-Hi and held up her other hand. "Five!"

We were in the elementary school playground, Caroline perched on the bottom of the slide, scrolling through her phone, and the rest of us in a séance circle in front of the swings. After the ordeal of getting over the fence, it had become pretty clear pretty quick that there was nothing else to do. We couldn't even walk around, in case we got caught by the security cameras.

"Yeah," Jamie said. "And so began the long and winding road to a lifetime of popularity."

"It impressed the hell out of my mom," Mika said. "It impressed the hell out of EVERYONE ALIVE!"

Jamie smiled down at his hands.

Mika had gone manic over Jamie, which probably wasn't good. Mika only got this crazy about something when she was in a bad mood about something else. Like that time her mom said she was wasting her academic potential and she challenged David to a soda-chugging contest and ended up barfing all over Yoyogi-koen.

David started digging around in the bottom of a plastic bag. "Did anyone bring cigarettes?"

"Not me." I tilted my head back to stare at the ominous sky, filling up with more clouds by the second. I wished I could see the stars. And I really wished I wasn't leaving so soon. (In four days, thirteen hours, and twenty minutes.) Dad would have told me not to think about that—to focus on what was happening right then because time only exists in the present moment. But it was hard to focus on the present moment when everyone in it was acting so weird. I felt like I was floating. Lost between this second and the next, between all these different versions of myself I'd left scattered across the globe.

"Okay!" Mika put down her can of Chu-Hi and stood up. "Okay! It's time to listen. Are we all listening?"

"Nope," David said.

"Everyone has to listen!" Mika shouted. "Does everyone know that Jamie is *famous*?"

Jamie jumped up and tried to cover Mika's mouth. "Okay. Mika. Stop."

She slapped his hand away. "No! Listen. Did you guys ever see *A Century Divided*?"

David pulled a crushed box of cigarettes from his pocket. He put one in his mouth and held it there like it was a toothpick. "Christ, Mika. We all know this."

"I don't care," Caroline said. She'd dropped her phone into her lap and was leaning forward on the slide. "I totally want to talk about this."

David and I glanced at each other. *Kill me now*, he mouthed.

Mika went on. "Everyone has seen *A Century Divided* because it's a big famous movie about the South after the Civil War and blah, blah, blah historical stuff. The point is, Jamie is the little boy! The little blond boy whose mom gets killed by her evil, drunk brother when he comes back from the war! That little boy is totally Jamie!"

"I know!" Caroline said. "David told me, and it is only, like, the most exciting thing ever. I've seen that movie ten times. And I've read the book! Wyatt Foster is my favorite author of all time."

"Yeah?" Jamie said warily.

"Yeah!" Caroline said. "My dad has a picture with him. He's such a cute old man. He even wears a bow tie!"

The air snapped and snarled with something that might have been thunder. Jamie obviously didn't want to talk about this. But Mika would probably bulldoze me if I said something she didn't like.

"Oh my God!" Mika said. "Yes! That old man! That cute old man is Jamie's grandfather!"

Jamie crossed his arms and hunched up his shoulders in embarrassment.

"Wait a second," Caroline said. "Wait a serious, freaking, serious second. Your grandfather is *Wyatt. Foster*?"

"Um . . ." Jamie said.

"He totally is!" Mika squealed. "He is totally Jamie's grandfather!"

Caroline pointed at me and then David. "You guys *did not* tell me that!"

"Must have slipped my mind," David said.

Mika hiccuped and giggled, trying to slick her hair back into a Mohawk shape.

"You know—" Caroline moved forward to ogle Jamie's face. Anxious red splotches appeared on his neck. "You do kind of look like him."

"Well, I don't see how that's possible," David said languidly. "Considering James is adopted."

We all turned to David.

Thunder. There was definitely thunder now. And rain splashing on the gravel. Everyone went silent, and I almost didn't know if it was because of what David had said or because of the cold shock of water against our skin. The sudden release of all that gluey heat from the air.

"That's not true," I said, half expecting David to laugh. For him to roll his eyes and say *Of course it's not true.*

Instead, he pulled a lighter out of his other pocket and fiddled with it. "And seriously, Miks, are you guys done yet? Because as much fun as this is, I think we could all use a break from watching you two flirt."

Jamie walked away from the group, to the other side of the playground. The rain picked up momentum, tapping a faster beat against the ground. Water sliced down the sides of my nose and seeped into the fabric of my shirt.

"Did you seriously just do that?" Mika hissed.

David tossed his cigarette over his shoulder. "What do you think, Sofa? On a scale of one to flirt, where do Mika and Jamie fall?"

"Fuck you," Mika said.

David raised one eyebrow but didn't back off. He leaned over and touched her ankle. "Come on, Miks. It's no big deal. Set your hormones free."

"Fuck. You." Mika kicked off his hand, and he sat back.

She was angrier than I'd ever seen her. Her fists were clenched at her sides, and her shoulders were squared like a boxer's.

"I think you're forgetting that tonight is about Sofa," David said.

"And I think *you're* forgetting to fucking control your jealousy issues!"

Jealousy issues? Why would David have jealousy issues with Jamie? He couldn't stand Jamie—he'd said so a thousand times. David was being such a jerk, and Mika was possibly going to punch him, and no one even seemed to care that the storm was getting worse or that Jamie might be picked up by the guard or a security camera at any moment.

"Guys," I said, sweeping my wet bangs from my eyes. "I don't think Jamie's on the playground anymore. We should go find him."

"Shut up, Sofa," Mika snapped.

I looked at her, startled. "What the hell, Mika? Is this because you're drunk?"

"Jesus! Is that your catchphrase or something? Stop asking if I'm drunk!" She kicked the swing set, drops of water flying like sparks. "And where the *fuck* is Jamie!"

David stood up, his eyes sorrowful now. "Come on, Miks."

Rain bounced off the playground equipment, hitting all the empty aluminum cans. It flattened Mika's fauxhawk and made David look thin and weak and sorry. He approached her and took her fingers between his own. He tugged her closer to him. And she didn't argue.

"I'm sorry, Miks," he said. "Okay? I'm a jerk. Everyone knows it."

"Yeah, you are," she said, but her voice was softer now, melting into liquid.

He stroked his thumb over her knuckles and held her hand to his chest. Mika lifted her eyes to meet his. Her mouth was open, like she wanted to say something and—

Oh my God.

"Oh my God," Caroline whispered.

Mika let go of his hand and jumped back.

My arms went numb and heavy by my sides. The rest of the night had collapsed into that one moment: the whisper of his thumb across her hand, the easy parting of her lips in return.

"*This* is why you've been acting so strange," Caroline

said, looking from Mika to David, from David to Mika. "*This* is why you ditched me last night."

David put his head in his hands and groaned. "Calm the drama, Caroline."

"*Fuck*," Mika said.

And all I could think about were David's "jealousy issues," and all I could think about was David and Mika hanging out by themselves, and all I could think about were the hundreds of times Mika had told me to get over David because he was a player, because he wasn't as miraculous as he pretended to be.

"You hooked up with her," Caroline said, "didn't you?"

"Oh, fuck!" Mika said.

"Jesus!" David said. "Am I the only one who wants to have fun right now?"

Lightning flashed across the playground, and I stumbled back, my ears ringing and my thoughts screaming that it couldn't be true.

They wouldn't do this to me.

Rain bled through my skin and into my bones, and everyone was still shouting around me. But I couldn't hear them anymore. Because Mika and David—they were my best friends, my focal point, the entire reason I was...me.

And just like that, they were gone.

CHAPTER 12
TUESDAY

———

04 : 12 : 36 : 22
DAYS HOURS MINS SECS

THE CEMETERY WAS DARK AND FAMILIAR in the rain. The worst kind of déjà vu.

I raced down wet paths, trying to ignore the ripped-open feeling in my chest. The feeling of being torn out from the inside.

Oh. And the crying. I tried to stop the crying.

I tried to believe this wasn't happening.

Mika wouldn't hook up with David, because she knew how I felt about him. And David wouldn't hook up with Mika because he was—mine. Not mine exactly, but my possibility. He saw me the way I wanted to be seen. He made me *feel* seen.

"Hey!" Someone was shouting, splashing through the puddles behind me. *"Hey."* Jamie grabbed the sleeve of my T-shirt. He was panting and his hair lay in damp, heavy strands against his neck. The rain fell in steady curtains now, separating us from the edges of the cemetery. From the rest of Tokyo.

"You followed me."

"Yeah," he said, still panting. "I saw you running across the football field. I went to see if Mika and everyone knew what had happened, but it was like the Council of Elrond up there. You know," he rambled, "before Frodo agrees to take the ring."

"Huh?"

"Jesus!" He bent over. "What did you do to your knees?"

I gazed down. Watery red streaks were running down my calves. "It was the fence. It's fine now."

"Yeah, it's really not," Jamie said. "We should get you some Band-Aids."

"Is there something you want?" I asked. He shook his head, and I realized he couldn't hear me over the rain. *"WHAT DO YOU WANT FROM ME?"*

"Nothing." He held on to his neck with one hand. "Just to help."

"Fine. Whatever." My feet were drowning in my shoes, and my clothes were suctioned to my skin, but I could barely feel it. I could barely feel any of it.

"Here." He shoved something at me. It was a candy bar, one of the Meiji milk-chocolate ones with the strawberry center. "This was in the pile of stuff Mika and I bought. I grabbed it for you."

"Thanks."

"Sorry it's kind of wet."

It was wet. The cardboard wrapper was so soggy, I thought it might disintegrate.

"Come on," he said. "Let's go to the train station. You realize you're going in the wrong direction, right?"

"I know where I'm going."

"Sophia?" He put both hands on my shoulders, and I blinked, surprised. It was strange that Mika and David were gone but that Jamie was here. Standing close enough that I could see his freckles and the green in his eyes. Their gold and brown flecks reminded me of calligraphy strokes. "Please try to think clearly," he said. "You're freaking me out a little."

"You don't get it." I squeezed the chocolate bar in both hands. "I knew this was going to happen. I knew I was going to lose them. But not"—my voice went hoarse—"not like this."

His face filled with pity. "It's okay," he said. "We all build someone up in our heads. We all fall for someone who hurts us."

"Is that what you did? Did you build Mika up in your head? Did Mika hurt you?"

"What?" He let go of my shoulders and took a step back. "Do you think I have a crush on Mika?"

"Please," I said. "Everyone knows you do."

"And by 'everyone,' you mean?"

"Me," I said. "David. And also Caroline."

He raised an eyebrow.

"You know what?" I waved the chocolate bar menacingly at his face. "I don't care. I don't want a detailed report on your feelings for Mika. They are what they are, and that's fine. But are you really telling me you don't have a problem with the fact that David and Mika have been sleeping together? *Sleeping together?*"

His tone was firm. "I'm telling you I don't have a crush on Mika."

"Well, why NOT? What's wrong with Mika?" Now I was yelling.

"Nothing." He pushed his hands all the way through his now soaking-wet hair. "Why are you mad at me?"

"I'm not mad at you."

He crossed his arms. "Bullshit."

"I'm not mad at you! You're harmless. You—you bring me candy."

"Which you should eat, by the way," he said. "It might make you feel better."

"Stop being nice!" I snapped. "You're making it difficult for me to express my rage."

"Seriously. I don't mind. Express away."

He sounded so earnest, it jolted me out of my anger. I wiped the mess of rain and tears from my face. "No," I said. "You didn't do anything wrong."

He started pacing. "Yeah, I did. I'm a total jackass. And I'm sorry, too. I'm sorry I chased you out here. Tonight and—and that other time. I'm sorry I was such a dick about you and David. I'm sorry I made you not want to talk to me for the last three years."

"It's fine, Jamie. Seriously."

He stopped pacing and stood in front of me again. His

eyes were pleading, and his cheeks were flushed. I wondered if his neck felt warm. I wondered why I was wondering that. "It's really not," he said. "I was pissed off because I thought you had a crush on David and that I was just some little dweeb you put up with because you had to. And then I sent that text, and it was all downhill from there because I went to boarding school, and then I got kicked out."

"How?" I asked. "How could you get kicked out? It just doesn't seem possible."

He sighed. "I got kicked out because I failed a couple of my classes. I failed *most* of my classes. And I did that because I've been fucking miserable for the last three years. Here's my summary of the last three years: They were the worst. And I'm sorry, all right? I really am sorry."

I could feel tears tracking down my cheeks again, the warmth of them dissipating in the cool rain. "But you were right. I did flirt with David. I was pathetic."

"Yeah, you definitely weren't." He nudged my hand with his. "Please. At least eat this. It's gonna melt."

I ripped back the cardboard and foil on the candy bar and broke off a piece. It did taste good. Like fake strawberry. Like the past four years in Japan.

"Is it true?" I asked. "What David said?"

He paused. "About me being adopted?"

I nodded.

He glanced down and scuffed the ground with his toe. "Yeah. That's true."

"How did David know?"

Jamie shrugged. "Mika must have told him."

"She never told me."

He shrugged again. I broke off another piece of chocolate and shoved it into his open hand. For a moment, the rest of the night felt vague, smudgy and uncertain compared with the vividness of my fingers on his wrist, of the rain falling between us, steady as a pulse.

"Jamie," I said, my hand still on top of his. "I think we should catch our train."

———

"Junior fucking year." Mika scrunches a plastic wrapper in her hands. "Well, this is gonna be a whirlpool of misery."

We're hanging out on the steps of the T-Cad station, eating breakfast and killing the last ten minutes of summer vacation.

David brought his new road bike, and he's riding it up and down the street.

"Bullshit!" he yells. "Two more years and we're out of here, kids."

"One more year for me," I say. I'm ripping my melon bread into pieces, dividing the parts with crystallized sugar on top from the ones without.

"Ugh," Mika scowls. "First Jamie, now you. You're all going to leave me alone with that asshole."

"You shut your dirty mouth," David says and turns the bike.

"We have to take the SATs this year," she says. "And my parents are making me take five goddamned AP classes."

"You should have my parents," David says. "They don't give a crap."

Mika flips him off.

"Hey!" He puts his foot down and stops in front of us. "You know what we should do this year? We should get Sofia a boyfriend."

"What?" I start blushing like crazy. "Why?"

"You need one," David says. "It's the law."

I try to think of something flirty to say back, but all this boyfriend talk has thrown me off my game. "Um, no, I don't date. It's too mushy, too needy, too"—I paw the air in front of me—"touchy."

"Oh no." Mika pushes down her sunglasses and peers at me over the top of them. "Not touchy."

I toss a piece of melon bread into her lap. "You know what I mean."

David sits on the step below mine. I resist the urge to fidget with my hair. Mika talked me into dyeing it platinum blond the other night, but I'm starting to regret it. I feel so obvious. So "look-at-me!"

Also, I'm pretty sure I smell like bleach.

"You have to at least make out with someone," David says. "Before the year is over." He puts out his hand like he wants me to shake it. I regard it warily.

"This can't honestly matter to you."

"Of course it matters! You're my friend, and you're cute, and you deserve to be made out with."

"You really are revolting, David," Mika says. "You know that?"

David takes my hand in his and moves it lazily up and down. My heart sputters pathetically. He wouldn't touch my hand like this if he was just joking around. He wouldn't hold on for these few extra seconds—his grip somehow loose and firm at the same time—if he didn't mean anything by it.

"And if I have to do it myself," he whispers, "then so be it."

CHAPTER 13
WEDNESDAY

———

03 : 22 : 53 : 07
DAYS HOURS MINS SECS

I WOKE UP ON TOP OF MY COVERS, still wearing all black. It was raining again. Not End of Days rain like the night before, but rain nonetheless. I held my watch above my head and stared at the seconds blinking uselessly away. It was one in the afternoon, but what the hell did that matter? A day isn't even what we think it is—the earth rotates on its axis every 23.93 hours, not every 24. My entire concept of this week was false.

Carefully, I climbed onto my desk, my scraped knees still throbbing, and pushed open the window. Drops of water smacked against the windowsill. I heard a train sluicing toward the station and a few indignant crows rustling their wings in the alley below. The skin of my arms prickled. It wasn't just raining—it was cold.

This is an alternate universe. I have discovered a wormhole.

When I was a kid, my dad would go on these long theoretical rants about wormholes, trying to explain them to me. I wished I could call him, even though it was practically the middle of the night his time. I wished I could ask him some basic physics question and listen as he launched into another lecture about time and the universe—explaining how time wasn't actually this all-powerful force but a variable. Something that could be changed.

I guess that's why I'd made this stupid countdown. Because I wanted to hold on to the time I had left here. Because I wanted to separate good-bye from all the moments—the *better* moments—that came before it. It was my own little scientific experiment, to try to contain that one second when everything I cared about would suddenly vanish.

But that was bullshit. I couldn't control losing Mika and David. I couldn't control how it ripped and altered the fabric of my universe. How it was like...like losing a leg. Like falling off the monkey bars. Like falling, period. They were my *best friends*.

They were.

And now I felt the way I used to feel before I met them. Empty and small.

Alone.

But on the other hand—the other seriously weird, confusing hand—there was Jamie. Jamie, who'd been gone for good. Jamie, who was freckles and moving limbs and a voice like warmed-up honey. When I thought about that, something inside my chest unclenched. The massive Mika-and-David-shaped hole in my life shrank as I thought about him riding the train with me to my station, talking to me the whole time. About boarding school, about his flight back to Tokyo, even about the movie.

"I wasn't supposed to be cast in it," he said. "That's fun fact number one. The book takes place in North Carolina, and they filmed some of it near my grandparents' place. Fun fact number two is that the director actually wanted my grandfather to have a cameo, but the Famous Wyatt Foster would have nothing to do with it. So they gave me a role instead."

It was way past midnight when we got to my station, which meant he couldn't get another train to his place. He had to take a cab home.

"I'll give you money," I said when we were standing near the station exit.

He shook his head. His hair had started to dry and turn back into curls. He shoved his hands in his pockets so I couldn't hand him the damp thousand-yen bills I was holding. "Can't let you do that, I'm afraid. Anyway, my parents gave me 'emergencies only' money."

"Your parents," I groaned. "It's already so late. They're going to kill you."

"It's fine," he said. "I'm alive and I didn't get kicked out of the T-Cad, so tonight is all victory as far as they're concerned. Besides, Mika and I have this deal where she won't make me go home alone. She'll wait for me in the lobby and walk me up, and my parents won't be able to freak out because they love her."

The thought of Mika waiting for Jamie, helping him,

made my stomach pitch. "Please don't tell her you were with me," I said.

He glanced down, sheepish. "I think she's probably guessed."

"In that case, don't tell her I yelled at you."

"Are you kidding?" He gave me a half smile. "That was my favorite part."

"Jamie," I said. "Please."

He paused, then held out a hand for me to shake. "I won't tell her a thing."

In a fit of madness, I'd almost told him to stay at my house. He could have slept on a futon on the floor, and the world wouldn't have seemed so empty and vast and terrifying.

I wrapped my arms around myself as cold rain splashed through the open window.

Mika and David were gone, and it was like I was losing air. I was losing gravity. I was already losing Tokyo, the lights fading around me one at a time.

Until I thought about Jamie—my hand on his, the strange, familiar sound of his voice in my ear—and the lights flickered back to life.

———

Mom had gone to work hours ago, but she'd left a note stuck to the fridge. *Cleaning out office—eat whatever you can find in the kitchen, miss you.*

I missed her, too. That was probably pathetic, but it was true—I missed my mom. I stood by the fridge, listening to rain hitting houses with paper-thin walls, to the distant ding of a bicycle bell. Dorothea Brooke came over and butted her head against my calf. I scraped my hands through my hair, fingernails digging at my scalp, and said, "I'm going to clean my goddamned room!"

I grabbed a box of trash bags from the linen closet and started filling them with stuff. A couple of old tests, a bottle of half-dried nail polish, a doodle Mika had drawn of stick-figure Sophia standing next to a unicorn. (At the bottom, it said, *happy birthday i got you a fucking UNICORN.*) The more I threw away, the more it started to feel—right. *Good*, actually. Like breathing clean air. Like pedaling a bike until it pedals itself. I hurled stuff in by the armful now. A FUTURE ASTROPHYSICIST T-shirt with a watermelon-ice-cream stain on it, a pack of Pokémon trading cards, a stack of torn Paris museum guides.

I was about six bags in when Alison burst through my door.

"You woke me up," she said. She was wearing fraying black leggings, a white T-shirt, and a pair of oversize tortoiseshell eyeglasses I think used to belong to my grandmother. Her skin was pale, and for the first time all summer, it occurred to me that she'd lost weight.

"Jesus," I said. "When did you transform into Edward Scissorhands?"

"You woke me up," she said again. "It sounds like you're herding *cats* in here."

"That actually makes no sense."

"God, and your window's open. Do you not realize it's freezing out?" She shimmied around my bed and crawled onto my desk.

I almost threw away a crumpled photo of eight-year-old Alison and six-year-old me playing with kitten Dorothea Brooke—but stopped myself just in time.

"Seriously." Alison yanked the window shut. "What are you doing with all that?"

"Downsizing," I said.

"Don't be stupid," she said, giving me her best Grown-Up face. "You've hoarded that junk for years."

"Exactly. It's junk. That's why I'm throwing it away."

"You sound like you're on something," Alison said. "Don't throw it all away. You just don't want to deal with it."

I stopped what I was doing and lay facedown on a pile of laundry.

"Are you hungover?" she asked.

"Not possible," I mumbled into the clothes. "I don't even drink."

"Good," she said. "You shouldn't. You're seventeen."

"*You* drink. You're nineteen."

"So? My friends are in their twenties. Your friends are twelve."

I rolled my eyes, then realized she couldn't see my face. I sat up, and Alison and the cat were peering at me. Intently. Alison adjusted her glasses.

"Are those even real?" I asked.

"Is that even the point?" she asked. "You're acting strange. You're throwing away your lifetime collection of useless crap. Did something happen to you?"

Yes. My best friend is screwing my other best friend, who, by the way, I have an enormous and unfathomable crush on, and they aren't my best friends anymore, and, if I really think about it, they probably never were.

"Nothing at all," I said.

"That's it." Alison reached for a bottle of sakura perfume and sprayed me with it. D. B. sprinted for the door. "We're going out."

I coughed. "We're not going out. You haven't left the house all summer."

"I've left the house."

"To go where?"

"Irrelevant." She sprayed me again. "Come on. Get up. Wash your face. Make yourself look less depressing."

"You're one to talk."

"No insults!" She sprayed me two more times. "I'm your goddamned sister."

CHAPTER 14
WEDNESDAY

————

03 : 21 : 13 : 36
DAYS HOURS MINS SECS

BEFORE WE WENT OUT, I changed into a red skirt, a white-and-red polka-dot blouse, and a black cardigan with a Totoro button pinned on it. (It wasn't the one Jamie had got for me, but it made me think of him.) Alison coerced me into sitting on the edge of the bathtub so she could put her favorite red lipstick on me as well.

"It feels like my lips are coated in Play-Doh," I said.

"Considering you have a fetish for dressing like a clown," she said, "it's amazing you've never worn this stuff before."

It was still drizzling when we got outside, so I put up my black umbrella with a print of green and blue birds on it. "Where are we going?" I asked as we walked to the train station. The city smelled fresh in the rain. Like all the stale humidity had been replaced with a pile of wet leaves.

"To be revealed," she said.

"Do you know how to get there?" I asked. "Do you remember how to buy train tickets?"

"This teenage sarcasm thing is already getting old," she

said. But when we got to the station, it turned out she *had* forgotten which station we were going to. I looked it up on my phone, calculated the price, and punched the location into the machine for her.

"Tokyo Tower?" I said, fishing out the magnetic strip of paper. "Really?"

"God, Sophia, I'm trying to be meaningful here."

Dad used to take us to Tokyo Tower when we were kids, on rainy days when we were bored and antsy. It's one of the few memories I have of the first five years of my life, when we all lived on the same continent together like an actual human family. He liked Tokyo Tower because it was modeled after the Eiffel Tower. Alison and I liked it because it was painted bright orange. We'd never been to Paris back then, and Dad used to describe it to us in detail. Cars whizzing around the Arc de Triomphe, gold statues of men on horses, bridges draped regally over a wide, curving river.

It was strange that Alison had chosen a place that reminded me—that reminded both of us—of Dad. But there we were, waiting in line for an elevator to take us to the observation deck. There were a decent number of people in line with us. Most of them tourists.

"Have you talked to Dad recently?" I asked.

"Yeah," she said, rolling the sleeves of her hoodie up to her elbows. "We talk every night. He reads me bedtime stories, and I call him if I have nightmares."

"Don't be so hard on him." I pulled my cardigan around my stomach.

We got in an elevator. A woman wearing a navy-blue uniform held the door and bowed as we walked in. I smiled awkwardly and bowed back. There were long windows in the elevator, so we could see the inner workings of the tower as we rode up. It was like being inside an orange spiderweb.

"Have *you* talked to him?" Alison asked.

"No," I admitted. "He didn't call the other night. There's probably no phone service at the vacation house."

"Sure there isn't. And I bet there's no Wi-Fi, either. Or a landline."

"I don't want to talk about this," I said.

"Fine," she said. "Me neither."

She sounded relieved. So was I. Alison and I couldn't talk about Dad—all it did was make us fight.

The windows in the observation deck were everywhere, forming a huge circle, a 360-degree view. There was a small glass panel in the floor where you could stand and stare at a very distant slab of sidewalk. A girl in high heels wobbled tentatively over it and clung to her boyfriend's arm while he laughed.

Alison and I stopped at a computer where you could bring up detailed pictures of the view. She tapped the screen a few times, then got bored. "All of this can be seen on Google Maps," she said. "We didn't have to go outside."

"Whatever you say, Howard Hughes."

She twisted her lips to the side. "How did you even make that reference?"

I shrugged. "Mika has a thing for young Leonardo DiCaprio."

I crossed my arms again and held my stomach tighter. The thought of Mika made my insides squirm.

"It used to be more impressive." Alison leaned toward the window so that her nose almost touched the glass. The city was saturated with buildings that were white and gray and brown with miniature streets gridded between and toy trees filling the gaps. A rainy haze gave everything indistinct edges.

"This place is mediocre since the Skytree opened," I said. "It's, like, twice this height."

"I can't believe we paid for a mediocre tower," Alison said. "Let's at least eat something."

There was a café one level below, where Alison got coffee and french fries and I got an ice-cream sundae. We didn't really talk once we were sitting and eating.

If David and Mika were here, we'd watch the people in line and try to guess what they'd order. David would kick me under the table and raise his eyebrows when I kicked him back. If David and Mika were here...

But then I remembered that particular "if" was impossible. A non-if. Tears pounded behind my eyes. I dropped my lipstick-stained spoon back into my bowl.

"Goddamn it," Alison said. "Are you going to tell me what happened or not?"

"Nothing happened."

"Like hell it didn't." Alison stabbed the air with a french

131

fry. "You're moping all over your ice cream. You look like crap."

"I look like crap? You're really going to lead with that?"

She fixed me with her most resolute stare, daring me to blink first. "You were fine yesterday, but today you're falling apart at the seams. Elaborate."

"Why don't you tell *me* what happened to you?"

She blinked. "This isn't about me."

"Really?" I balled up a napkin in my lap. "You spend all summer being *Girl, Interrupted*, and this isn't about you? You get a free pass from talking about your shit?"

Alison sat back. "This is about you. I took you out. I'm making an effort."

"So make an effort," I said. "Tell me what happened with your girlfriend. Or tell Mom, at least. Do you even realize how much she worries about you? You completely cut us off!"

She crossed her legs, one foot banging the underside of the table. "I did not."

"Please," I spat. "What about your friends at the T-Cad? What about Dad? You cut people off all the goddamned time."

"Jesus," she said. "Just back off, okay? We can't all live in naive little Sophia World. Sometimes you leave people, and then you move on."

I laughed, but it came out harsh. "Because look at you. Moving on like a champion."

"At least I know when to let go. God, have you seen

yourself recently? You idolize Dad even though he *abandoned* us. Which is pretty much the number one thing a parent isn't supposed to do. And! You wear that ridiculous watch like you're still a—"

"A kid?" And now I was shouting. Loud enough that the two women having lunch at the next table flinched. "I'm still a kid? Because I don't want to lose everyone who loves me? Because I don't want to spend my whole fucking life finding people and then *moving on from them*?!"

The muscles on either side of her jaw twitched. "I don't understand why you're doing this. I was just trying to find out if you're okay."

I wasn't okay—of course I wasn't okay. The tears had broken down the doors. I was really crying now. I was, as a matter of fact, falling apart. At the seams.

"Why did you even bring me here?" I asked. "Are you trying to make me upset about Dad, too? Are you trying to remind me how worthless and alone I am?"

"Don't be selfish," Alison said, more annoyed than frustrated now. "I'm here, too. Worthless, check. Alone, check."

"No." I wiped tears from my mouth, and my hand came back smudged red. "I'm not like you."

"What do you want me to say to that?" Alison said.

I stood up and pushed my tray across the table. "Nothing, okay? I just—I don't want you to say anything."

I went into the bathroom, found an empty stall, and sat on top of the toilet seat. There was a speaker mounted on the wall to my right—an Otohime—and I waved my hand in front of it until the polite sound of running water began. I cried so hard, holding my Musée d'Orsay tote against my chest, curled over it. I cried until my throat was scratchy and my head throbbed. Until I was sure Alison wasn't coming to get me.

Until I was sure I was alone.

CHAPTER 15
WEDNESDAY

———

03 : 18 : 54 : 29
DAYS HOURS MINS SECS

MY PHONE STARTED RINGING.

I sat up and rubbed my eyes. It was probably Alison, calling to tell me to grow up or pull myself together or some hypocritical bullshit like that. I dug around in my tote and gripped the phone in my hand, waiting to see if the muffled ringing would stop.

It did. Thank God. I'd already had my daily quota of my sister's judgmental self-righteousness. She'd been like that practically my whole life, ever since Dad left. Although, in fairness, it was better when we were little kids. She was more protective of me then. We'd walk hand in hand through Charles de Gaulle airport every January, Alison shooting death glares at anyone who tutted at me for crying. But as we got older, things got worse.

She said she was sick of how I put up with Dad. She said he was a Russian nesting doll of disappointment, each disappointment leading to another even when you thought it wasn't physically possible. The phone calls that never happened, the sporadic e-mails, the summers he said we could come stay with him until he decided to visit friends in Vienna instead. The angry whispered phone calls we'd overhear Mom having with him late at night. The way she punctuated every word when she said he was *letting. Us. Down. Again.*

Things changed after he got remarried. He moved into a house outside the city center, in an area full of small brick houses and kids who'd bike around the quartier all day long. He never backed out of having us to visit. He called us once a week. At least.

And then, four years ago, when Mom said we were moving back to Tokyo, my parents gave me a choice: I could go to Tokyo with Mom, or I could live in Paris instead. Dad and Sylvie had a decent-sized house, and there was an American school I could go to, and that way I could stay in one place until I graduated.

I'd chosen Paris. Because it was the only thing that hadn't changed since my parents got divorced. And I had this theory that maybe—*possibly*—it could also be home. Until the babies. Until Mom had to sit me down and explain it wasn't going to work out. Not then, anyway.

And even though I wished it wouldn't get to me, it totally got to me. I'd wanted a life in France. I'd wanted to slice out the times I'd spent with Dad—watching Hitchcock movies, eating falafel in the Marais, hanging outside cathedrals in the evenings waiting for the bells to ring— and make those times last beyond four weeks a year.

And that, Alison couldn't understand. She couldn't understand why I'd pick Dad, why I'd even imagine picking him.

"You realize he's not our actual parent," she'd say for the hundredth time. "Just because he acts like this Cool Guy, that doesn't mean he is. That doesn't change the fact that he ditched us in the first place."

"He didn't," I'd reply. "He left Mom. They left each other."

Someone else came into the bathroom, yanking me from my thoughts. I took a deep breath and walked out. Thankfully, Alison wasn't in the café anymore, or on the observation deck. I stood by a window and closed my eyes, imagining the gray buildings and the traffic and the rain outside, all of it utterly silent behind glass.

A part of me wanted to go find Jamie, even though I knew that was crazy. But I could feel the strings connecting me to my life snapping one by one. I was floating in the air, untethered, and I needed something to grab onto.

My phone started to ring again. This time, I scrambled to pull it out of my bag, Jamie's name thrumming in my thoughts. But it wasn't him or Alison or Mika or even my mom.

It was David.

———

By the time I got to Shibuya, it was after six. *The real reason you're here,* I told myself, *is you don't want to be alone, you pathetic, needy loser.*

When I'd answered David's phone call back at Tokyo Tower, the plan had been to hang up on him in twenty seconds. But then he told me that Caroline had dumped him. Then he told me, in an even sadder voice—one that was shaky and nearly transparent—that he wanted to see me. That he missed me.

And that had broken down my last defense.

David was at Smiley's, an America-themed restaurant that served a plethora of huge drinks and many-layered hamburgers and had black-and-white photos of old Hollywood stars covering the walls. It was in a knot of narrow streets too small for cars to drive down and crowded with konbinis, karaoke places, cafés, and boutiques.

David was on the second floor of the restaurant, at a table with his back to the window. A glass of something pink and frothy sat in front of him—and Jamie sat across from him.

I actually gasped. This had to be an alternate universe. Jamie would never hang out with David, because a) David was a jackass and b) he was a jackass who'd just blabbed to everyone that Jamie was adopted.

Thinking about last night, I felt a fresh plunge in my stomach: *My best friends lied to me; they aren't my best friends anymore.* To ground myself, I focused on Jamie. He was wearing a short-sleeved red T-shirt, and there was a black coat thrown over the back of his chair. The rain had dampened his hair, which was both endearing and frustrating.

Did he consistently keep his hair half-dry? Was that how he made people like him?

"Sofa!" David waved frantically with both hands even though I was standing next to him. "I'm not drinking, see? This is a nonalcoholic smoothie. James has one, too!"

"There's fruit in it," Jamie said. "It's nutritious." He stirred his drink with a straw and smiled up at me. I tried to smile back but ended up glowering instead. I mean, Jesus Christ. It was like they were on a tropical cruise together.

"Sit down," David said.

"Can't." I pointed at the two-person table. "No chairs."

David grabbed one from the next table and dragged it over, patting the green plastic seat. "All fixed!" There was a cigarette behind one of his ears, and he didn't look miserable. He didn't look like he'd recently had his heart torn from his throat and smashed to pieces.

I shoved my umbrella under the table and sat with my bag in my lap. A few tables down, an American couple kept saying "Oh my God!" and taking pictures of their elaborate sundaes with upside-down waffle cones sitting on top.

I felt clunky and awkward. Makeup sat in sticky clumps on my face, and my hair was frizzy from the rain. Jamie kept tapping his fingers against the dark wood of the table.

"So," David said. "What should the three of us do this evening? Karaoke?"

"I thought you were upset," I said.

David snorted and leaned back on his chair, tipping it onto two legs. "Because of Caroline?"

"What about Mika?" I asked.

"Pah." He waved his hand like he was swatting away a bug. "She's just pissed off. Or not talking to me, or something."

"She seemed pretty angry last night," I said.

David shrugged, but his grin was good-natured enough. The restaurant was dim, and rain fogged up the windows, making the lights and all the buildings blurred and hazy.

"Do you want something to eat?" Jamie pushed his menu across the table.

"Thanks," I said. We briefly made eye contact, and my heart jumped. This whole situation was seriously unnerving. To my right was the boy I'd obsessed over for the last four years, the boy I'd tied up in my hope and longing until he'd hacked through all of it. To my left was—Jamie. I could feel his tentative gaze on my cheek.

David dropped his chair back to the ground. "Anyway," he said, leaning forward to make eye contact with me, "you're all dressed up, Sofa. And look. Look at your lipstick."

The couple near us held up their phones to take more pictures of the restaurant. I fiddled with the laminated corner of the menu. "Can't. It's on my face."

He clapped his hands and laughed. He was trying to banter, but I couldn't match his enthusiasm for it. I examined a picture of an avocado-topped cheeseburger instead.

"You see?" David said. "This. This is why you can't leave."

"Why?" I asked.

UGH! STOP ENGAGING WITH HIM, SOPHIA! Why was four years of secret pining so hard to snap out of?

"Because," he said, "you're smart as hell. Because you get me."

"Yeah, well. You'll survive."

"Life is about more than surviving."

"Actually," I said, "I'm pretty sure that goes against the entire evolutionary principle of existence."

"Trust me on this, little Sofa," he said. "Life is about other people. It's about finding people you love and holding on for good."

"Yeah, because you're really skilled at that." I flicked my eyebrow up, challenging him to respond. A small smile played across his lips, and a thrill raced through me. And even though I knew it was stupid and pointless and wrong, I still loved the way he craved my attention. He reached out his hand and touched his thumb to the corner of my mouth. All the heat rushed from my cheek to my lips. "So, so weird. Sofa in lipstick—"

Crack!

David leaped out of his chair. I sat back and blinked hard. Jamie's glass was lying on its side. It had fallen and knocked into David's glass, which had knocked into David's lap. The American couple turned to gape at us.

"Fuck!" David yelled. His black pants and green polo were soaked through with smoothie.

Jamie started pulling napkins from the napkin dispenser. "Sorry. I'm an idiot."

David glared. Pink liquid pooled on the table, pieces of wilted fruit floating in it.

I pushed back my chair. "I'll get more napkins."

"I'll come with you," Jamie said.

"Not both of you," David snapped. "Sofa, you stay here."

"Jesus." Jamie gripped the back of his chair with both hands.

"What?" David asked.

Jamie leaned back, and the muscles in his throat tensed. He looked like he was bracing himself for something. "Just stop. Stop saying that."

"*What*?" David asked.

" 'Sofa.' Stop calling her that. It's offensive. It's like saying, 'Hey, you, piece of furniture, carry all my body weight for me.' "

David curled his lip. "Lay off, James. No one asked for your input."

"Jamie, please. Stop," I whispered. That American couple seemed really interested in what we were doing now. Their ice cream was starting to melt.

A waitress came by and asked if everything was okay. Jamie said something apologetic to her in Japanese, and she nodded reassuringly at him. *(Stupid, wet-haired Jamie.)* She took a dish towel from the pocket of her apron and started wiping at the mess. Jamie asked for a handful of new napkins and helped. David stormed off to the bathroom.

I shoved my hand in front of Jamie. "Give me some."

Worry filled his eyes. "Are you okay?"

"Fan-fucking-tastic." I shook my upturned palm at him. "Gimme." I started wiping up David's side of the table, keeping my head bent so the American couple couldn't see how red my face was.

I couldn't believe I'd flirted with David like that. In front of Jamie, of all freaking people! The humiliation of being duped by David (yet again) was bad enough without adding Jamie-as-witness to the mix. *I mean, what the hell is he even doing here?*

David came back from the bathroom just as the waitress was leaving. "I have to go somewhere and change," he said. "This pink shit is staining."

"That's fine," I said. "I'm going home."

"Why?" David asked. "What's wrong? Don't tell me you're pissed off at me as well."

"You probably shouldn't yell," Jamie murmured.

"I'm not yelling!"

Jamie crossed his arms and shrugged. He was standing a little bit in front of me. "You're not not-yelling."

"Oh." David glanced between us and sneered. "Oh, *now I get it.*"

"Get what?" I asked.

He pointed at Jamie. "All this fake chivalry. All this

bumbling good-guy crap. I should have noticed. Baby James still has the hots for Sofa."

I stared hard at the table, at the wet, glossy swirls where the smoothie and stranded strawberries had been. A Beatles song was playing over the restaurant speakers, and I wished someone would turn it up.

"That's not—" Jamie said.

"Any of your business," I said.

"Don't take his side, Sofa," David snapped. He rubbed his temples like he was exhausted. "God. Girls and their drama. It's all so stupid."

I sucked in a sharp breath. "*Girls* and their drama?"

David threw up his hands. "You, Mika, Caroline—you all do it. You're incapable of hanging out and having fun without making it about some boy who likes you, or doesn't like you, or whatever. All this pointless, dramatic bullshit."

My jaw clenched. I saw the last twenty-four hours in snapshots: Caroline crying as she walked through the cemetery, David telling us Jamie's biggest secret, satisfaction in his voice. I saw Mika telling me not to trust him. And I saw all the girls he'd broken up with over the years, how some of them had sought me out to ask me what they'd done wrong, why they'd lost him.

"David," I said quietly. "Please know that when I say this, I do not say it lightly. You. Are. *Deluded*."

He raised one eyebrow.

I jabbed Jamie's shoulder. "And you're an idiot!"

"Me?" he asked.

"Yes! You knocked that milk shake over on purpose."

"It was a smoothie," he said timidly.

"Whatever!" I turned back to David. "But you. You listen. Because this is important. You can't hurt people and expect them to take the hit. You can't call them *dramatic* when they get upset *because you used them and lied to them.* That is not a girl thing. That is a you thing!"

"Hey," David said, lowering his blue eyes and then looking up at me again. All contrite and placating. "Sofa..."

"No." I took a breath, deeper than the one before. "I'm the one who had a crush on you, and you're the one who led me on. But whatever. Joke's on me, right? You're covered in smoothie, but I'm the idiot in this scenario. The biggest freaking idiot for—for ever thinking you could like me back. And, whatever, it's exhausting. This is all exhausting."

I tossed the used napkins onto the chair and walked away, swerving around tables, ignoring stares, heading to the door that led down to the street. The music over the loudspeakers changed to something new: Elvis.

As I got to the door, I spun around. "For God's sake, Jamie!" I shouted. "Are you coming or not?"

CHAPTER 16
WEDNESDAY

———

03 : 16 : 17 : 52
DAYS HOURS MINS SECS

"WOW," JAMIE KEPT SAYING. "WOW. That was incredible. Really incredible. You were like an Avenger or something! You *avenged* yourself."

We were on Inokashira-dori, the main road that ran toward Shibuya Station. I could see the crossing in the distance. It wasn't raining anymore, but the streets were dark and slick. Water sprayed out from under the tires of passing cars, and the air felt cool and metallic.

"Hey." I stopped walking. "I have a question for you."

"Okay."

I shoved him. "Why the *hell* were you hanging out with David?"

Jamie seemed embarrassed but didn't answer right away. We were standing outside H&M, a steady rush of people going in and out of the fluorescent entrance even though it was after seven. Someone walked past us in a black raincoat, which made me realize that Jamie had forgotten his. And that I'd forgotten my umbrella.

"He called," Jamie said finally. "Mika wasn't picking up her phone, and he wanted me to check on her. I told him she wasn't home, and then he invited me out."

"That doesn't explain why you went."

He rubbed the palms of his hands together. There was an anxious crease between his eyebrows. "I figured you'd be there."

I pulled my bag around me and hugged it tight. We were blocking people's way on the sidewalk, but I didn't care.

"Was she really not home?" I asked.

"No," Jamie said. "She just didn't want to talk to him."

I relaxed my grip on the bag. "She doesn't want to talk to me, either. She hasn't tried to call me all day."

"I think she's worried you're mad at her."

"*Duh*. But she could at least try. I don't want to leave things like this."

"You won't." Jamie nudged the tip of my shoe with his own.

A bus flew past us, hurtling toward the crossing. Speakers attached to it blasted a new J-pop hit that warbled and distorted as it moved away. I pressed my lips together and tasted lipstick, which creeped me out.

Jamie nudged my shoe again. "How are your knees?"

"My knees?"

"Yeah, they still look sore. Do you need more Band-Aids?"

I shook my head.

"Well, okay," he said. "But you must be hungry, what with all the kicking ass and taking names."

"I don't know," I said. "I'm a little hungry. I guess."

He grinned, and in the incandescent light of the store behind him, his green eyes seemed to flash. "This is a hunger only ramen can cure."

———

Jamie, as it turned out, was pretentious about ramen.

"That place is way too big," he said when we passed a restaurant with floor-to-ceiling windows and two long counters with rows of plastic seating. "It's industrial. A ramen shop shouldn't seat more than five people at a time. The steam from the kitchen should get into your sinuses."

We found a small one tucked around the corner from the station, beneath an overpass. It was windowless with only one booth and three counter seats.

"This," Jamie said as I pulled the paper-screen door shut behind us, "is what I'm talking about."

We put money into a machine at the front of the shop and pressed buttons for everything we wanted to order. It spat out tickets for each item. A miso ramen for me and a miso ramen with extra seaweed and two plates of *gyoza*— vegetable and chicken—for Jamie.

The booth was free, so we slid in.

"This is officially what I missed the most," Jamie said. He started pouring glasses of water from a plastic jug on the table. "Well, almost the most. You can have some of the gyoza if you want. Or if you want to order anything else..."

I sat back against the plastic of the booth and rubbed my eyes. The air was warm and salty, and I could feel it in my pores. Jamie was right; ramen shops were better this way. But they weren't what I would miss most. Ever since the Imperial Palace, I'd been cataloging the thousand small things I wished I didn't have to leave behind. The Christmas lights at Takashimaya Times Square, the small row of persimmon trees growing in one of the alleys behind my house, hot *yakitori* from the stand by Yoyogi-Uehara Station.

An older woman wearing a heavy blue apron came out of the kitchen to take our tickets.

"I have a question," I said as soon as she walked away. "And just tell me the truth, okay? Is it a southern thing?"

"Is what a southern thing?" He pushed a glass across the table. I caught it and took a sip. The water was cold, and it made my teeth buzz. I drank it all in two gulps, so Jamie poured me another glass.

"You know," I said. "The chivalry thing. The being-the-good-guy thing. Is it because you're southern?"

He snorted. "You wouldn't say that if you knew the rest of my family."

"You don't have to do anything for me," I said. "I'm not going to have a meltdown, you know."

"I know that." The worry crease appeared between his eyebrows again. That crease was starting to become familiar. "And you're wrong. You and David are both wrong. I'm not the good guy."

"Of course you are."

His voice dropped. "If I were the good guy, I wouldn't have sent that stupid text. I wouldn't have left without talking to you again."

I shook my head. "That wasn't all your fault, Jamie. I'm the one who said all that stuff about you. About how you were a—"

"A twitchy little loser." Jamie cleared his throat. "Yeah. I remember."

"Exactly! And I threw your good-bye present, like, right in your face."

He smirked, and his eyes skirted the Totoro pin on my sweater. This weird, tingly warmth rushed through me.

The waitress came back and set two small blue-and-white cups in front of us. They were filled with hot tea that smelled like rice and autumn leaves. I leaned over and let the curling steam evaporate on my face. When I glanced up, Jamie was still watching me, his eyes thoughtful and searching. I could have pretended not to notice, but I met his gaze full on. My pulse started pounding in my ears.

"Can I ask you something?" he said, leaning across the table.

"Yeah," I said, leaning forward a little to meet him. "I think you've earned the right."

"That watch you've been wearing—is it the same one you had when we were kids?"

"Oh." I sat back and grabbed my wrist.

"Crap," Jamie said. "Sorry."

"No," I said. "It's no big deal."

He nodded, clearly relieved.

"It was a gift from my dad." I placed my hands back on the table and stretched out my fingers. "You remember how he lives in Paris?"

Jamie nodded again.

"When I was a kid, I hated going back and forth. I used to be really—depressed about it, I guess. That might not be the right word. I don't know how else to describe it."

Depressed. Or maybe just sunk so far inside myself that no one could get to me. Not my mom, not my teachers.

Nobody.

Like how I'd felt when I found out Mika and David had been lying to me. Like the floor was dissolving beneath my feet and there was nothing I could do to stop the fall that would follow.

"So your dad got you a watch," Jamie said carefully.

"Yeah." I shook off the dark and sticky feelings and clicked the button that switched the display. "Dad would set it so that it told me how long I had until I saw him again. That way, when I got sad, I'd know time was bringing us closer together, not further apart. I think he was trying to make me feel less powerless or something. But honestly, the only thing I wanted was to go live there."

"Really?" Jamie said. "In Paris over Tokyo?"

"I don't know." I folded and unfolded the corner of a chopstick wrapper. "I'd definitely pick Tokyo now. But when I was little, I would've gone to Paris in a heartbeat. I used to tell all my teachers I was from there, even though I couldn't speak French."

Jamie laughed.

"And I've visited every year since I was five. Since—my dad left."

Discomfort crept across his face. "Parental abandonment, I definitely get. Why'd he leave?"

I twisted my watch, hard. I hated talking about this. It always made Dad sound like the bad guy. "We were moving to the States—my parents met here, in Tokyo. Mom had a job at a foreign university, and Dad was teaching English. He'd just graduated from college—he's, like, seven years younger than she is. They got married here, and Alison and I were born here, but then Mom got a job at Rutgers and Dad didn't want to go." I couldn't stop twisting my watch. A small blister was starting to bloom on the sensitive skin just below my palm. "But it wasn't just that. Dad didn't want to live outside France forever, and Mom didn't understand that. You know what, though? I think I do. If you had one place you totally fit, wouldn't you go? Wouldn't you *have* to?"

Jamie took hold of my wrist and gently pulled it away from my other hand.

He wasn't touching my skin or anything. Just the watch. He had smooth, trim nails and a wide thumb.

I swallowed so loud, I was sure he must have heard it. I'd definitely told him more than I'd meant to. I never really talked about my dad, and no one other than my mom and sister knew the whole watch story. Maybe I'd only told him because I was leaving—because it didn't matter as much.

Jamie held up the watch so he could read it; I moved to the edge of my seat. "Is this how long till you see your dad again?" he asked.

I shook my head. "That's how long till my flight leaves Tokyo."

The waitress came back, this time holding two deep bowls filled nearly to the lip with brown broth, noodles, and meat. She put one in front of me and the other in front of Jamie. I grabbed a set of wooden chopsticks and broke them apart. Jamie and I didn't say anything for a minute as we mixed the ingredients together: slender bamboo shoots, bright green onions, dark seaweed, and long, crimped noodles.

"I know it's weird," I said eventually. "Alison's always telling me to stop wearing it. And I really should. It's a little kid's watch."

The waitress set the plates of gyoza in the middle of the table. Jamie drizzled them with soy sauce and pushed the plate of vegetable ones closer to me.

They were delicious—warm and crispy dumplings with a filling that was almost too hot and too sweet. We polished off both plates without talking. Jamie looked like he was trying to hold the gyoza in his mouth for as long as possible. He looked like he'd been waiting to eat them for the past three years. Which, I guess, he had.

"It's not a little kid's watch," he said, swallowing his last bite. "You're not a little kid."

———

After dinner, we walked to Shibuya Station. Mom called to say she was still cleaning out her office. I said I was walking around Shibuya with Mika. I couldn't help the lie—the truth felt way too weird to say out loud. *Alternate universe*, I reminded myself. *None of this counts.*

Everyone around the station was dressed to go out. A girl with a bow on her head the size of a small street sign, a guy in bright yellow combat boots and pinstriped pants. They clustered around the Hachiko statue, then broke off into the night like satellites tracing new orbits. Jamie and I stopped at the crossing and waited for the light to change. Cars shooting by, one after the other after the other.

I studied him. Lit up by the surrounding buildings, he was blue, white, pink, and yellow. A neon constellation. He caught me staring and his face brightened. I was grateful he didn't ask if I wanted to go home then. I wouldn't have known what to say.

CHAPTER 17
THURSDAY

———

03 : 11 : 50 : 39
DAYS HOURS MINS SECS

JAMIE AND I WENT TO TOWER RECORDS and rode the glass elevator all the way to the top floor. We went to a fast-food restaurant and ordered french fries, spilling them over a tray and counting them out so we each got the same number of crispy and non-crispy ones. We stood on a street corner where the air smelled like the memory of rain, and Jamie touched my elbow and said, "So. What next?"

Midnight came and went, but we didn't catch the last train.

We didn't even try.

———

The arcade was three stories high and packed with hundreds upon hundreds of games. Best of all, it was open all night.

Jamie and I hung out by the UFO catchers. UFO catchers are those claw-machine games, the ones that are a total con in the States and slightly less of a con in Japan. With a little strategizing, I'd seen people actually win some of the vast array of prizes: Rilakkuma stuffed animals and Hello Kitty toasters and enormous boxes of candy. Jamie decided we should try to win a box of chocolate Pockys bigger than my TV.

"Don't you think we've eaten enough?" I asked.

"Still not everything in Japan, though," he said. "We must forge ahead."

"Right, of course," I said. "Win us those Pockys or the mission will be compromised."

He spared a glance from the machine to give me his biggest grin. When he turned back again, he furrowed his brow in concentration. I let my eyes trace the small bump on his nose and then move to his eyelashes, which were as pale as his hair. The game must have been frustrating, because he'd started chewing on his lower lip.

"Isn't that your phone?" he asked.

"Huh?"

"Your phone." He pointed to my bag, which was buzzing.

"Oh." *Crap! Why do I keep ogling him?!* "Yeah. It is." It was my mom, saying good night. I'd texted her a little while ago to tell her I was staying at Mika's and that I'd be back in the morning. The constant lying to my mom didn't feel like the best decision I'd made all day. But it didn't feel like the worst one, either.

I tried to hand Jamie my phone. "You should call your parents."

"Nah," he said.

I frowned. "They're going to be so pissed. They're going to excommunicate you."

He gave me a wry, amused look. "They're not the Catholic Church. I'm not Henry the Eighth."

"How can you be so casual about this?"

Jamie shrugged and pressed the red button on the machine. A claw zoomed forward from a corner of the glass case. "My parents were upset about the whole flunking-out-of-boarding-school thing, yes"—he pressed the button again and the claw whizzed to the side; it was hovering over the box of Pockys now—"but at this point, they kind of expect me to fuck up. I don't even think they mind that much. I guess they would if I were actually theirs."

The claw touched the corner of the box and scraped it. But it didn't grab on.

"Jamie," I said. "You don't mean that."

"I don't know." The game finished, and he dropped his hands by his sides.

"If you really mean that, you're stupid. Because you are theirs. Because they're *your parents*."

"Come on," Jamie said, nodding his head in the direction of another aisle.

Even though it was bizarrely unpopulated that night, the arcade still hummed with its own energy. Jamie had gone quiet. I hoped he wasn't upset with me for saying that. I hoped he didn't want to go home. Although, to be honest, it might have been better for both of us if he did. It might have saved me from feeling all these...*feelings*. The ones that made me want to stay out all night with him. To stay in this pocket of the week where time stopped breathing.

Jamie stopped at a machine, and I figured he'd fish out a few hundred-yen coins to play the game. Instead, he sat down on the floor. I sat next to him, close enough that I could smell the laundry detergent on his T-shirt. I inhaled deeply.

"I'm sorry," I said. "I shouldn't have talked about your parents like that. It's obviously none of my business."

He shrugged. "I asked about your dad. You can ask me whatever you want."

I shoved my phone into my bag, and my hand scratched against the canvas. "So tell me about them. Your parents, I mean."

He leaned his head back and closed his eyes—I could see his eyelashes moving against his cheeks. "My parents got married in their thirties. They wanted kids, but they couldn't have kids, so..." He lifted his hands helplessly. "Voilà."

"Did you ever meet her?"

"My birth mother?" he asked.

I nodded.

"Yeah, a couple of times. Once when I was three, right after the movie came out. And once when I was six."

"Did your parents know her?"

"Sort of. It was an open adoption. Lauren—that's her name—is from a town not far from where my parents grew up. But her family threw her out when they found out she was pregnant. She was seventeen."

"Jesus," I said. "That's, um, my age."

"I know," Jamie said.

I shifted uncomfortably. The stiff purple carpet felt like Styrofoam against my bare legs.

Jamie went on. "Every year, my parents sent Lauren pictures of me, and she sent me birthday cards and stuff. But my parents wanted to help her as well."

"Help her?"

"Yeah. They wanted her to go to college and make something of herself, I guess."

"So what happened?"

He knotted his hands together and held them between his knees. Jamie had always been so light and open, like he couldn't contain his emotions even if he tried. But now he seemed small and closed in. This was Jamie from a new angle, through a hidden door, and I wanted to do something for him. To help him.

"Lauren couldn't handle it," he said. "It was too much me. Me in pictures, me in a movie, for Christ's sake. Plus my parents breathing down her neck all the time." He went silent for a moment. "Anyway. She moved to Oregon. She's a dental hygienist now, I think."

"Do you talk to her at all?"

"Nope." He cleared his throat. "No one heard from her. Until last year."

"Wait." I scooted toward him. "You mean you met her again?"

He sighed. "She contacted my parents' lawyer and said she wanted to visit for Thanksgiving. She was supposed to come to my grandparents' place from the airport, but—she never showed. She freaked, I guess, and couldn't handle it."

I thought about Paris. About how much I'd wanted to live there and how heartbroken I'd been when I'd found out I couldn't. But no matter how weird things were in my family, I never doubted for a second that my mom and dad loved me.

"I'm sorry," I said, placing my hand next to his on the ground. "I can't imagine doing that. I can't imagine cutting off someone you're supposed to love."

Jamie turned suddenly to face me, his expression resolved. "But that's the thing. She wasn't supposed to love me. That's my parents. And they do, but they have all of these expectations. After last Thanksgiving, I skipped class and I totally bombed my exams. Honestly, I should have been kicked out at winter break, but the headmaster gave me another shot because my *glorious* grandparents donate so much money. Anyway, he didn't have a choice when I failed next semester, too...." He sat back again, miserably. "My parents said I didn't deserve that school. And it's like—I don't deserve their family, either. I know I don't."

A speaker nearby kept playing the same twenty seconds of a song over and over. I focused on how close our hands were, only a sliver of purple carpet separating them, and wished I could close the gap.

"Okay," he said, sitting forward. "Okay. This is important. Tell me where you want to go to college."

"What?" I laughed. "No."

"Why not? Are you worried I'll apply? Because you shouldn't worry. I already failed out of school. I'll never get anywhere in life."

"*No.*" I knocked his shoulder with mine. "I'm not worried about that."

"So you think I couldn't get in?"

"Jamie! This isn't about you."

"But still."

I tugged nervously at the bottom of my skirt. "MIT."

"Wow! Really?"

"Yes, *really*. I mean, I'll apply. But that doesn't mean I'll get in. That doesn't even mean I've got a shot."

"What do you want to study?"

"I don't know."

He raised a disbelieving eyebrow. "Liar."

I sighed. He was right, but I was used to not talking about this. David and Mika got bored whenever I tried. "Astrophysics," I said. "I guess I've just—I've always been fascinated by the universe, about all the things we don't know and just by how *malleable* everything is..." I trailed off. "Okay. That was super dorky. I'm stopping now."

"Don't," he said.

I blushed. "It's really not worth thinking about. I'll have

to get a scholarship because my parents can't afford the tuition. If I go to Rutgers, I'll get reduced tuition because of my mom."

"No," he said. "You won't need to do any of that. You'll get a scholarship and go to MIT."

The firm way he said it—like he didn't doubt for a second it was true—made my gaze skitter down to the floor. Whenever I told someone about MIT, they'd usually give me a spiel about having backup options. I felt like one of us should be practical. "Do you have any idea how difficult it is to get a scholarship to M-I-freaking-T?"

"No? Very difficult? You'll still do it."

I shoved his knee, and he shoved mine. His impossibly bright smile was back, and it made me feel light-headed. This was the Jamie I remembered, the one who couldn't contain what he felt or believed in. I was so relieved to be with him and so overwhelmed by his belief in *me*, I wanted to reach over and touch him one more time. Just to make sure this was really happening.

He threaded his leather wristband around his index finger. "Anyway, Mika told me how you kicked everyone's ass in that AP Physics class. If you don't go to MIT, you'll do something else awesome. I know this for a fact."

"For a *fact*?" I shoved his knee again, lightly this time. "Are you a visitor from the future or something? Did you cross the boundaries of space and time to be here, Jamie?"

His eyes warmed up ten degrees. "*That* is exactly what I did."

———

Outside, the heat was crawling back into the air.

Music slid out the windows of karaoke places. People glided in and out of nightclubs, out of konbinis, out of *izakaya*. Some entrances were shuttered, but others were thrown open to the street, spilling light onto the sidewalks.

In fact, all I could see was light. Unfurling on the ground, bursting in windows, glowing on the vertical signs that ran all the way up the sides of buildings. Shibuya fizzed with light, pushed back the darkness.

"What should we do?" I asked.

Jamie walked a few steps in front of me and then walked back again. "What do you want to do?"

"I really have no idea."

"Karaoke?"

I tightened my ponytail. "Don't feel like it." The thought of being inside made my skin feel itchy. The thought of Jamie and me in a small, dark room…I couldn't even begin.

"Let's walk," I said. "I want to see it all before it disappears."

The roads were bright passageways. All of them strange and new in the middle of the night. Even the people seemed different, less inhibited than they did during the day. They were taking pictures with their phones, checking their reflections in darkened windows, sitting on the curb outside the 24–7 McDonald's eating hundred-yen ice-cream cones.

"I'm not sure how to proceed," Jamie said. "I feel like we have to talk about everything just because we can."

"We can't talk about everything," I said. "We have a limited number of hours."

He contemplated it for a moment. "That is some serious pressure."

We reached a quieter, narrower street. I was startled when a group of people sprinted out of an alleyway and crossed in front of us, a blur of glittering colors and loud voices.

Jamie and I stood still. We briefly made eye contact and then looked away at the same time, which made me feel all weightless and fluttery. I was falling for him. That was why I was so determined to stay out with him all night. That was why I kept moving toward him even when I didn't have to. It was daunting and it was scary, but I was drawn to him, like he had his own gravitational force.

"My first question," he said, "is where are you from?"

I touched the strap of my watch. "Um. France, Japan, Poland, New Jersey."

"Never mind. Next question." He stepped in front of me. We were by an Internet café pumping techno music into the street. Black lights lined the stairs that led up to the entrance, giving us both a blue glow. It heightened the curiosity on his face. "My question is, do you even know how intimidating you are?"

I pulled my cardigan around my rib cage. "Intimidating?"

"Yes. From the moment I met you, you intimidated the hell out of me. You're so cool. And terrifying."

"Terrifying?"

"I don't mean it like that," he said. "You're terrifying in a good way."

"Obviously. Like spiders or serial killers or life-threatening diseases."

"You're terrifying the way a book is right before it ends. You know? When you have to put it down because it's too much to take in at once. You are the most terrifying person I know."

He was smiling at me. Even in that aquarium light, I could see the freckles dispersed across his nose and cheeks, and the gold flecks like matching freckles in his eyes.

"My question for you," I said, "is why do you have all those Japanese books in your room?"

"That's easy," he said. "I want to be a translator."

"Like you want to work for the UN or something?" I asked.

"No," he said. "I think I want to translate books. Novels, actually. It sounds pretty stupid, I know."

I gave him a mock scowl. "No. It's amazing. I can't speak Japanese. I still can't speak any French."

He lowered his eyes self-consciously. "Trust me. I have to get a lot better. Right now, I wouldn't have a shot in hell of translating a street sign."

"You're smart."

"Right. Of course. And ruggedly handsome and able to leap buildings in a single bound."

"I remember the way we used to talk about those movies. You made everything seem so—"

Beautiful. Jamie made the world seem more beautiful than it had ever seemed before. And bigger. Like it was a dark sea I wanted to swim in. Like it was a place I wanted to explore.

I needed to say it to him. Even if it connected us in a way I couldn't take back. Even if it meant I would inevitably get hurt. "You make everything beautiful. And—you made me feel less like life was going to swallow me whole. And you made me feel the opposite of small and stupid and alone. For the first time maybe ever."

As he was looking at me, his eyes flicked back and forth. Like he was reading a book. Like he was memorizing a passage. "I don't feel like tonight is real," he said. "Do you think we're both sleeping?"

"Ha," I said. "Maybe sleep*walking*."

"Sophia?"

"Yes?"

"Don't wake up."

CHAPTER 18
THURSDAY

---

03 : 08 : 39 : 06
DAYS   HOURS   MINS   SECS

"SUMIMASEN!" THE GIRL TOTTERED a few steps away from me and bowed.

I shook my head. "Sumimasen." At the very least, I could say sorry in Japanese.

We were standing on a street corner fed by the traffic from various nightclubs. The sidewalks were hectic, and I was tired, and the heat was getting more intense by the second. Maybe from all the walking and walking and walking. The girl smiled at me. She was wearing bright red platform heels and a black dress. *"America jin desuka?"*

"Um, *hai.*"

"Nai!" Jamie said, grinning. *"Tokyo ni sundeiru."*

The girl's expression became elated. *"Eh—! Nihongo sugoi desune."*

Jamie blushed so hard, I was amazed all the blood vessels in his face didn't burst. The girl asked him a few more questions, and I stood to the side, following most of what they were saying but too self-conscious to join in with my own basic, T-Cad level-two Japanese. The sounds of Tokyo transformed into a gentle murmur, and the night grew warmer and hazier and— was my head against Jamie's shoulder? I pushed myself away.

"Tired?" he asked. The girl was gone. There were patches of sweat around the neck of his red Anpanman T-shirt.

"You speak Japanese good, Jamie. So good. Can we stop walking now?"

"I'm not sure how to break it to you, but we're not currently walking."

But we had been walking. For so long. A little while back, we'd tried to go to a bar. Jamie ordered a beer, but neither of us drank any. It was too loud to think. Or talk—I wanted to talk. So we walked instead. Outside, in the imperfect dark, we could talk as much as we wanted to. There was all this space above, all this room for our voices to go.

"Jamie." I blinked through the glue in my eyes. "I need to sit down."

"We need coffee." He raked his hands through the sides of his hair. The sweat made it into a disheveled mess. I sort of wanted to run my fingers through it. Sleeplessness was giving me all kinds of irrational desires.

"There's no coffee here," I said. "You're hallucinating."

He looped his hand around my wrist and gave me a small tug. Then he started to run. We started to run. All the lights blotting and blurring, the roads unraveling in a familiar way. There were fewer people out now, everyone weighed down and listless, like we were in a distorted version of the bustling city Tokyo usually was.

We didn't have to run for long till the street deposited us on the edge of Shibuya Crossing. My eyes opened wider. It was like racing through the solar system and stumbling on the sun. All the signs and the screens and the people and the cars. Light and sound crawling up, up, up.

"Wow," I breathed.

Jamie squeezed my wrist. "Look behind you."

I already knew what was there, of course. The building had huge paneled windows that faced the crossing. Advertisements flashed across its glass exterior, and a sign in all caps ran along the facade of the second floor.

STARBUCKS COFFEE.

"*Coffee*," I said.

Inside, everything was exactly what I needed. The air-conditioning, the whirring espresso machine, people in green aprons smiling. There was light folky music playing over the speakers and, as soon as we walked in, all the baristas chorused, "*Irasshaimase*."

"It smells like life," I said, feeling a little teary. "This is where life comes from."

Jamie dug into his pockets for change. "I have a plan. I'm going to get two enormous green tea lattes with all the whipped cream and sprinkly things they've got, and you're going to go upstairs and steal the couch."

"The couch?"

"It's the only couch," he said. "It's in front of a window. You're going to steal it and we're going to stay there till the trains start. This is our destiny."

"The couch," I repeated.

Jamie joined the surprisingly long line. Somehow, my dead legs carried me up the stairs to the second floor. An array of insomniacs crowded around the small tables and counters that ran along the floor-to-ceiling windows. The entire room hovered over Shibuya Crossing like balcony seating. As Jamie had predicted, there was a maroon couch situated in the center of all the windows, wedged between two counters.

I shuffled over. The couch was occupied by the sleeping body of a guy wearing skinny jeans and a leather jacket. There was no way I was going to be able to steal it. How does one steal a couch, exactly? I waved down at him. "Um. Hello?"

He didn't respond. Presumably because he was asleep.

"Okay." I nodded, and my head felt like it was bobbing in water. I was swimming. "Okay. Desperate times call for desperate measures."

I lay on the ground in front of him, in the small sliver of space between the couch and the window. I put my bag under my head for a pillow, and then I fell asleep. Right there, right in the window, where everyone in the whole wide world could see me.

———

"Sophia?"

It took a minute for everything to come into focus. Jamie was floating above me, holding a huge white paper cup.

"Issit morning?" I asked.

"Yeah, technically," he said, with more energy than I could have dreamed of mustering. "Get up. There is a couch to sit on."

I closed my eyes. Bright green spots popped behind my eyelids. "I can't. Someone's there."

"He left."

I propped myself up on my elbows. Jamie was right. There was no one there anymore. No man in skinny jeans. "Did he leave because of me?" I asked. "Did I scare him off?" And more importantly, had I been snoring? Or drooling? I wiped my mouth with the back of my hand just to make sure. It came away with a final, faded smear of red.

"No," Jamie said. "He left because I gave him a green tea latte. By the way, I've only got one left. We'll have to share." He reached down to help me up. Jamie's hand was warm. And he must have shaken out his hair because it wasn't pushed off his face anymore. It fell in a rumpled mess of curls around his ears, making him look cozy and tumble-dried.

I collapsed onto the soft maroon cushions. All the bones and muscles in my body ached, and sitting down was miraculous. I was about to say that to Jamie when I realized my hand was still tangled with his. Neither of us had tried to let go.

My heart pounded. I quickly checked my reflection in the window and—yikes. Orange hair escaping from my ponytail, shirt dank and crumpled, and blobs of mascara beneath my eyes. Not to mention the fact that I probably smelled like a sticky floor.

But when my gaze found Jamie's, none of that mattered. The distant hiss of the coffee machine and the sleepy conversations at surrounding tables faded. All I could see were the lights of the crossing below and Jamie sitting next to me. I wanted to keep touching him. Maybe the exhaustion was finally taking over, but I didn't care. I imagined touching the spot where the hollow of his neck met the collar of his T-shirt. Tracing the line that led from his jaw to his ear with my fingertips.

"Jamie—" I said.

I'm falling for you.

My watch emitted one quick chirp. I jumped in my seat.

"Everything okay?" Jamie asked.

"Yeah," I said. "It just does this sometimes. When the hour changes." I let go of his hand and fumbled with the buttons on the side of my watch. The display blinked. It was four in the morning.

Three days.

I had three days left—and then I was gone. Just like that, all the awful feelings, the ones I'd tried so hard to ignore for the past few hours, came rushing back.

"God," I whispered. "This is so pointless."

"What is?" Jamie sounded worried. He put the latte on the ground and inched toward me.

I focused on the crossing below. It reminded me of a living tide, all these people moving over it in waves.

The trains hadn't started yet, but there were some early-morning commuters mixed in with the remains of the night crowd. The same ebb and flow that would go on week after week after week. Without me.

"It's almost over," I said. "This night, this week. All of it."

"It's not over yet," he said softly.

I sat forward, agitated. "But it will be. And I keep telling myself to deal with it. I should be able to deal with it, right? I've left places before. I've left *people*."

He shook his head. "It still sucks, though. It always does."

"And the worst part is there's nothing I can do about it. I want so badly to stay, but I can't. And I know this is going to sound dumb, but I keep thinking about—about black holes. About how I'm stuck on this trajectory, being pulled toward something I can't stop and eventually I'm going to get—" I squeezed my hands into fists; the words caught in my throat.

"Crushed," Jamie said.

"Yeah." I slumped back. "Crushed."

We both watched the crossing for a minute. Jamie had his hands on his knees and was twisting the leather band on his wrist around his index finger. He twisted it and let go, twisted and let go. It was the longest we'd gone without talking all night. But I was still so *aware* of him. His knee rested against mine. And his hair smelled like rain—like our whole night together.

But the night was almost over.

"In three days, I'll be gone, and it'll be like the last four years never happened," I said. "Every time I feel like I belong somewhere, it goes away."

"Not always." He pushed his leg against mine.

I shrugged and rubbed my eyes—they were undoubtedly bright red.

"And at least you know you belong somewhere," Jamie said. "I'm not sure I've ever felt that way."

"I'm sorry," I said, pushing the heels of my hands into my forehead. "I shouldn't have brought all this up. I'm just making us both miserable."

"No." His tone was insistent. He turned to me and didn't try to look away. "What I was going to say is, I never really felt like I belonged anywhere. I always felt like I was half in one place and half somewhere else. Like I was never exactly where I should be. Except—now. Except being here, with you."

I closed my eyes, and a few tears spilled down my cheeks.

"I think you choose," he whispered. "I think you choose where you belong, and those places will always be there to remind you of who you are. You just have to choose them."

I opened my eyes again, and I saw green taxicabs washing over the crossing and a city that burned like a glowworm cave and Jamie's reflection laid over it all. I reached out for his warm hand at the exact moment he reached for mine. "I think I already have."

CHAPTER 19
THURSDAY

———

03 : 06 : 18 : 51
DAYS HOURS MINS SECS

A LITTLE OVER AN HOUR LATER, the sun was up.

No more insomniacs at the counters next to us. Just businesspeople in snappy outfits, sipping lattes and reading the newspaper. Jamie stretched. His eyes were barely open. He was a puffy, confused kitten.

"Why does it sun?" I asked, rubbing my face.

"Don't ask me," Jamie croaked. "I didn't do it."

The trains were up and running again. Jamie bought a ticket, and I dug out my Suica card, and we idled in front of the barriers. I was headed for the Fukutoshin line; Jamie was taking the Hanzomon.

"I'll probably spend the next three days sleeping," I joked.

Jamie laughed, but he seemed distracted. He pushed his hand though the front of his hair and shook it out.

"You won't miss your flight," he said. "You've got an alarm."

"Ha. Yeah."

We stood for another second or so, swaying on our feet. The electronic board above me flashed one minute until my train arrived, and I checked my watch to make sure it had the same time. "Well, guess I'll see you later."

"Later," he agreed.

I went through the barrier and down to the train platform. I tried to smile, but the corners of my mouth were way too tired for that.

———

I unlocked the front door as quietly as I could and stood in the genkan, peeling off my shoes. They were still damp from walking through puddles all night. *Guilty shoes*, I thought, and dropped them on the ground.

The genkan was a dark, peaceful cave, and I was still so tired. I sat on the floor, on top of a pile of pizza and sushi delivery flyers someone must have shoved through the mail slot. I closed my eyes and came dangerously close to falling asleep.

Wake up, I told myself. *Go upstairs.*

Upstairs. To my room. Where I could put on my favorite pajamas and sleep all day and dream about last night. That was all I wanted to do. Hold on to last night for a little bit longer, keep it from becoming morning and afternoon and evening.

I thought about Jamie, pushing the hair off his forehead. About the warmth radiating off his skin, like the steam that evaporates from sidewalks after the rain. I missed him. Even though I'd seen him less than an hour ago. Even though I would probably see him again soon. If I missed him now, how would I feel when I actually left? But I couldn't care about that yet. The memory of him was better and stronger than the fear of anything else.

I stood up and pushed open the door to the rest of the house. Mom was sitting at the dining room table talking on the phone. When she saw me, she said, "I'll call you back." She set the phone on the table, and then she was standing up, and then she was hugging me, pulling me to her stomach. Her grip was tighter than I'd anticipated.

"Sophia," she said. "What have you been doing all night?"

"I was—" I was a mess. Rain-encrusted and makeup-smudged and Starbucks-scented. "I was with Mika. We stayed up all night, but it's okay. I'm not drunk or anything."

"Why didn't you tell me what happened?"

I squirmed out of her grasp. The paper screens were pulled back from the windows, making everything in the house look garish and overexposed. "I don't know which 'what' you're referring to."

"Your sister said the two of you had a fight. She said you stormed off and disappeared somewhere all day."

"Technically, she's the one who stormed *off*. I just stormed to the bathroom. And when did she tell you all this?"

The worry lines on Mom's face were more pronounced than usual. "She woke me up a couple of hours ago. She was frantic because she hadn't heard you come home. She told me you were really upset earlier."

"I was with Mika," I repeated. "I texted you and you texted me back. We do this all the time. There's nothing to worry about."

In the apartment buildings around us, doors were opening and closing. People were waking up. Mom smoothed the hair that had fallen out of my ponytail behind my ears. She really did seem concerned. There were dark circles under her eyes and a tea stain on her shirt. She picked up her phone from the table. "I have to get ready for work, but we still need to talk. Do you want any breakfast?"

I shook my head numbly and followed Mom to her bedroom. It was much bigger than my room or Alison's. She had her own bathroom and enough space for a queen-size bed. It seemed even bigger now because she'd cleared out so much stuff. There was nothing left on the nightstand, nothing hanging in the closet.

I collapsed onto the bed while Mom shoved her laptop into a leather satchel. She stood in the bathroom and brushed her teeth and pinned her hair back with a tortoiseshell clip. It was warm in the room, but I wrapped myself up in my grandmother's quilt and lay down on a pile of dark green throw pillows. The quilt smelled like my mom's almond-scented moisturizer and reminded me of being a kid. From the window, I could just make out the purple peak of Mount Fuji.

Mom sat at the end of the bed.

"Are you mad at me?" I asked.

"No," Mom said, fiddling with the ends of her scarf.

I propped myself up but kept the blanket bundled around my shoulders. "I'm not drunk. Or on drugs."

"That was your dad on the phone."

"What?" I scooted down the bed. "Why did he call so early? Did something happen?"

"I called him," she explained. "I couldn't sleep after Alison woke me up. We were talking about you. About how hard all of this has been for you."

"Duh, it's hard. Going back to New Jersey isn't exactly a dream come true."

Mom placed one hand on my knee. "I meant this whole arrangement, all this living between places. You haven't had much time with your father, and that hasn't been fair."

I worked my fingers through the knitted loops in the blanket. I hated this. When Mom talked about Dad, it made her sad. I'd once seen a picture of Mom and Dad walking around Kamakura when they were first married. She was laughing at something Dad said, her head thrown back, swatting playfully at his arm. I'd never seen Mom laugh that way.

"Mom," I said. "I almost lived there, remember?"

She looked pained. "The timing wasn't right then."

"I know," I said. But the truth was, I didn't know. Not really. I knew that I'd been happy in Tokyo and that I loved my mom and that it would have sucked leaving her behind. But I'd never forgotten the feeling of thinking I could go to Paris and stay there and then having it swept away.

"Besides," Mom said, "no other arrangement made sense. The two of you living with him half the time and with me the other half of the time? That would have been a disaster. Especially when he had that apartment."

"I liked his apartment."

Mom squeezed my knee. "When you were over there, I could barely sleep at night. He was so young, he barely had his life together. But it's different now. He's got a good job and a family and a house."

"You have a good job and a family and a house."

Mom adjusted the clip in her hair and took a steadying breath. "If you want to move to Paris this year, you can."

I let go of the blanket. "Mom. Is this a joke?"

"The Paris American School doesn't start for another three weeks," she said. "Your dad said he could register you. You'd live in his house, and there's a bus nearby that would take you straight to the school."

I tried to process what I was hearing. To my surprise, a thousand objections sprung to mind.

"I don't speak French," I sputtered.

"You'd learn fast enough. And you'd be at the American school."

"The babies don't speak English," I said. "Am I just supposed to live in their house and gesture at them all year? Or talk to them about pieces of fruit?"

"Pieces of fruit?"

"Some of the only French words I remember are the ones for pieces of fruit. I don't know why."

Mom laughed.

"Mom," I said firmly. "Did you seriously decide to send me to Paris at six o'clock in the morning? *Over the phone?*"

"No one's sending you anywhere," she said, choosing her words carefully. "All your stuff will go to New Jersey, and the plane tickets are already booked. We'll go back together, and if you decide you want to be in Paris, we'll pack you a couple of suitcases."

"Suitcases?"

"You've got some stuff over there," Mom said. "And a room."

That was true. Sylvie had decorated it with pink lacy lamp shades and floral curtains that Alison said made her feel like a young Miss Havisham (whatever that meant).

"You don't have to decide anything now," Mom said. "It's up to you, and whatever you decide is okay." She touched the back of my hand. "I have to go. We can talk more about this later."

She stood up and put her satchel over her shoulder. I went to my room. Dorothea Brooke was asleep on my pillow, shedding gray fur all over it. I lay down beside her and turned on the fan on my bedside table. It whirred to life, sending my pile of postcards and pictures flying to the floor.

I closed my eyes and thought about Paris, trying to pull up an image of it with as many details filled in as I could.

It had always been a fairy-tale city to me. A city of rain-drenched boulevards and bakeries full of almond croissants and parks with hidden nooks where I could curl up and stare at the centuries-old buildings looming above. It was my anchor, the place that stayed constant even when the rest of my life was racked with seismic shifts.

Mom said Dad wanted me there. In Paris.

And I'd get to go to the American School. Maybe the type of friends I'd have there were the type I wanted. The T-Cad type, with Mika's biting sarcasm and better fashion sense. And I'd have a stepmom and a little brother and sister. That could be cool. I could be the big sister. The big sister who knew a lot about fruit.

But, I don't know—I hadn't thought (*seriously* thought) about living in Paris for years. The possibility seemed sudden and strange and impossible. I mean, my siblings were toddlers who spoke French. And screamed. Could I seriously keep up my GPA living with French-speaking toddlers who screamed? Would Dad invite me on family outings? Would people think Sylvie was *my mom*?

I'd miss my mom. She loved me. She cooked cheese-and-onion pierogi on Thanksgiving because it was my favorite, and she always remembered to make my dental appointments.

What if Dad doesn't know how to make dental appointments?!

I sat up and held my hands in front of the fan, the breeze moving between my fingers.

I guess Paris still trumped New Jersey.

It trumped Edenside High and the same kids who'd ignored me in middle school and weekend parties I'd never be invited to. Paris could be somewhere I fit—somewhere I belonged. That's how I'd always thought of it, anyway, ever since I was a little kid.

———

Alison sits on my bed with me, her hand fiercely clutching the sleeve of my pajamas. "I'm gonna Skype Dad. Give me Mom's tablet. I'm Skyping him right now."

"Don't," I whisper and sob at the same time. Alison pulls the sleeve of her sweatshirt over her hand and wipes at my face.

Between my curtains, I see the curled and beckoning finger of an oak tree. And even though it's one in the morning, I hear a group of people walking down the street, their laughter cracking through the night.

It's June. A few months from now, we'll be leaving New Jersey for Tokyo. But I wasn't supposed to go there. I was supposed to go to Paris.

"He's such an ass," Alison hisses. "He said you could live there."

I rub my face into the fabric on my shoulder. "It's because of the babies. Mom said they'd drive me nuts."

"She's looking out for you." Alison scoffs.

I pick up the small Eiffel Tower key chain perched on my windowsill and grip it till it bites into my palm. "But Paris is home," I whisper. "I really thought it was supposed to be home."

Alison tips her chin up. "Mom is our home."

"It doesn't work that way." I sniffle. "Home has to be, like, a place."

Alison sighs and turns to the side, her profile illuminated by the glow of the streetlights. "No," she says eventually, still staring out the window. "It really, really doesn't."

CHAPTER 20
THURSDAY

———

03 : 01 : 20 : 26
DAYS   HOURS   MINS   SECS

I ONLY SLEPT FOR A FEW HOURS. Even though I was exhausted, even though the thing I wanted to do most was sleep. But I couldn't. I kept waking up every five minutes, convinced it was already nighttime. The air was stale and humid, and my room felt smaller than ever.

I checked my e-mail in case Dad had written to say I should definitely come to Paris. But he hadn't. I dialed his cell, then remembered it was three in the morning his time and hung up.

I paced the room.

Usually if I stayed out all night, Mika and I would spend the next day in her enormous bed with the curtains shut. We'd eat the chocolate ice-cream bars her mom kept hidden at the back of their freezer and watch episodes of *My So-Called Life* on her computer.

I slumped back onto my messy bed. Dorothea Brooke purred and groomed my hair. My watch was damp and itchy, so I took it off and tossed it on top of my dresser. Then I went to the kitchen.

Someone was knocking at the front door. Which was weird.

Really weird.

The only people who ever knocked at our front door were the NHK man coming for our unpaid TV subscription or our one English-speaking neighbor, this Canadian guy who brought us Reese's Peanut Butter Cups whenever he went to North America on business trips. For a wild second, I thought it was Jamie. He wanted to do something else. Tour Japan on the Shinkansen. Fly to Sapporo and back again. Something that could be accomplished in a whirlwind seventy-two hours. I opened the door.

It was Mika.

My hand froze on the doorknob.

"Hey," she said, lifting her chin in a stiff greeting.

I wanted to slam the door in her face. I wanted to lock it and bolt it and tell her to *GO. AWAY.*

"Can I come in?" she asked.

I hesitated before opening the door wider. She walked in and stood uncomfortably in the genkan, like she couldn't decide whether to take her shoes off.

I crossed my arms and tried to seem angry. But I was so tired and confused, and the anger grew numb—a blunt blade. "You cut your hair," I said.

"Yeah," she said, touching the side of her head self-consciously.

But she hadn't just cut it; she'd *buzzed* it. Right down to the quick. It made all her features stand out: piercing eyes, small nose, thin lips. Her eyebrow stud became a cold slash of metal.

"You look like Debra in *Empire Records*."

"My parents said Annie Lennox."

"Were they pissed?"

She smirked. "Yeah. Inevitably. But I don't know, also mildly amused."

I nodded. "You can take off your shoes. If you want."

Inside the living room, everything was sloppy and chaotic, the gray carpets and the frayed couch pillows and the furniture pushed into disarray. Mika played nervously with a hole in the cuff of her dark green shirt.

"You want coffee or something?" I asked.

"No thanks," she said.

"Okay. I'm going to make coffee. And breakfast. I'm assuming you don't want breakfast, either." She followed me to the kitchen, where I hunted through cabinets for something to eat. There wasn't much. A couple of bags of rice, orange juice, two browning bananas on the windowsill.

"Dude," Mika said. "Are you okay? Have you been sleeping in a gutter?"

No. I'm just recovering from spending all night in Shibuya with Jamie, and also I might be moving to a different continent than was originally planned, and ALSO the thought of you and David together still makes me feel like the world is tipping out from under me.

"Okay," I said. "I am, I mean. I am okay."

"Uh-huh," she said. "You're being kinda weird right now."

I opened the fridge and spotted a box of leftover pizza, probably Mom's dinner from last night. There were two slices of veggie inside, and I wolfed one down in a few bites. "How so?" I asked through a full mouth.

Mika scratched the side of her new head. "I don't know. I figured you'd call me a traitorous bitch or something. I figured you'd throw me out."

"Do you want me to?"

"No."

I ate another slice of pizza. There was a stool shoved in the corner, but Mika didn't sit on it, and I didn't offer it to her. I took a coffee mug from the drying rack. I needed to do this before I chickened out completely.

"Did you and David really hook up?"

She seemed to think it over. Which was so ridiculous. It was a yes-or-no question.

"Yeah," she said finally. "We did."

I swallowed the lump in my throat. "I'm angry you never told me."

"It wasn't a big deal," she said quickly. "We hooked up a few times, but then we'd talk about how dumb it was. I'm not his girlfriend or anything."

I put the mug down on the kitchen counter. My hands were trembling a little. "A few times? How many times?"

"Do you really want to know?"

"No. But if you don't tell me, I'm going to assume it was every day."

"Christ. Clearly it wasn't every day."

"How many times?"

"Five." She picked up the mug and held it. She was probably worried I would smash it on the floor. Or throw it at her. "Four times last summer. Once this summer."

"By 'once this summer,' you mean Monday, right? The night the three of us were hanging out? The night before David and Caroline broke up?"

She tugged on the silver hoop in her left ear. "It was dumb."

"Then why'd you do it?" I asked.

"Agh!" She started rubbing the top of her head with both hands, like she was checking all her hair was really gone. "I don't know! Because he's not hideous? Because I was bored? Sometimes you feel like hooking up with someone, and it's better to do it with a friend because that way you can laugh about it later."

"That's space talk," I said. "*Hooking up* is not eating pizza. Or watching every episode of *Buffy* in a row. Having *sex* is not a casual activity."

She snorted. "Oh, right. Because you're an expert?"

I gripped the pizza box against me like it was a shield. "I really liked him. You knew that."

She rolled her eyes. "He uses people. Everything he touches turns to stone."

"Well." I shrugged. "I'm not the one who slept with him."

Mika stopped rubbing the bristles on the top of her head. She really did look awesome with short hair. Sharp and androgynous. She reminded me of the girls I sometimes saw in Paris, standing on sidewalks in leather jackets and oversized wool scarves, smoking cigarettes and glowering a lot.

The thought of Paris made me feel even more out of control. I was still mad at Mika, but I also wanted to talk to her. I needed my best friend.

"He likes you," I said, putting down the pizza box. "I think he wants to be your boyfriend."

"That's his fucking problem," Mika said. "I'm here because I'm worried about you. I don't want you to hate me forever. Not over an idiot like David."

"You lied to me. You lied and you were my best..." I spun around and started pawing through a cabinet, searching for coffee grounds. Mika came behind me and pulled at the fabric of my tank top.

When I turned around, she looked shyer and smaller than she had a few minutes ago. "I hope you'll still come to our birthday–going-away thing tomorrow night," she said tentatively. "That's what I came here to say."

For a few seconds, I just let myself breathe in and out again. All I wanted was to forgive Mika. All I wanted was to sit on the kitchen floor and drink coffee and tell her about last night and Jamie and Paris. I wanted to trust her again.

But then I thought about her and David, saying they were going out but going to her apartment instead, flicking off her bedroom light, pressing their mouths together. My stomach heaved.

"I'm not sure I can forgive you," I said.

Mika blinked. "So you're really going to let David do this to us? You're really going to let him get between us?"

"It's not just David," I said. "I can't forgive you for—for other things, too. For the way you treat me like I'm a little kid sometimes. For telling me to stay away from David and making fun of me because I don't drink or have sex or whatever. That's why you slept with him, right? Because you guys are the experienced ones, and I'm just the dumb, innocent little *Sofa?*"

Mika's expression went carefully neutral. "You're not actually mad about that."

I held back a scream. I grabbed the empty pizza box and jammed it into the full garbage can.

"Come on," she said. "You know that dating David would have been a catastrophe. On a government-intervention level. He doesn't deserve you. He deserves someone who— will divorce him. And take all his money."

"I don't care if it would have been a mistake! It was my mistake to figure out!"

"Jesus!" she said and then softened her voice. "Just— please. I never wanted you to hate me. I never wanted everything to explode like this."

I scoffed. "Oh, it's way past exploded. *Way* past."

"*Please*," she said again, something that could have been anguish filling her eyes. "I'm not abdicating my position as best friend yet. We can still talk about this. We can come back from this. Right?"

I crossed my arms and didn't say a single word. Neither of us moved a muscle for a minute. The cicadas outside were so loud, it felt like the noise was filling up the room, crowding up my head, drowning me even more.

"Fine," Mika said. "You know what? That's fine. Have it your way. I'll see you later, or maybe I won't. Or whatever." She left the kitchen.

I heard the door to the genkan open and then close. Followed by the front door.

Opening. Closing.

CHAPTER 21
THURSDAY

___

02 : 22 : 35 : 12
DAYS HOURS MINS SECS

___

From: jamiethinksyourecool@foster.collins.net

To: sophia_wachowski@tcad.ac.jp

Subject: I drooled on some guy's shoulder on the train :-/

___

Good morning! (Sort of.)

So I have no idea if this is your e-mail address anymore. Or if you still use e-mail. I probably should have sent you a message by carrier pigeon. That would be more my style.

I hope this isn't stupid. I would have tried to call you, but we don't have a house phone and Hannah won't lend me her cell. She says I'm "up to something." Of course I'm up to something. I wouldn't ask for her phone if I weren't.

What I'm trying to say (attempting to articulate) is that I'm going to Meiji Shrine. I just Googled it, and it's open till sunset. So I'll be there around fourish, and I guess I'll loiter around the entrance, and if you're there, then cool. If you're not, also cool. You should sleep. I should sleep.

No. I'm lying. WAKE UP, SOPHIA!! I WILL BE LOITERING!

CHAPTER 22

THURSDAY

—

02 : 20 : 16 : 05
DAYS HOURS MINS SECS

TO GET TO MEIJI SHRINE, I took a train to Harajuku and walked along an avenue of kitsch boutiques that became a row of cubed apartment buildings that became Yoyogi-koen.

Inside the *koen*, everything melted to green. Trees replaced buildings. The sound of traffic grew more and more muffled until it was drowned out by thousands of cicadas singing. The entrance to the shrine was a tall wooden torii, a Japanese gate shaped like an enormous, elegant pi sign. That's where Jamie was. At Meiji Shrine, loitering outside. Wearing a Studio Ghibli T-shirt and a pair of sunglasses with square red frames. His hands were stuffed in his pockets, and he was watching the milling crowds.

Every time I saw him, it was different. This time, it was waking up. My fight with Mika, the conversation with my mom, those things didn't exist anymore. The night Jamie and I had spent in Shibuya burned back to life. It was real. It was the only thing in the whole world that was real.

"Hi," I said when I reached him.

"Hi." He pushed his sunglasses onto his head. There were pink grooves under his eyes. "You're here."

He was smiling. And it was such a warm smile, such a relieved smile, that it made me want to kiss him. To kiss the shy nervousness right out of him. To kiss him under his eyes, in the cool, delicate place that should have been hidden by his sunglasses.

"You seem tired," he said.

"The opposite," I said, tugging on the sleeve of his shirt like it was a kite string. "I'm the opposite of tired."

———

Oh. CRAP.

We'd passed through the torii and were snaking our way down a long, curving path toward the central building of the shrine. And I had no idea what to do. Was I supposed to hold his hand again? Was I supposed to touch him? He wasn't touching me, which did not compute at all.

I knew he liked me. Or, at least, I thought he did. He'd said all that stuff about belonging with me, but maybe he'd meant, like, belonging *in our friendship*. The way I'd belonged with Mika.

That wasn't how I felt, though. I felt about him the way I used to—only times ten thousand. To the nth degree. We weren't touching, but the energy between us fizzed and popped. And I was such an idiot for ever thinking he was *cute*. Puppies were cute; the tiny cakes they sold at Kinokuniya were cute. Jamie was—electric.

When I looked at him—all lawless hair and anxious hands—I felt a lightning storm in my skin. When I looked at him, I wanted to kiss him. It was an automatic response. Like smelling a cookie and wanting a cookie. I tried to remind myself of all the things that were awkward and goofy and not-in-any-way-attractive about him. *He's a nerd. He's read* The Lord of the Rings *and* Harry Potter *at least twenty times each. He makes jokes about history and literature.*

Every single one of those things just made me want to kiss him more.

But maybe kissing Jamie was a terrible idea. For one thing, it would make leaving Tokyo completely impossible. (Like, physically impossible. I would just hug Jamie around the waist and refuse to let go.) For another, it would take my soul and leave nothing but a warm, liquid center.

Kissing Jamie...

It would be Harry finding his wand. Frodo taking the ring. It would turn this week into something I couldn't even fathom.

———

"Why'd you want to come here?" I asked, my voice a lot louder than I'd meant it to be. The path was cool and quiet, with cicadas cooing and trees eclipsing our shadows. This was a place to be peaceful.

And I was blabbering like a nervous weirdo.

"Because it's historical," he said, "and also it's not my apartment."

"I thought maybe you'd want to go to a cat café," I said.

"A cat café?" He laughed. Loud, infectious laughter.

"I don't know," I said. "It's a café. Full of cats. We could—hang out with some cats."

He was finding all this very funny. But I wasn't joking. I was talking about cats because I needed to talk about something. Cats, dogs, parakeets, the unpredictability of the weather. I needed to distract my twisted brain from noticing that we were surrounded by trees. Dark and shadowy places...

Christ. I was so inappropriate. Who imagines making out with someone *at a shrine*?

"Did you get home okay?" Jamie asked.

"Yeah," I said. "I mean, I guess. Mom was waiting for me when I got there."

"Yeah?" He sounded surprised. "Was she pissed off?"

"I don't think so. She was just worried because Alison and I had a fight yesterday."

"You had a fight with your sister?" He seemed concerned, which was so unfair. A genuine display of emotion was the last thing I needed from him. *Don't look at his lips...or his neck...or both! You idiot! You idiot! Don't do both!*

We walked over a wooden bridge.

"My sister and I fight all the time," I said. "We're like

pairs figure skaters. But instead of skating together, we fight. At an Olympic level."

"Uh-huh." He gave me a sidelong smirk. "My sister and I don't really fight. But that's because we're the delinquents of the family. We have to band together."

"Right. So I guess your parents weren't thrilled when you came home this morning?"

His grin faded a little. "You could say that. But they're both gone all day, and Hannah said she'd cover for me if they came back early, so…" He lifted his hands, palms tipped up. "Here I am."

There he was.

And I could not stop STARING at him. I wondered if he'd noticed. I wondered if he was picking up on my swoony vibes. No way was I the first person to crush so hard on him. Maybe he'd even had a girlfriend. That thought made my stomach start to eat itself. Mika had never mentioned a girlfriend, but she'd never really mentioned him in general. Not around me, anyway. She'd once joked to David that he usually went for "older women."

Older women.

I tried to imagine that. Older women with driver's licenses and dark lipstick. Older women who gave him cigarettes and rolled around on his bunk bed with him.

I was eight months older than Jamie, so technically I was an "older woman," too. But my hair was twisted into two braids, and I'd never had a boyfriend, and the thought of kissing someone made me want to breathe into a paper bag.

So. I probably didn't count.

"Anyway," he said, "what happened with your mom?"

"Huh?" I blinked. Like I was trying to clear my vision of him. (Because *that* was possible.)

"You said she was worried?"

"She was," I said. "She talked to my dad this morning. Apparently I can move to Paris if I want to."

"Like for college or something?"

"Like, next week."

"Shit." He rubbed the back of his head. "That's—short notice."

"You could say that."

"Do you think you'll go?"

I touched my wrist, but it felt bare and strange. I'd forgotten to put my watch back on. "Yeah? I mean, I should go, right? It's *Paris*."

"I can imagine you there," he said. "Drinking wine, wearing scarves, going to museums. You could pull that off." He grinned and his sunglasses fell down onto his nose. He pushed them back up again.

"Mom would be alone, but not *alone*-alone," I said. "Alison would only be one state away. I don't know. It still feels pretty strange. When I was a kid, all I wanted was to move to Paris, and now it might really happen."

I breathed the heavy air, which tasted earthy and bitter. Maybe, in a few weeks time, I'd be in Paris, dunking *pains au chocolat* in bowls of hot chocolate and hunting for dresses at my favorite flea markets. Maybe I'd be somewhere I actually wanted to be.

I tried to focus on that instead of the way I was unraveling from the inside, my molecules breaking apart and rearranging every time I glanced at Jamie.

"So," he said, the corner of his mouth twitching up. "The question is, are you sure you still want it?"

———

We arrived at the torii that marked the entrance to the central area of the shrine. Before we went in, we had to wash our hands and mouths at a fountain, a *temizuya*. I ladled water into my left hand, then my right, then my left again and rinsed out my mouth.

"My mom comes here for New Year's," I said. "She always e-mails us pictures of the thousands of people waiting in line to get in."

"You don't go with her?"

I felt a tiny twinge of guilt in my stomach that I quickly suppressed. "Alison and I go to my dad's for New Year's. In Paris. She spends it by herself."

He nodded. People around us were washing their hands at the temizuya. I'd been to shrines with my mom and for school trips before, but I still worried I would embarrass myself. "I feel so noticeable here," I whispered. "Do you think we seem like loud, obnoxious gaijin?"

"First of all," he said, "you're currently whispering. And second of all, this is one of the most famous shrines in Japan. We're not the only foreigners here, I promise."

We walked through the torii—bowing as we went—and then we were in the middle of a broad square paved with striated gray stone. The square's edges were marked with low wooden buildings with slanted green roofs. We were facing a building that was slightly taller than the rest, its roof curled up at the corners. The shrine. Or the outer hall of it, according to Jamie. Groups of people stood in the archways, clapping, bowing, and throwing coins for good luck. More people hovered in the center of the square, taking pictures and consulting guidebooks. Jamie was right. We definitely weren't the only foreigners there.

"What should we do?" I asked.

"We should walk," Jamie said. "It's our thing."

At the various stalls around the square, you could buy charms, woven amulets that hung from thick, colored string and promised health or safety or success. Jamie tried to read the painted kanji signs that described what each charm was supposed to do. I liked the way he blushed and laughed at himself when he messed up. I liked the way he laughed at himself, period. I thought about David, who strutted and crowed and dragged the spotlight with him wherever he went. Jamie was the kind of person you could talk to all night without getting bored, who was funny in a quiet, observant way. And now that I'd noticed it, I couldn't un-notice it. I couldn't imagine paying attention to anyone else if he was in the room.

We came up to a tree with three walls propped around it sitting in the far-right corner of the square. The tree's branches spilled over the walls, and the walls themselves were covered in hooks with small wooden tablets hanging from them. Hundreds of wooden tablets, all inscribed with handwritten messages.

We stopped there.

"They're called *ema*," Jamie said, reading a nearby sign.

My eyes scanned the tablets. Some had neat vertical rows of kanji on them; others had pictures of flowers or anime characters drawn on.

"What do they say?" I was half tempted to touch one. There were so many of them, layered on top of one another. Some tablets were hung precariously over the others, their woven threads barely catching the hooks. I wondered if they would drop to the ground, like acorns.

"They're wishes," he said. "Do you want to write one?"

"What would I say?" I asked.

"How about 'I wish I could stay in Tokyo forever'?"

"Ha. Is that what you'd wish for?"

He took a breath. "If you did."

I turned away, my cheeks burning. I wanted it to be true—it was terrifying how much I wanted it to be true.

"I'd wish you weren't moving," he said, the words tumbling out. "If I could wish for anything."

"Jamie." I couldn't face him. My ears were ringing.

"I'd wish I were going to Paris next year," he said. "I'd wish I'd never gone to boarding school. I'd wish—"

"Jamie," I said. "Stop."

"Okay." I felt him take a step back from me. I could hear the letdown in his voice. "I'm sorry."

I turned around, and before he could take it back—before the moment could turn to glass and shatter into pieces—I kissed him.

CHAPTER 23
THURSDAY

———

02 : 19 : 04 : 21
DAYS HOURS MINS SECS

IT WAS BARELY A KISS. My lips on the corner of his mouth, my hand on his neck. There was a warm pulse against my palm. When his throat moved, I felt it in my skin.

He stayed still, eyes closed, hands lightly touching my waist. I stepped closer to him, and he brushed the back of his fingers against the bottom of my T-shirt.

He pulled back, just enough so that our mouths lost contact. But I wasn't ready to let go. Not yet. I grazed my lips against his and held the back of his hair. My breathing had gone all weird and shaky. My heart was beating so loudly, and all I wanted was to kiss him more. To kiss him completely. To press into him, and open my mouth, and feel his whole body move against mine. I leaned forward an inch, and my shirt hiked up at the back—his hands skimmed the surface of my skin. I gasped and jumped out of his grasp.

"Sorry," I said. My lips were tingling like crazy.

"Sorry," he repeated, his neck turning red. "I shouldn't have—"

"No, I didn't mean—" I wanted to kiss him again, but I was conscious of the fact that we weren't alone. People were still tossing coins into the shrine. A sudden breeze rustled through the branches of the tree, making the ema clack against one another.

I grabbed him by the fingertips. We stayed like that for a moment, our hands linked between us like a jump rope. "I just meant, that wasn't planned," I said.

He blushed. "No. I guess not."

I studied him. The corners of his mouth, his eyebrows— they were light brown. I took him in, piece by piece. The broken line of his nose, the white spots on the tips of his teeth.

"Is this okay?" he asked, glancing nervously at our hands. "Do you want me to let go?"

Instinctively, I stepped forward. Our hands moved together.

"No," I whispered. "No thanks."

We stayed like that as we walked to see the inner square of the shrine. It was quiet and I felt sleepy. Not tired, but sleepy. Like I was in that moment when you lie down in bed in the dark and everything feels warm and safe.

We walked back through the sacred forest, back into the gray city. I was waiting for the spell to break, for Jamie to pull away or touch his hair or something. To give me an apologetic shrug. *Well, I think we can both agree that that was weird. Am I right?*

But he didn't.

We kept walking, past Harajuku and all the way up to Omotesando. The sky was starting to darken. The trees running up and down the *dori* sparkled in the light from glass shopping centers. It made me think of a thousand twinkle lights. It was the Champs-Élysées in Paris and Fifth Avenue in New York all rolled into one. My stomach lurched as I remembered that soon I would be flying toward one of those cities. In fact, the movers were coming tomorrow—

I dropped Jamie's hand. "Oh shit!"

"What?" he asked. "Is everything okay?"

"It's fine." I dug through the mess of receipts and flyers and purikura in my tote until I found the plastic cardholder with my Suica card inside. "Except it's not. I have to go. I have to pack. Like, I'm beyond the point of having a choice in the matter."

"Sure," he said. "That's fine."

"Right." I hoped I didn't sound as heartbroken as I felt. I hoped he couldn't hear the catch in my voice. "I guess I'll see you around. Tomorrow maybe?"

"No." He opened his hands and flexed his fingers. I wanted to grab them again. Or kiss him. Maybe I could kiss him good-bye. Maybe I could kiss him good-bye and start running down the avenue and then we wouldn't have to deal with a real good-bye later. That was probably the best idea I'd ever had. Bravo, Sophia—

"I mean, that's fine. I'll come with you. I'll help you pack."

I stepped closer to him. "You do not want to help me pack."

"Of course I do." He was smiling. "I'm a great packer, and anyway, what else am I going to do tonight?"

"Uh. Something that doesn't suck."

"You're ridiculous." He wrapped his hand around mine and whispered in my ear, "I'm coming with you."

———

At my front door, I let go of Jamie's hand again. It was bizarre and sudden—all that space between us.

"Sorry," I said. "It's just, my mom's probably in there. And my sister. She'd be merciless."

The curtains were closed in most of the apartments around us. It was dark but not silent. Someone was listening to a news broadcast. Someone else was practicing a Yann Tiersen song on the piano. Our house had a small front yard closed in by stone walls, and a part of me wanted to stay there, in the dark, with Jamie and the halting city music.

"No worries," he said. "My sister would be exactly the same. She hated the last girl I dated. They met over the summer. I think Hannah might have stolen twenty dollars from her wallet." He paused. "Honestly, I think she's probably the more delinquent of the two of us."

"Oh." I took my key out of my bag and rubbed my fingers over my plastic panda bear key chain. So I was right. There had been a girlfriend.

An *older woman.*

I wondered if I was in over my head. Five days ago, Jamie had showed up in Tokyo and I'd been convinced he was there just to make my last week miserable. Five days ago, I'd wanted him to get on another plane and leave me alone forever. Five days later, and I didn't even like it when he wasn't touching my hand. In some ways, it was wonderful. But another part of me kept freaking out over these really terrifying things.

Like, for example, what were the chances that Jamie was a virgin?

I mean, he'd been at boarding school, for Christ's sake. *Boarding school.* There are no parents at boarding school. Just unlocked dorm rooms and teenagers marinating in their hormones. And why was I even thinking about this? If I had more time, I probably wouldn't be. I'd be thinking about practical things, like whether I had any breath mints in my tote. But the week was tightening its grasp on me, and the panic portion of my brain had seriously kicked into gear. *Where is this going? Are you going to kiss him again? Are you going to do MORE than kiss him? Don't you realize how unprepared for this you are, Sofa?!*

"We should go inside," I blurted, pushing the door open and charging through the genkan. Mom and Alison were in the dining room, and I was almost grateful to see them. Grateful and then—horrified.

"What the hell!" I gasped.

The inside of the house had been scraped clean. No more papers and books scattered around the floor, no more stereo or piles of CDs. Instead there were boxes. Boxes stacked against the windows and in towers in the center of the living room. The only things left out were a few fans, some half-melted votive candles, and Alison's laptop, which was connected to a set of portable speakers playing Joanna Newsom.

"We packed," Alison said.

"You packed *everything*?" I asked.

"I came home early," Mom said. The sleeves of her T-shirt were rolled up to her shoulders, and she was eating sushi and tempura from a lacquer box.

There were no pillows or throws on the couches, no books on the bookshelves. The ceramic frog we used to prop open the door to the genkan had completely vanished.

"Where the hell have you been all day?" Alison asked. She wasn't using chopsticks, just picking up pieces of tempura with her forefinger and thumb. From the pissed-off look on her face, I could tell she was still upset about yesterday. But this was so not the time to deal with that. Not with Jamie standing behind me, frozen like a kid at the edge of a pool, terrified to jump in.

"I've been out with…" I faltered. "I went to get Jamie. He's helping me pack."

Alison crinkled her nose in disdain. "God, why? Are you paying him?"

Mom lowered her glasses onto the tip of her nose and gave Jamie a once-over. "Hello," she said. "Do you want sushi? I ordered tons. You two can have sushi, and then you can pack."

"I don't know him," Alison said. "Do we know him?"

"He's Mika's friend." Mom shifted in her chair so she was facing us. "You're back from boarding school, aren't you?" She seemed surprisingly cool about all this, like maybe she'd been sitting around waiting for me to turn up with a strange blond boy.

"That's right," Jamie said. He reached up to touch a curl at the back of his hair, then let it go. "I flew in with my parents last weekend."

"I'm sure Sophia would trade places with you in a second," Mom said casually enough, but I knew she was thinking of our conversation about Paris. Which made me realize I *hadn't* thought about it in hours. Which made me feel totally guilty. "Both of you eat," Mom said. "Have whatever you want. We're almost done."

"I'm not done." Alison dunked a deep-fried piece of sweet potato into a plastic container of tempura sauce.

"I'll have a little," Jamie said. "Thanks so much."

I figured Jamie and I would sit there and quietly shove a few *nigiri* into our mouths before escaping upstairs. But Jamie was determined to make conversation. He asked my sister what her major was; he asked Mom if she was looking forward to going back to Rutgers. It was crazy. Maybe this was something his parents had taught him. *Chew with your mouth closed. Ask polite questions, and make sure your hosts feel at ease.*

Mom answered his questions, and then she asked him about boarding school. He gave a seemingly straight-forward but evasive answer. "I wouldn't go back. Which is lucky, I guess, because I don't have to."

Alison kept staring at me in this horrified way, like she was trying to send telepathic messages: *Oh. My. God. Can't you make him stop?!*

I'm not sure how long we sat there for. Longer than I wanted to, that's for sure. My mom and Alison were not easy people. David, for example, avoided them at all costs. But here was Jamie, not avoiding them at all. Treating them like they were guests at a cotillion or something.

After dinner, Mom said she and Alison were going to take a bunch of garbage bags to the trash spot by the station and buy some more packing tape at the konbini. Before they left, Mom offered us herbal tea and Jamie accepted. As soon as she handed us our mugs (mine had a picture of a cat chasing a mouse on it; Jamie's said THIS IS MY CUP OF TEA), I jumped up. "We'll drink these upstairs."

Halfway up the stairs, I heard the back door open. At the top, I heard it swing shut. Jamie and I paused. It was quiet, like the house itself had drifted to sleep. We went into my room, and I switched on the lights and closed the door behind us.

"Before you ask," I said, "yes, it is always like that."

"Like what?"

I gave him my best *oh please* expression. "Dial back the southern charm, Colonel Sanders. I'm talking about my mom and Alison and me. We're like—we're the three witches in *Macbeth*."

"Huh?" He laughed and shook his head.

"You know. We're three moody women who sit around lighting candles and drinking tea."

"So?" Jamie hitched his shoulders up. "I like tea. You know what else I like? Incense. And Enya. That song from the first *Lord of the Rings* movie—I love that song!"

"You're defying all kinds of gender norms right now," I said, smirking a little.

Jamie looked at the wall behind me. When he spoke, it was with an exaggerated southern accent. "Well, well. Look at that! Big Ghibli fan, huh?"

I glanced at my *Spirited Away* poster and Totoro toys. "Yeah, yeah. Don't blow this out of proportion."

Jamie didn't stop smiling. He walked over to my night-stand and put his mug down. "Do those work?" He pointed up at the twinkle lights on the ceiling.

I gestured at his feet. "Yeah. That's the extension cord."

He plugged it in, and I turned off the main light. The ceiling began to glow.

"Cool," Jamie said.

I put down my mug and cleared a spot on the floor by my bed. We sat down on my rainbow-patterned throw rug.

"Is it just me, or is it hot in here?" he asked.

"What?" I giggled. "What do you mean? Oh, the air conditioner. Yeah, it doesn't work. Hold on. I'll open the window."

I opened it but kept the curtains closed and sat down again. It was like being trapped in a jar of fireflies. Trapped with a beautiful person who wants to kiss you.

And he did want to kiss me; of that, I was 100 percent certain. And I wanted to kiss him. That's why I'd closed the door. That's why I'd sat with him in the dark. I was creating the optimal make-out environment.

Creating the optimal make-out environment. I really didn't know what I was doing. Like, not at all. I wished I could press pause on all this and let myself hyperventilate for a minute. Or call Mika so she could tell me that what I was feeling was perfectly natural and to just go with it. Not that I could call her anymore. Not after our fight this morning. If I'd tried, she probably would have told me to fuck off and leave her best friend Jamie alone.

No, not her best friend Jamie. Just Jamie. Sitting right there, his cheeks slightly pink from the sun. "I like your mom," he said. "I like how she trusts you. You guys are so comfortable with each other."

"Of course she trusts me." I picked up a stuffed puppy dog and tossed it onto the bed. "That's why she lets me go out all night. That's why she doesn't care if my laundry smells like cigarettes and booze."

He took his sunglasses off his head and ruffled the top of his hair. "She trusts you because you're not the one smoking the cigarettes or drinking the booze."

"She trusts me because I'm smart. Smart is all the currency in my family."

"Not in mine," he said bluntly. "We Fosters are big on appearances."

"Just the Fosters? What about the Collinses?"

"My dad's family has been absorbed into the orbit of the Famous Wyatt Foster. They're all big on the manners thing. Use *ma'am* and *sir* when talking to adults. No fighting in front of strangers or, worse, in front of the Famous Wyatt Foster. Go to the gym. Smile a lot." He smiled as an example.

"You definitely win in the manners category," I said. "You were horrifying down there."

He drew back, affronted. "Horrifying? How was I horrifying?"

"I'm just glad you didn't call my mom *ma'am*," I said. "If you'd called my mom *ma'am*, this would all be over."

He scrunched up his eyes in adorable confusion. His sunglasses were sitting between us, so I put them on the nightstand. When I lowered my arm, he reached over and brushed his fingers against the back of my hand. Goose bumps traveled up my arm. And then I actually couldn't take it anymore. I grabbed his hand and rubbed my thumb over his knuckles, again and again and again.

He closed his eyes.

"How many girls have you kissed?" I whispered.

"What?" He opened his eyes.

"How many girls have you kissed?" I asked again.

"You want to know that?"

"Of course I want to know that. Jesus. Who wouldn't?"

He chewed his bottom lip. "I feel like the number is misleading."

"Oh God," I groaned. "What does that even mean?"

"It means I've kissed people for stupid reasons." He sat closer to me. "I went to *boarding school*. If you didn't have a car, you might not leave campus for months. There was a lot of let's-pass-the-time kissing going on."

"Let it be known that you are currently confirming all my worst fears," I said.

"Damn." He dipped his head forward. "I was trying to make it better."

"How many girlfriends have you had?"

He seemed to think about this for a while. I imagined him tallying up the numbers. Twelve, thirteen, fourteen, fifteen...

"Three," he said.

"Three?"

He nodded. "My last girlfriend was the one I was talking about, the one Hannah hated. Her name was Sam. We dated for a year and a half."

"That's exactly one-half of your teenage life."

He pulled my hand into his lap with both of his, then turned it over and started tracing figure eights on my palm. Every part of me shivered.

"We broke up last January," he said. "But we were really done six months before that. When she went to the University of Florida. Long distance. We were doomed."

Long distance.

"The girlfriend before that," he said, "was one of my first friends at that school. We dated because everyone else in our tiny friend group was dating. She dumped me after two weeks."

"And the one before that?"

His fingers stopped moving. "Mika."

"Mika?"

"Not seriously or anything." He pulled me a little bit closer so he was holding me lightly by the wrist and forearm. "When I started at the T-Cad, I was in kindergarten and Mika was in first grade. She saw that other kids wouldn't play with me, so she told them all that she was my girlfriend. We used to walk around the playground holding hands."

I thought about me and Jamie—walking around Tokyo, holding hands. I shimmied back a little. "Was that it?"

"Not exactly," he said. "We did *kiss*. Once. When I was in sixth grade."

"What?" I jerked my arm away. "The year before I moved here?"

A crease flickered briefly between his eyebrows. "It was on the train one night. Afterward, Mika made me swear I wouldn't tell anyone, and she said it would never happen again. I was disappointed, but I got over it."

I crossed my arms. "But she's still your best friend. You still talk to her all the time."

"Yeah, but honestly? Mika and I have never been great with the serious stuff. I mean, we joke around, and we grew up together, so I guess she knows a lot about me. But hey, listen." He reached out and held me carefully by the elbows. "She's not my *best* friend, okay?" We were leaning into each other, like there were magnets in our shoulders. "Since we're on the topic of past romantic lives," he whispered, "I have to ask you a question."

"What is it?" I whispered back.

"Shit. Okay. I have to ask if you *really* liked David? Before, when we used to...hang out a lot?"

I paused. "Yes. I mean, I did. And I'm sorry. I'm sorry I led you on."

He ducked closer still; our foreheads were nearly touching. "Listen to me, Sophia. You didn't lead me on. We were friends. You treated me like a friend. It was my problem that I wanted it to be different."

"I really liked you, Jamie," I said. "But, I don't know, I liked David, too. He was so...self-assured, and funny, and charming—"

"Thanks," Jamie said. "I got it."

"No." I rolled my eyes. "I mean, he was imposing. I

thought, if someone like him paid attention to me, I must be special. Turns out he was just addicted to the confidence boost."

"He liked you," Jamie insisted. "But you're too much awesome for his brain to handle."

"Uh." I snorted. "Am not."

"You are," he said. "Sophia. I like you. The last three years haven't felt as real to me as the last three days. I like talking to you. I like listening to you talk. I don't want it to end."

I shifted forward. Our knees connected.

"That's because I'm good at talking," I said. "You may think my only strong suit is science, but I have a bunch of other skills. I can talk, I can listen and look serious at the same time, I can nod knowingly."

Jamie lifted my left hand and pressed it between both of his. He brought my exposed wrist to his lips and kissed it, once, where my skin was nearly sheer and charged with nerves.

I really hoped it wasn't sweaty or smelly or something. I really hoped he didn't hate it. I really hoped he didn't think it was embarrassing when I gasped.

I sat up on my knees and ran both of my hands around Jamie's neck, tilted his face up to mine. His lips parted easily, and his eyes closed. When he opened them again, I said, "I don't want it to end, either."

His mouth found mine, his arms wrapped around my back. Kissing. I was kissing someone! And it—it made my mouth feel instantly numb. It was like plunging into

219

ice-cold water. My body was all, *I have no map for this! Help!*

I took a quick, shallow breath and our lips disconnected. I sat back on my feet, trying to fill my lungs with oxygen. Jamie leaned forward, one hand sweeping away the hair that had gotten stuck to my lips. "Is everything okay?"

All those shadows and the curves of his face. All that concern in his magic green eyes. *Okay. I am okay.* My hands held on to his face. And then...

And then we were kissing again.

I opened my mouth wider and his tongue pushed gently against mine and I tasted tea leaves and mint. His hands slipped under my knees and he was pulling me into his lap. My stomach touched his. My mouth opened a little more and his teeth clicked against mine, which Mika had told me was bad, but it didn't feel so bad. It didn't feel like a disaster.

He shifted back so he was resting against the bookshelf. I sat back and ran my hands down his shoulders and up his arms. His eyes were closed, and his eyelashes beat furiously against his cheeks, sending out all kinds of Morse code. It made me want to kiss him more.

So I did.

I wanted to coil all the way around him. I wanted to take all his air and give it back to him and take it again. His arms adjusted around my waist, and he twisted his mouth away. He touched his nose to my cheek, then my jaw. "You're pretty good at this, too," he whispered.

I kissed his ear and rested my nose there, in the dappled sunlight of his hair. I whispered, "MIT will be glad to hear it."

He laughed with his mouth against my throat, and the nerves in my body disconnected, one by one by one.

CHAPTER 24
THURSDAY

———

02 : 05 : 15 : 00
DAYS HOURS MINS SECS

JAMIE WAS RIGHT. He was good at packing.

"This is the advantage of being repeatedly shipped between nations," he said. "I am a Jedi master of packing."

"If that was true," I said, "I'd be one, too. But I totally suck."

"You"—he pointed at me with a pack of *Pingu* stationery—"are just denying your potential."

It took three hours to pack my room. It should have been weird between us after the marathon make-out session, but it wasn't. I was too floaty to be anxious. Too effervescent, like I'd been filled to the top with something carbonated.

Kissing Jamie had made time stop. Or, at the very least, slow down. Every second was too alive to worry about the next. I couldn't even think about getting on a plane in two days, because there were hundreds upon thousands of seconds between this moment and that one. Seconds I could potentially spend with Jamie. Kissing.

We'd only been making out for ten minutes or so when

we heard the back door open again. My house was small enough that I could *feel* if someone else was inside it. The floor in my bedroom actually shook when Mom and Alison walked into the kitchen.

I jumped up, flipped on the light, and threw open the door. By the time I turned around, Jamie had started packing. We made boxes, we labeled boxes, we filled boxes. Jamie was a Grade A folder of clothes. And he wrapped all my science books in old T-shirts and carried them with both hands before putting them gingerly into a box. Which made me want to nudge my way between him and the box, to nudge my nose against his neck and kiss a line along the back of his ear. (My imagination was being way more active than I had realized it could be.)

Soon my room was nothing but boxes. They sat around my bed and under my desk and in front of the closet. We packed a suitcase for me to take on the plane, since the rest of my stuff was being shipped to the States.

I stood next to my bed and tried to wrap my head around all the change. The walls were stripped of posters and pictures, the rainbow rug was gone, and the twinkle lights were coiled in a box instead of hanging from the ceiling. I went downstairs to get a glass of water and put our tea mugs away while Jamie finished taping the very last box. When I came back, it was done.

"It looks so small," I said.

Jamie flipped my stuffed puppy into the air and caught it. "It looked small before."

223

I knocked my arm against his, and he bopped the top of my head with the puppy. It was hard not to kiss the side of his neck, but I could hear Alison moving around in her room next door, listening to cello music.

"Hey." Jamie put the puppy on top of my suitcase. "Don't forget this." He picked up the watch from the otherwise empty dresser and handed it to me.

"Right. Thanks." It felt almost hot in my hand. Staring at its faded purple-and-white face sobered me up for a second—the inevitable was coming. The only reason Jamie was here was to help me pack my room. So I could get on a plane and leave.

I dropped it on the suitcase. "You're going to miss the last train," I said. "I'll walk you to the station."

Mom was sitting at the desk in her room, typing on her laptop. I knocked and said I was taking Jamie to the station. "Okay, good." She pushed her glasses onto her head and gave us a weary smile. "Still miles to go for me. Thanks for all your help, Jamie." Jamie nodded and tugged his leather wristband. I stared intently at some loose plaster on the wall.

Going downstairs felt like walking into a crime scene, everything neat and square and cordoned off. And then we were outside, and Jamie was reaching for my hand again. The night opened up around us: a breeze rustling the laundry on someone's balcony, cicadas croaking in the trees that curled around buildings. I could smell *yakisoba* and the vague perfume of persimmon trees, all of it float-ing up to a dark smear of hazy sky.

Since it was just before midnight, every store we passed was shuttered, but a few vending machines lit our way down the hill. Someone biked past us with a small dog sit-ting on a cushion in the basket. But then they were gone, and we were alone.

Jamie lifted our joined hands and pointed them at the sky. "Check it out," he said. "There are exactly four stars up there."

I looked up. "Those are probably airplanes."

"So cynical," he said. "Those count."

He stopped walking, so I did, too. "Stupid question," he said, sounding nervous all of a sudden. He was swinging my hand back and forth. "Did you miss me? When I was in the States?"

I frowned. "That doesn't sound like a stupid question. That sounds like a trick question."

He laced his other hand with mine, like we were going to start dancing up and down the empty street. Like we were in one of those cheesy movies from the 1950s with big, long dance sequences at night under the stars. I could see Jamie in one of those movies. All that goofy charm and that wide, expressive face.

"Actually," he said, "don't answer that. I'm gonna stop talking before I embarrass myself some more."

I turned away. There was a cat sitting in an alleyway

between two stores, its flashlight eyes blinking at us. "I don't know what to say. I thought we'd fucked things up so much when you left. I thought you were living proof that I was a loser with no ability to make genuine connections with other human beings."

"Wow." Both of his eyebrows quirked up. "That's quite a compliment."

I rolled my eyes and shoved him a little. For the past three years, I'd tried so hard not to think about him. When I sat in the courtyard at lunch, when I watched my favorite movies, when I checked my e-mail and knew I'd never see his name there again. "You were my first real best friend," I said, realizing with each word that it was true. "Of course I missed you. Every single day."

He didn't say anything or even smile. He just kissed me, with all those airplanes twinkling above.

CHAPTER 25
FRIDAY

---

01 : 18 : 38 : 11
DAYS HOURS MINS SECS

I DIDN'T GET UP WHEN MOM knocked on my door, but I did when Alison came in and tore the sheet off me.

"Get your shit together," she said. "The movers are here."

"I'm up," I mumbled, burying my face in my pillow. "My shit is together."

Alison snorted. "Yeah, you seem real alert. Change your clothes."

I grabbed the first things I found in my suitcase. A green-and-black striped T-shirt, a pair of skinny jeans, a plastic belt covered in pictures of comic book covers, and my toiletry bag. There were people downstairs. I heard furniture scraping across the floor and boxes bumping into doorframes.

Seeing the house picked clean was even worse in the morning, sunlight and dust filling up every empty corner. None of this belonged to us anymore—it belonged to a stranger.

"Don't think about it," I whispered. I went into the bathroom and brushed my teeth with a miniature toothbrush and a tube of travel toothpaste. As I pulled my shirt over my head, I smelled mint on my shoulder. Memories of last night sparked in my nerve endings—Jamie's mouth and the careful loops he'd drawn up and down my arms.

The iron fist gripping my stomach loosened as I reminded myself that whatever else happened today, I was going to see Jamie. He didn't have a cell, so I couldn't call him. But last night, before he'd gotten on his train, we'd agreed to meet at Hachiko at four. That thought was like putting on a coat of armor. It was like putting on headphones to drown out the racket downstairs.

I practically skipped out of the bathroom and back into the chaos of boxes.

The movers were there all morning, Alison and me swooping around them, and Mom directing them in Japanese. It was noon, and then one, and then, somehow, it was after two.

The last few boxes huddled in small groups by the genkan. The rest of the house had transformed into nothing but blank walls and spongy carpet. Mom shouted at me from the top of the stairs that we'd be leaving for the hotel in an hour.

And after that, I'd go to Hachiko.

My stomach growled. I escaped into the kitchen to see

if we had any food left and almost collided with Alison, who sat near the back door pulling on shoes. "Mom gave me money. She said we should get lunch at Mister Donut before we leave."

I twisted my belt so it sat in the right place. "You're talking to me again?"

I could hear Mom in the hallway now, explaining something to one of the movers. Alison stood up. "Captain's orders."

Jamie had left his red sunglasses in my room, so I wore them on the way to the station. My sister eyed me suspiciously.

"You're smiling a lot," she said. "Did you knock your head on something?"

"The other day you thought something was wrong because I was sad," I pointed out. "Now you think something's wrong because I'm happy."

"Yeah, yeah," she said. "Your face is warped with a new and unique emotion every time I see you."

Mister Donut was a donut shop in Yoyogi-Uehara Station. I waited in line with Alison, overwhelmed by how familiar everything was. The glass cases of donuts and the cheerful yellow decor and the rumble of the trains overhead. I used to hang out here with Mika and David on boring Sunday afternoons. We'd sit at a table in the back, and they'd laugh and tease each other for hours, maybe flirt with each other, now that I really thought about it....

"Hello?" Alison snapped her fingers in front of my face. "Are you ordering or what?"

Alison and I ordered two donuts each. She got black coffee, and I got a creamy latte and dumped three sugar syrups into it.

"Blech," Alison said when we were sitting down. "This coffee tastes like garbage."

"But they give you free refills." I gestured at the employees in bright yellow shirts who walked briskly between tables, topping off everyone's cups. I ripped my pink frosted donut into halves and then fourths. I wished I hadn't let myself think about Mika and David. Now I was obsessing over how much I missed them. How I would never karaoke with them again or go to purikura booths after school or text them nonstop when I stayed home sick.

I sipped my creamy coffee and tried to concentrate on Jamie instead.

Alison stared at me. "So. You're still pissed at me, right?"

"Nope." Since I wasn't wearing my watch, I reached for my cell to check the time. But I didn't have it anymore. Mom was taking it to the Docomo store to cancel my contract.

Alison took a bite of her jam donut and chewed. "But you were pissed at me. At Tokyo Tower. You were royally pissed at me."

"I'm not pissed at you." It must have been almost three. Which meant I needed to hurry. I needed to get to Shibuya so I could meet Jamie. So I could hear his voice and touch his skin. Because when I did, I didn't feel like everything was ending. I didn't feel the future dragging me toward something I couldn't control.

Alison leaned over the table, and a curtain of dark hair dangled near my latte. "Where did you go that night? After Tokyo Tower?"

I sighed. "Mom told you. I was with Mika."

"No," she said, "you weren't."

"Yes," I said. "I was."

Alison frowned. Deeply. "I heard you and Mika in the kitchen yesterday. You guys didn't sound like you'd just had a fun little slumber party together."

I felt a rush of annoyance. "You were listening to us?"

"God, Sophia. Have you been to our house? I can hear when you freaking breathe."

I thought about last night and about Jamie, which made my face blaze all the way up to my forehead. "Look," I said. "It's nice that you care. Weird, too, I guess, but nice. Do me one favor, though. In the future, if you find yourself worrying that I've locked myself in a public bathroom for the rest of my life or something, call me. Don't wake Mom up in the middle of the night. Don't panic her."

Alison sat back and made a *tsk* sound. "You're not an adult yet. You were acting crazy, and Mom should know when you're acting crazy."

"Well, she does know," I said. "And that's why I'm moving to Paris."

"Wait... what did you just say?"

"Yeah. Mom called Dad, and they said I can live in Paris this year. If I want to."

Alison didn't seem fazed. "But you're not going."

"You actually have zero say in this. Zero."

"You're not going," Alison said. "What the hell, Sophia? You're not seriously considering this?"

I shoved two large hunks of pink donut into my mouth. "I have considered it." I swallowed. *"Seriously."*

"Sophia," she said, angry now. Angrier. "You can't do that. You can't leave Mom alone."

"Why not? She already said I should go."

"Fuck!" Alison slammed her hand on the yellow tray, making me jump. "Are you kidding me? She's our *mother.* You can't abandon her. Not for someone who walked out on us because he was too French or we weren't French enough or whatever bullshit reason he had for doing it."

"He didn't..." I shook my head. "He was young. And I know he used to be unreliable, but he's not like that anymore. He has a family now."

"Yeah, the family he wants. A real family."

"Stop saying stuff like that!" I shouted and then lowered my voice. "Just stop talking about us like we can be replaced."

"Fine." Alison jabbed the air with her finger. "Then why don't you go to Paris? Why don't you go find out how *reliable* he is? Part of me really wants to watch this whole goddamned scenario go down in flames, to be honest."

I bristled. "Why do you always get so bitchy about this? The last time I almost went—"

"He didn't want you there! Don't you get that? He's the one who decided it wouldn't work. *He's* the one who said you shouldn't go. Mom didn't tell you, because she thought it would wreck you."

My stomach and chest clenched. It didn't make sense— Mom had explained why I couldn't go to Paris then. She'd talked it over with Dad, and they'd decided, together, that I should come to Tokyo instead. "That's not what happened," I said.

"Of course it is! God! Do you have any clue how hard this is? Watching you cling to all these ridiculous ideas of him? You want to think he's this normal dad to us, but he's not. And if you go there, you'll see that. You'll see how little you matter to him."

I dropped my gaze to the table. I couldn't believe it—I *wouldn't* believe any of it. "It isn't like that," I insisted.

"Sophia, I'm begging you," Alison said, her voice cracking now. "If you go to Paris, he won't treat you like you belong there. You're going to get hurt."

Confusion engulfed me. I wanted to argue with her but didn't know how. She was lying. She was saying this to scare me out of going.

Wasn't she?

"Please," I whispered. "Can we please stop talking about this now?"

"So when do you want to talk about it?" she shouted, a sob breaking through her words. "When you're boarding a plane to freaking Paris?!"

One of the servers carrying coffee stopped short near our table.

"Don't do this to us," Alison said. And now she was crying. My sister was crying. "Please don't leave us."

CHAPTER 26
FRIDAY

———

01 : 12 : 49 : 38
DAYS   HOURS   MINS   SECS

THE HOTEL HAD A PANORAMIC VIEW OF TOKYO, of gray buildings, red billboards, and a smudgy sky. Alison and I didn't talk as we dropped our stuff on opposite sides of the room. Probably because everything was broken. Beyond repair. Just beyond everything. My sister hated me, and we were leaving, and this week was catching up with me, grabbing me by the heels.

Alison snatched a key card and left the room again, the door slamming behind her. I let cranky Dorothea Brooke out of her airplane carrier and raced to the nightstand to pick up the chunky hotel phone. I would call Dad. I would call Dad, and he'd tell me that Alison was wrong.

But as I held the plastic handset, I felt something tightening the screws of my rib cage, making it harder and harder for me to breathe. I was supposed to have met Jamie—I was supposed to have met him ten minutes ago. The realization hit me, sudden and sharp, but I couldn't worry about that now. The only thing I could do was push the thought down as far as it would go and sit on the edge of the bed, the phone cord stretching and uncoiling behind me.

"*Allô*, Philippe Moignard." It surprised me to hear him answer in French, but I guess that made sense. It's not like my number would have popped up on his phone.

"Dad," I said. "Hi."

"Sophia? Is everything okay?" He sounded harried. I could hear the twins arguing in the background and Sylvie snapping at them. There were other sounds as well—traffic pouring down a busy road, car horns beeping.

"I'm fine," I said. "I was just calling because—"

"Is your sister okay? Your mom?" His voice went distant, and he said something else to Sylvie, something in French.

"Dad," I said, raising my voice. "Everyone's fine. Seriously."

"Emmanuelle," he said to my half sister. *"Calme-toi."*

I pulled my legs onto the bed. All that coffee and sugar from Mister Donut was pulsing in my veins. There was a cardboard sign advertising cheap deals to Tokyo Disneyland on the nightstand, and I reached over to press my thumb into the corner of it.

"Sorry," Dad said after a moment. "Maybe we can talk later? We're on our way to the market, and Emmanuelle says she has a stomachache."

"Dad," I said. "I wanted to tell you something. I wanted to tell you that—that I've decided to move to Paris. I know Mom said I should think it over, and I know it's a big decision, but I have thought it over. Like, a lot. And I wanted to tell you and Sylvie first."

Another pause. I heard Emmanuelle's small voice breaking into a scream, Luc joining her with a scream of his own.

"We should talk about this later," he said. "When you're back in America."

His tone was off somehow—more clipped than usual. Something cold and prickly crawled across my skin. "But you have talked about it," I said. "You talked about it with Mom yesterday."

"Sophia." Dad sounded stern. Almost like Alison actually. "We need to think everything through."

Think everything through?! "But. Mom said it was my choice."

"Of course," Dad said. "But it would be a lot of change, yes? You coming here."

No, I wanted to say. It would be the opposite of change. It would be the same bakeries and parks I visited every Christmas. The same Metro stops and the same walks along the Seine and the same museums, shoes squeaking on the same glossy floors. It would be the place I'd wanted to live since I was five years old when my dad first explained that he was moving back there.

But I didn't say that. He didn't mean it would be a lot of change for me.

"Fine," I said, embarrassment surging through me, making my face and neck feel numb. "Sorry to bug you."

Dad said something else—bye, probably—but his voice washed over with static, and the call went dead.

For a moment, I sat completely still. It was like my vision was shifting. It was like, in that moment, I could see things the way Alison must have. The e-mails he'd send a few times a week that felt rushed and superficial. The phone calls he'd cut short because of the time difference. And excuse after excuse after excuse for why I shouldn't live there.

I put the phone back in its cradle. Then I picked it up and slammed it down, hard. Dorothea Brooke bolted out from under the bed and into the bathroom. I stood up and sat down and stood up again. I leaned against the nightstand, wishing I could do something. Wishing I could scream so loud, everyone in the hotel would hear me. Wishing I could find my mom and put my arms around her neck and sob into her shoulders for hours.

Wishing I could pick up that phone again and smash it to pieces.

He was my dad. His home was supposed to be my home. I was supposed to just—fit there. Like I was supposed to fit in Tokyo. Like I was supposed to fit with Mika and David. But they'd let me down, too. And I didn't get to keep Tokyo—I didn't get to keep any of this.

So I wasn't going to try anymore.

Seconds and minutes and hours came and went. The sun was starting to set, and I was on the floor between the beds. But I didn't know how I'd gotten there. Or how long

I'd been sitting for. There was movement in the hallway, and my heart screeched into my throat. If that was Alison, there was no way I could talk to her. No way I could tell her anything Dad had said. I grabbed the spare key card and ran to the door, desperate to get out before she came in. Desperate to get somewhere I could be entirely alone. I pushed at the door—just as someone started knocking on it.

"Sophia?"

"Caroline?" I opened the door and there she was, in a purple tank-top dress and hot-pink flip-flops. Her eyes lit up the second she saw me. "Hey!"

"What?" I stumbled back, wishing I could impose reason on this seriously unreasonable situation. "What are you doing here?"

"Oh." She held up her phone. "I texted you."

"You texted me?" I shook my head emphatically. "I didn't get it. I don't have a cell anymore."

"I know. Your mom called when she saw my message. She said she was canceling your phone contract, but she told me where you guys were staying." She blushed and started fiddling with the strap of her blue-and-white check purse. "Anyway, I was thinking maybe we could go together tonight? I know it's lame, but I'd feel better if I didn't show up alone."

"Go where?" I asked.

She cocked her head, confused. "Your good-bye thing. Mika's birthday. You didn't forget, did you?"

My stomach roiled. Oh God. Mika's birthday. My good-bye thing.

"No," I said. "I'm not going."

"What?!" Caroline stepped into the room. "You have to go! It's your last night in Tokyo!"

"Technically, tomorrow night is my last night in Tokyo."

"Were you asleep or something? It's super dark in here." She was right—the room was growing dimmer by the second. Outside the window, buildings were turning into something bigger and stranger, something with thousands of greedy eyes. She walked toward the lamp in the corner of the room, and I felt my temper fraying. What the hell was she even *doing here*?

Why couldn't I be left alone?!

She flipped on the light and turned to examine me. "Are you sure everything is okay?" She narrowed her eyes. "This isn't about David, is it?"

"Oh God." I crumpled into the chair by the window. My head was aching, but I wasn't thinking about David. I was thinking about Jamie.

About how he must have been waiting for hours.

About how I'd never tried to contact him.

And how I didn't want to.

"Sophia?"

I crammed my hands into the pockets of my sweatshirt and pressed my forehead into my knees. "Can't you go by yourself?" I asked. "What does it matter if I'm with you or not?"

"Are you kidding?" she said. "Of course it matters. You're, like, my only friend here."

My head jerked up.

"I mean"—Caroline licked her pink, glossy lips—"I have friends in Tennessee and everything. But not *here*."

"I'm your friend?" I asked, and then realized how harsh that sounded. "I mean, of course I'm your *friend*." I slumped back and rubbed both hands over my face. "Sorry. I'm having a seriously shitty day."

"Yeah." Caroline sat on the end of my bed. She was being sympathetic and understanding even though she had no idea what had just happened.

"I was just surprised," I said. "About the friend thing. It's just, you're so—popular."

She laughed a little. "What makes you think I'm popular?"

I pointed at her phone, which she was now clutching in both hands. "You're always texting people."

"Yeah, people in Tennessee. And sometimes I think they just text back out of pity. I don't really have friends in Tokyo. Well, except for you. You're kind of my best friend, actually."

"Please," I snorted.

"No!" she said. "I'm serious! I've never had super-close friends. I went to this ginormous public school outside of Nashville, and I was really shy. My only friends were the ones I did tennis and swimming and stuff with. And they kind of treated me like an outsider."

"I'm sure that's not true," I said, a wave of guilt washing

241

over me for all the times I'd treated her the exact same way. She shrugged, and her cheeks went red. And, much to my surprise, my icy feelings toward her started to soften up.

Still, she couldn't possibly think of me as her best friend. I'd always seen Caroline as a character from an American teen movie. The Homecoming Queen. The perfect, pretty popular girl. She was David's girlfriend, and I was the dorky sidekick she found semi-amusing.

But maybe that wasn't true. Maybe we had more in common than I'd thought. Both of us lost in huge American schools, both of us wondering if our friends liked us as much as we liked them. And I guess she'd been dating David since she moved to Tokyo a year ago. Which meant I was one of the few people she hung out with on a regular basis. On an everyday basis. Which meant...

Holy shit. We really were friends.

And I'd been a bastard to her from the second I met her.

Caroline said, "I'm not going to miss your last night here because of stupid David. After tonight, we might never see each other again."

Someone was walking down the hall, and panic exploded inside of me again. What if it was Alison this time? What if I had to talk to her?

"Fine," I said, standing up.

"Fine?" Caroline stood up as well. "It was that easy?"

"Yeah. Let's get out of here."

Caroline threw back her shoulders and looked me over. Suddenly, she was the American Homecoming Queen, and all I wanted was to crawl into my bed, to hide under the covers until I had to catch my plane.

"What is it?" I asked. "You're giving me a look."

"No offense," she said, crossing her arms, "but if we're going out, you seriously have to change."

———

Caroline picked out an outfit for me: a black stretchy skirt that I approved of because it covered my still-scabbing knees and a loose blue shirt that was slightly sheer. The shirt, I approved of less. I could kind of see the outline of my bra, which was *neon green*.

It was way too much, but whatever, I didn't care.

The only thing I cared about was going somewhere crowded—somewhere I could be absorbed into the blare of music and the crush of bodies. Somewhere distinctly *not here*.

After I got dressed, Caroline insisted on French braiding my hair.

"I didn't even know people still did this," I said.

"I love French braiding!" Caroline said. "My sisters and I do it for each other all the time."

"I think you and your sisters have a very different relationship from me and my sister," I muttered.

Alison didn't come back, thank God, and I didn't knock on Mom's door to tell her I was going out. Even though I probably should have. But she would have known I was upset—she would have stood in the doorway, tapping a pen against the palm of her hand and looking worried, and that would have defeated me. I would have told her everything.

I texted her from Caroline's phone to say I was going out for Mika's birthday. She texted back and told me to have fun.

CHAPTER 27

SATURDAY

———

01 : 04 : 12 : 23
DAYS HOURS MINS SECS

"THIS PLACE IS INFESTED," MIKA SAID, wrinkling her nose.

"Infested with what?" Jamie leaned one hand on the bar, then yanked it off and wiped it on his jeans.

"T-Cadders." Mika held her drink over her head and shouted, "This whole fucking place is infested with fucking T-Cadders!"

"Watch it." Jamie took the drink from her and put it on the bar. "You could have spilled that on your head."

"*Psh*. Or on yours." She flashed him a manic grin.

I swirled the tiny plastic straw in my melon soda. The ice had melted, and the glass was warm and sweaty.

This was our third club of the night. So far, my plan to distract myself was *not* working out. Everywhere we went was too obnoxious. Overrun with T-Cadders and saturated with monotonous techno music that ground over the speakers like a chorus of dental drills. Since I didn't have my watch or my phone, I had no idea what time it was.

Probably after midnight? And I was still waiting for something to change, for everyone to suddenly grow comfortable with each other.

Which was never going to happen. David had gone all sullen and broody when he realized I was with Caroline, and Mika barely acknowledged my existence. But Jamie was the worst. There was so much uncertainty in his voice when he'd said "hey," like he was waiting for me to explain where I'd been all day. Why I'd never shown up.

But I couldn't. I couldn't explain how pointless everything seemed. Couldn't even think through the noise in my head.

And now David had wandered off somewhere, and Mika was ignoring me, and Jamie was barely looking in my direction. (At least he was slightly more comfortable now; he'd had two beers.) The only person I could even begin to tolerate was Caroline, and she'd gone to the bathroom.

I stood on tiptoe to see if she was coming back, but I couldn't make out much in the thick, beer-foamy crowd. There were some black walls covered in cracked paint and wilting flyers. A few glow sticks waved lethargically in the air. Mika was right. It *was* infested with T-Cadders. Not just this club in particular, but Roppongi in general. T-Cadders loved Roppongi, even though it was seriously sleazy. The streets were crowded with nightclubs and bars, gaudier and seedier than the nightclubs and bars in other parts of Tokyo.

Mika would have probably told me I didn't like Rop-pongi because I was so *innocent*. If she was still talking to me. Which she wasn't. She wasn't talking to anyone except Jamie and the T-Cadders we'd been running into all night. The ones who went on and on about their summer vacations and bemoaned the start of school and happily introduced themselves to Jamie. Some of them hadn't just introduced themselves. A few girls had touched his arm. They'd said they *hoped to see him around sometime*.

Caroline came up behind me and grabbed my shoulders. "Hey!" she said.

"Hey," I said, exhaling.

Jamie was still watching Mika, smiling at her in this lazy, relaxed way.

"They opened the dance floor upstairs," Caroline said. "We have to go! We have to dance!"

"I have to finish this," I said, stirring the straw in my soda.

"I'll come," Mika said. She took a swig of her drink and handed it to Jamie.

"Oh," Caroline said, sizing her up.

So far, the two of them had seemed okay with each other. Not friendly or anything, but okay. Caroline didn't even seem *that* annoyed with David. She didn't talk to him, but she didn't cry or hurl drinks in his face, either.

Caroline threw back her shoulders and looked at Mika like she'd just decided something important. "Great! Let's go!"

They threaded their way through the crowd toward a rickety metal staircase already teeming with uncoordinated teenagers.

That left Jamie and me.

Alone.

A part of me wanted to lean into his chest, to touch his cheek. But another part of me—a stronger part—couldn't put myself through it. Couldn't try to hold on to another thing I knew I'd have to lose.

I put down my soda. After a strained minute, he said, "How'd the moving go?" I forced my gaze up, forced myself to take him in. He was wearing a maroon hat and a gray T-shirt with the phrase PAST LIFE printed on it. I could almost count the honey-colored freckles on his nose and cheeks.

"Fine," I said.

"So," he said, his tone abrupt. "Are you going to tell me what I did to piss you off?"

I traced my index finger through a patch of condensation on the bar and shrugged. The words were right there in the center of my mouth—*you didn't do anything*—but I didn't say them.

"God." Jamie ran both hands through his hair—his hat fell off, but he didn't pick it up. "I don't know what to do here. I waited for you all fucking afternoon."

I squeezed my eyes shut. He sounded so angry, I almost hated him for it. Didn't he understand how impossible this was? Didn't he see how much it hurt, just standing there with him?

"I was moving," I said. "I was busy."

"You were busy." Jamie kept his hands in his hair, gripping it. "That's it? That's all you've got?"

I picked up a tiny plastic straw and wrapped it around my fingers. "Screw you," I whispered. "You have no idea what I'm going through."

"Christ." He thumped his fist against the side of the bar, making the countertop vibrate. I jumped a little. "Of course I know what you're going through. I've moved, too, Sophia."

"Then you should get it! I'm leaving in two days, remember? One day, actually, because it's officially past midnight. Why do I have to hang out with you? I don't *want* to."

He fell into a stunned silence. A girl standing on the other side of me started laughing so hard she fell against my back. I shrugged her off. The pulse in my temples was thudding in time with the obnoxious music. I crushed the straw in my palm and tried as hard as I could to blink back the tears. I didn't want to say any of this, but I was just so—*furious*. Furious at Jamie for tricking me into thinking this could work. That this week could end in anything but disaster.

"You're being pretty goddamned selfish," he said eventually.

"No," I said. "I'm being realistic."

He recoiled. "You're not the only one who's been dealing with stuff this week."

"Oh, whatever," I snapped. "You left North Carolina. I'm about to leave everything that matters. Tokyo and my friends and my life here. *You* get to stay. And you get my friends. *And* you get my life!"

He turned away from me, but I couldn't seem to stop talking. "And to top it all off, you want me to like you! You want me to *miss* you. What? Is this some kind of revenge? Make me like you so I can see what it feels like to leave with a broken heart, so I can feel as awful as you did…" I trailed off. Inside, I was screaming at myself for saying what I'd just said. Inside I was begging him, *Please know that I'm lying, please know that I'm lying, please know that I'm lying.*

But outside I wasn't saying anything at all.

And neither was he. His usually expressive face was completely closed off. He was standing right in front of me, but he was a thousand miles away.

The T-Cadders around us whooped and hollered. Jamie pushed himself back, took Mika's drink, and started picking his way toward the stairs.

The ringing in my ears became a roar—a crashing as violent as a storm. The guy next to me vigorously fist-pumped the air and spilled his drink on my foot. *Oh God, oh God, oh God*, I was going to fall apart, right there, right in front of all those drunk T-Cadders.

"Shit," I said quietly to myself. My temples continued

to throb. This was it. I'd done it—I'd officially and completely ruined everything. Jamie would never forgive me after this. And he shouldn't; I didn't deserve to be forgiven. And even if he did forgive me, it didn't matter now, because this was over. I was over. I was practically gone.

"*Shit.*"

I fell away from the bar and forced my way through the masses until I got to the bathroom. There wasn't a line; thank God there wasn't a line. I locked the door and leaned against it with all my weight. I closed my eyes and saw an image of a black hole. Something powerful and massive, something that destroys anything it touches. It was all around me. It was a snare trapping me; it was pulling me in.

Okay, okay. Deal with this, Sophia. Deal with this.

There was money in my wallet, which meant I could take a cab to the hotel. Which meant I could sit in the air-conditioning with my cat and my suitcase and pretend none of this had ever happened.

Go outside and find a cab. Deal with this.

I stumbled back from the sink and shoved open the bathroom door and . . . it collided with someone's face.

"Jesus!" David toppled back.

"David?" I stayed in the doorway for a second. "What the hell are you doing here?"

"Jesus." He tipped his head back and pinched his nose, like he was trying to stop it from bleeding. (It wasn't bleeding.) "Is that any way to treat someone trying to help you?"

I slammed the door behind me, and it vibrated in its frame. "What did I need your help with? I was in the *bathroom*!"

If his nose was broken, I wouldn't have cared.

"I was about to knock," he said.

"On the door to the girls' bathroom?!"

"I saw you running in there. I figured maybe you were crying, so I came to check on you." He was smiling like he expected me to fawn all over him or hand him a Sensitive Boy of the Year award or something. What I wanted to do was punch him.

"Well, here's some good news," I snapped. "I'm not crying."

A girl wearing a yellow dress and high heels was trying to get past us, so I grabbed David's sleeve and dragged him to the side. We were standing at the edge of the crowd, right where all the drunken arm-waving began.

"So," he said, nodding his head slightly to the music. "What's going on? Did you chunder? Are you sure you're not crying?"

"I'm fine," I said. "I just can't stand this place."

He tilted his chin up in agreement. "Pretty rank, isn't it? I went outside for a smoke and decided to stay there— away from the feeding frenzy." He gestured at the mob of T-Cadders.

I pulled my skirt over my scabby knees. He was such an ass, but I couldn't bring myself to ditch him. Everything about this night felt wrong; at least he was being his normal d-bag self. "Why are you talking to me?" I asked. "I'm still unbelievably mad at you. You realize this, right?"

"Jeez, Sofa. When did you get so mean?"

"Stop trying to be cute." I jabbed his arm with my index finger. "Did you not hear what I just said?"

"Yeah, yeah," he said. "You're mad at me." His posture slumped a bit. Which reminded me of when I used to hang out with him after gym class. How I'd get Ramune candy from the vending machine and he'd dip his head down and pout at me until I shared them with him. How he'd pick me up and spin me around when I agreed to give him just one.

"*Still* mad at you," I said.

He raised an eyebrow. "Why? Because of what happened with Mika?"

"That! And other things. Lots of things! Things I outlined to you two nights ago!"

"This is about you having a crush on me, isn't it?"

"Oh God!" Mika had been right. She'd been right all along. Telling David that I liked him was a terrible idea. I'd spent so long keeping it secret from him that I'd tricked myself into believing he would welcome the news. That he would tell me he liked me back.

But now we were talking about it, and he didn't seem shocked at all. He seemed sorry for me.

"I don't want to talk about this," I stammered, and surged forward, bumping into two guys drinking dark brown liquid from shot glasses. One of them clapped me on the back and tried to clink his glass with my nonexistent one. I veered away. The whole claustrophobic room was sticky with booze and sweat and perfume. I kept moving, toward the entrance.

David followed me. "Come on. This is no big deal. You had a crush on me! It's totally normal!"

"Argh! Stop! I'm not listening!"

"Hey." He brushed his hand against my shoulder. "Hey. Sophia."

I froze. Everyone in the bar was being loud and horrible. But David seemed somber. A dark slice of hair fell between his eyes, and he didn't push it back.

"What is it?" I asked sharply.

"Wow," he said. "You're really gonna make me work for this, aren't you?"

I crossed my arms.

"Okay," he said, his tone suddenly businesslike. "Okay. We should stop fighting. You should stop hating me right now."

I snorted.

"Hold on!" he said. "I'm not done yet. You shouldn't be mad at me because you're—you're Sofa! You are the one and only Sofa. You're the one I talk to about stuff. And you're funny in a not-on-purpose way. And you make me comfortable. And"—he poked my shoulder—"I really, really like you."

"Okay," I said.

"And!" he said. "I'm not in *loooove* with Mika as everyone seems so inclined to believe. And also, I might have cheated on Caroline, but she cheated on me first, so I'm not the World's Biggest Asshole, okay?"

I narrowed my eyes at him. "Caroline cheated on you?"

He nodded his head. Big, exaggerated nods. He was a bobblehead toy. "When she went home last Christmas, she hooked up with her Tennessee boyfriend." He tried to say "Tennessee boyfriend" with a southern accent, which was so ridiculous I laughed. His face brightened. David really loved making me laugh.

"When did you find out about this?" I asked.

"She told me the other day. Whilst she was dumping me."

"Well," I said. "Just because she cheated on you, that doesn't cancel out you cheating on her."

"True." He touched my shoulder one more time. "But it doesn't seem like a significant indicator that we were destined for each other, either, now, does it?"

I sighed. "Whatever."

Some guys from the T-Cad varsity basketball team stampeded past, knocking David off balance. He stumbled and I reached out to take his arm. He grinned, showing off toothpaste-commercial-ready teeth. "Thanks."

I let go.

"Hey. Sofa." He tugged the strap of my tote bag. "You heard what I said, right? About how I really, really like you?"

David's voice had grown quiet, but I was standing close enough that I could hear him. Despite the raucous environment, his eyes were fixed on mine. His deep, inky eyes. "Yeah," I said eventually. "But you made me think that you *liked me*-liked me."

He didn't let go of my bag. "Oh, come on, Sofa. We both know I make a terrible boyfriend. And it's not like you ever asked me out. I could have been sitting at home every night in my party dress, waiting for you to ask me out."

"Please. You would have laughed in my face."

He scoffed. "Would not have."

"Whatever," I said.

David's face was wolfish again. He wasn't somber David anymore. He was the one who sought attention like sunlight, who got all his kicks from being the most charming person in the room. In every room. As usual, he'd dressed up for the evening. New shirt, dark jeans, sleek shoes. This sophomore had once accused David of being gay because he put so much care into his appearance, and David had just smiled and said, "Sexuality is a sliding scale, my friend."

God, I'd really liked that response. I'd really liked *him* for that response.

The music changed from techno to some hardcore rap. David started bouncing a little. "Hey," he said. "Hey, Sofa. I like this song. You wanna dance?"

"Nope," I said.

"Of course you do." He gave me a mischievous grin. "But first, I'm buying you a drink."

CHAPTER 28
SATURDAY

———

01 : 02 : 50 : 47
DAYS HOURS MINS SECS

BACK WHEN DAVID AND MIKA used to drink and I didn't, I'd wonder what the point of it all was. Drinking made people drowsy and mean. It made them laugh at things that weren't funny and cry at things that weren't sad. It made them say things most preschoolers would find nonsensical.

But as it turned out, it also made them feel good. Great, even. I felt greater than great, like my worries and cares had been filed down. Like I had less of a neurotic edge. When people bumped into me, I didn't notice. When I thought about Jamie, I didn't feel like lying facedown on the ground and weeping.

God. I was practically edge-free.

David ordered me a melon soda with vodka. It tasted different from a melon soda without vodka. "It's like someone dumped toxic chemicals into it," I said.

"Exactly!" David said. "That's exactly what happened."

I drank two toxic melon sodas and ate the ice cubes out

of the bottom of each glass. "Come on." I grabbed David's hand. "Dancing time."

"Dancing time?" he asked. "You want to dance?"

"Yes! Dancing time!"

The metal staircase was a lot spinnier than it had been an hour ago. My feet didn't feel attached to my legs anymore, and I grabbed the railing with both hands. "Don't remember how to do this," I grumbled.

David put his hands on my waist and murmured into the back of my neck. "One step at a time, little Sofa."

When we reached the top, I couldn't believe how many people were up there. Probably a thousand T-Cadders, all writhing in an enormous mass, singing along to some song I didn't know. David was singing, too. He dragged me into the belly of the beast, and the two of us started jumping up and down.

Yes! Jumping! Jumping is great!

David was super cute with his spiky hair flapping all over his forehead. Since he was tall and I was short, I had an excellent view of his stomach and chest. He was long and thin and, from all the times I'd hugged him, I knew how he felt, too. Flexible and strong.

I thrust both hands into the air and started singing some lyrics I'd just made up for this song I didn't know. Something about badgers wearing top hats. David broke out laughing and grabbed my hand, knotting his fingers with mine.

Holding hands! Yes! This is great!

David was my friend. He was my friend because we were both bastards and we could be bastards together. Remove all sexual desire from the equation, and we were just two bastards. Two bastards enjoying each other's company.

David let go of my hand and looped his arms around my waist. He lifted one eyebrow and smirked. I imitated him, which made him laugh again and lean into me. He had a really cute laugh.

I spun out of his grip, and that's when I spotted her. Bald head and black shirt ripped at the collar. Mika was standing at the top of the stairs, scanning the crowd. Jamie and Caroline weren't with her, which made me feel panic under all my other feelings. My happy, swimmy feelings. She homed in on me, and then she was waving like crazy.

I bounced up to David's ear and pointed at Mika. "WE ARE SUMMONED!"

David stopped jumping. He squeezed my hand and pulled me back down the stairs to follow her.

"It's cold!" I said as soon as the bar door closed behind us.

"No, it's not!" David said.

I rolled my eyes. "I meant relatively speaking."

Jamie and Caroline were standing by the brick exterior of the bar, talking to each other. They had serious looks on their faces. Serious, *boring* looks.

The bar was right in the middle of Roppongi-dori. The street stretched away from me on either side, a long, straight blur of neon. The people going up and down it were zombies. Vacant-eyed, shuffling zombies. The whole street...a blur of neon. Really blurry...

I fell into David's shoulder, and it was like falling into a warm, solid pillow. I felt his muscles react as he steadied me. "Whoa," he said.

"Everyone in there is a moron," Mika declared. "Austin Cormack just tried to rub my head for good luck, and that was the last fucking straw, as far as I'm concerned. We're going."

I kept my head resting against David's shoulder. "I kind of like it in there. It grows on you."

"Like a foot fungus," David said, and we both started giggling. I was still holding his hand, or maybe he was holding mine. I let go.

When Caroline saw me, she walked over and linked her arm through mine, steering me away from David. Her hair was in a bun on top of her head, and her neck and cheeks were flushed. "Where were you?" she whispered. "Is everything all right?"

"I'm great," I said. "Edge-free."

The door of the bar opened again, expelling a gush of loud music. A group of kids staggered out. More zombies, so blurry.

Caroline scrunched up her nose. "Oh my God," she

said, still whispering for some strange reason. "Are you drunk?"

"*Duh*," I said. "Isn't everyone?"

———

David made us stop by a konbini so he could buy those little bottled drinks that prevent hangovers. He was right; it wasn't cold out. Walking around Roppongi was like walking around in a giant steam bath. Everyone's clothes were clinging to their skin.

Mika said she couldn't stomach another club, so we went to karaoke instead. We got a room with a window and red plastic couches. David sat down next to me and put his arm around my shoulders.

"You better not mean this in a romantic way," I said.

Jamie and Mika and Caroline stayed on the other side of the room. They weren't talking to me anymore, not even Caroline. Jamie's face was so sad—stupid, sad-faced Jamie. Just because he was in a movie once didn't mean he could act sad whenever he felt like it. I glared at him. But he wasn't paying attention to me. He kept tracing the lip of his beer glass with his thumb. Stupid, sad Jamie and his stupid, sad thumb.

Mika was singing something. Shouting it, actually.

I had no idea how many songs we'd sung or how long we'd been there. Every second careened into the next; they all crushed together until they became one monstrous, unending *thing*. Not a second or a minute or an hour anymore. This night wasn't something I could measure. It was bigger and much more terrifying, as unimaginable as infinity.

Jamie was singing a Radiohead song—his voice low and mumbly—and David whispered, "What a downer."

I'd been drinking another toxic melon soda, but it was watered-down and tasteless. I needed to go to the bathroom.

"Bathroom," I said.

I climbed over David's legs on my way to the door, and he wrapped his fingers briefly around my wrist.

In the bathroom, I washed my face with cold water. My reflection was confusing. It was someone else entirely.

What time is it? Why am I even here?

I opened the door, and he was leaning against the wall across from me.

"What's up?" I asked, fanning my neck.

David didn't answer. Just took my face in his hands, pressed me against the door to another karaoke room, and kissed me to the sound of someone singing "Manic Monday."

I didn't kiss him back. But I didn't stop him, either.

CHAPTER 29
SATURDAY

———

01 : 01 : 22 : 56
DAYS HOURS MINS SECS

"WHAT THE FUCK?!"

Someone was shouting at us.

I put my hands on David's chest and managed to shift him away from me, to give myself some breathing room. He had a dazed look on his face. His eyelids were heavy, and his mouth was still sort of open. I turned my head to the side. Mika was standing in the door of our karaoke room. With Jamie.

"What. The. Fuck!" Mika said again. Her new haircut brought out the intensity in her face. The stern set of her jaw, the fury in her eyes.

"What's up, Miks?" David said placidly. "We're just hanging. Everything's fine here."

"What are you even *doing*?" Mika yelled.

"Mika," Jamie said. He sounded distant, like the real him was shuttered and closed off. Like he was somebody else. "Don't."

Caroline came to the door. "Is someone hurt?"

"Out!" Mika said. She was pointing at David. "I want you out. This is my birthday, and I'm pulling the birthday-girl card, and you can get the hell out. *Now!*"

My knees buckled. I steadied myself against the door, which was shaking from the music. Not "Manic Monday" anymore. "Bohemian Rhapsody."

"It's not his fault," I managed to say.

"Damn straight it's his fault!" Mika stormed over and shoved David. "Do you think it's funny to do this to her?"

David reached into his pocket for a cigarette. His nervous tic. "Calm down, kiddo. We're all having fun here."

Fun. Was it fun? Was it even good? My lips felt cold and wet. My chin felt wet, too.

"Sophia?" Caroline asked. "What just happened?"

I took a deep breath. Jamie was standing next to her, only a few feet away.

"Jamie..." I said.

He turned around and punched the door to our karaoke room so hard it blew back on its hinges. "Fuck," he said. And then louder. *"Fuck."*

Caroline flattened herself against the wall in surprise. Piercing music hovered in the hallway.

"Jamie..." And now I was crying, *really* crying. Sliding down the wall and dissolving completely. I couldn't fix this. There was no way on earth I could ever make this right.

"Don't." Jamie turned around. "Don't talk to me."

I swiped the back of my hand over my eyes and tried to think of something I could do. Something other than cry and feel numb.

But he was already going, head down. Disappearing down a stairwell, and disappearing in general. I pulled my legs into my chest. Mika and David were still yelling.

"You can't decide who I kiss," David said. "This doesn't have anything to do with you."

"Oh, screw you!" she shouted. "Just because I won't date you doesn't mean you can mess around with Sophia. Because you can't! Not on my fucking watch!"

David said nothing.

"This isn't a joke," Mika said, spitting out every word. "I want you gone. I want you out, now!"

I put my face on my knees. The tears were sliding out easily, a few of them running down my calves. Caroline crouched down beside me, studying my face with obvious concern. She was holding a glass of water. "You need to drink this."

"Fine," David said. "You want me gone? No problem. Happy friggin' birthday to you."

He didn't say anything to me as he walked away. And I didn't watch him go.

"Hey? Sophia?" Mika and Caroline were lifting me up. "Sophia," Mika said again, pushing some sticky hair out of my eyes. "We have to get you home. Or to your hotel, or whatever."

I hugged her tightly, my face pressed to her shoulder. She hugged me even tighter than that.

———

Before we left karaoke, Mika and Caroline made me drink three whole glasses of water. Mika ordered them from the bar downstairs. I drank and I cried, curled up in a corner of one of the couches. I cried until my sinuses went raw and scratchy, until my tear ducts actually burned. Mika got out her phone and started texting.

"Are you texting David?" I asked, lifting my cheek from the plastic seat.

"Hell no," she said. "I'm telling Jamie to leave."

I rubbed my nose on my shirt, which was so disgusting I'd have to throw it out. "I think he left already," I said, miserably. Wretchedly.

"No," she said. "He was waiting downstairs in case I needed someone to take me home."

That made me cry all over again. Which made Caroline hug me and cry as well.

"You two are fucking ridiculous," Mika said.

Caroline and Mika came to the hotel with me. When we walked through the door to my room, Alison said, "Good. God. It's worse than an MTV reality show in here."

Mika laughed and smirked approvingly.

It was late, and we were all tired, so they decided to stay

over. I lent them T-shirts, and Alison lent them leggings. There was Advil in my toiletry bag, so I took some of that.

"I didn't drink that much," I said when we were all crowded in the blindingly white hotel bathroom. Caroline was sitting on the edge of the bathtub while Mika and I washed our faces.

"You drank enough," Mika said, scrubbing her face with a towel. I gaped at drops of water near her shorn hairline, still mesmerized by her new haircut.

"I could never have a shaved head," I said.

"Nope," Mika agreed. "I'm more punk rock than all you chumps combined."

I laughed, and then hiccuped.

Caroline drew one leg up and rested her chin thoughtfully on her knee. "I don't get why everyone drinks so much here. It makes you do such stupid stuff."

"Meh," Mika said. "Being stupid is what we do best. But for the record"—she turned off the sink in one dramatic motion—"I drank exactly nothing tonight. Nothing but soda."

I dropped my washcloth on the marble countertop. It landed with a wet, slopping noise. "Well, I feel pretty damn awful."

"How awful?" Caroline asked.

"I don't know. I think I'm still tipsy."

"Tipsy," Mika snorted.

"My head feels like someone's pushing it. And I mean,

look at my face—I look like Jigglypuff from Pokémon. Oh, and my mouth's all *grunky*."

"Brush your teeth," Mika said, flicking some water at me.

I flicked some water back at her. "Jamie was drinking," I said, picking up the washcloth again and folding it over in my hands. "Do you think he's okay?"

"Yeah," Mika said. "I think he just holds beers. He doesn't really drink them."

Talking about Jamie made me feel peeled open; it made everything awful that had happened that night come rushing to the surface—what Alison had said, what Dad had said, what Jamie had said. And what I'd done. I tried to push it aside, but I must have looked worse for wear because Mika was watching me in the mirror. She met my eye and hitched up a single eyebrow, like she was trying to answer my unasked question. *How much does she know about me and Jamie?* I thought about how Jamie trusted her, how they'd been talking to each other all night. If Mika knew what he thought of me now—I didn't want her to tell me.

"Anyway, Tipsy." Mika grabbed one of the hotel glasses from the side of the sink and filled it up for me. "Time for bed."

I slept in Alison's bed, and Mika and Caroline shared the other one. In the middle of the night, I woke up. Alison was sitting bolt upright, staring at me. My head felt like it was trying to crack itself open, and my mouth was *grunkier* than ever. *So this is sobering up.*

"What is it?" I rasped.

Alison sighed. "If you choked on your own vomit and died tonight, I would never, ever forgive myself."

"I had three drinks," I said. "They were mixed drinks! There wasn't *that* much alcohol involved."

"You've never drunk before, baby sister. That's practically a bottle of tequila."

I turned over. "God, Alison. Stop being so overdramatic."

"Good," she whispered. "Stay there. That way if you vomit, it'll come out the side and you won't die."

CHAPTER 30
SATURDAY

———

00 : 19 : 21 : 44
DAYS   HOURS   MINS   SECS

I WOKE UP.

With a hangover.

Oh. Dear. *God.* So much of a hangover. It took a minute for the various sensations to settle over me—headache, nausea, putrid taste in my mouth. I pulled the comforter over my head and *gagged*. The bed smelled like booze. No, I smelled like booze. The smell made me queasy, but I already felt queasy, so then I just felt like throwing up.

Which was so the opposite of awesome.

I burrowed under the covers. Alison wasn't next to me, and it didn't sound like anyone else was in the room. I couldn't even hear anything outside. No morning news broadcasts, no creaky doors being thrown open. The morning was silent and dull. I lay there for a while and felt sorry for myself. Sorry I wasn't home anymore. Sorry this was my last full day in Tokyo. Sorry that my head was trying to detach itself from my body.

But mostly, I felt sorry about Jamie.

"Hey," a voice said from the other side of the room.

I threw the comforter back and sat up. The bed spun; it was like I was on one of those horrible fairground rides Alison and I rode whenever we went to the Jersey Shore. Mika was there, sitting in the chair by the window and reading a room-service menu.

"Hey," I squawked.

"You awake?" She licked her finger and calmly turned a page. She was very clearly not hungover, and I got the feeling she was savoring the role reversal.

"Maybe. I feel—not good."

"Yeah, I figured. This entire room smells like an old towel soaked in sour milk."

I grabbed my stomach and doubled over. "Less. Vivid. Descriptions. Please."

"Baptism by fire, dude." She closed the menu. "Let's get you some breakfast."

———

Caroline had left a note for me, scribbled on the pad of hotel stationery on the nightstand. *Had to lifeguard! Have fun in America! E-mail when you get there? XO*

"You are so going to e-mail her." Mika was reading over my shoulder. "Aren't you?"

I tucked the letter into the front pocket of my suitcase. "Shut up. You like her, too."

When I moved, my body screamed at me. There was

a stale, syrupy taste in my mouth that wouldn't go away. I sat on the edge of the bed and drew my legs up to my chest. The feeling-sorry-for-myself had not abated.

Mika grabbed me some clothes from my suitcase. My T-shirt that says SCIENCE IS AWESOME. THAT IS ALL. My pink cotton shorts. "You own pink clothing?" Mika said, tossing me the shorts.

I picked them up, slowly. "Don't judge. Anyway, you're forgetting that my watch is sort of pink."

Mika glanced at my bare wrist but didn't comment on it. She told me it was a miracle I hadn't puked and that Alison had gone out for a walk with my mom. "To keep her off the scent," she said. "Like, the literal scent."

I threw one of my socks at her, and she laughed.

Outside, it was hot but not punishing. The sky was clear, and there was an actual breeze. I couldn't decide if the world was mocking me or trying to cheer me up. We walked to a konbini and I ambled down the aisles, contemplating how this was the last time I'd be in one of these. The last time I'd browse shelves upon shelves of green tea jellies and individually wrapped *kare pan*. Mika grabbed some *onigiri* and two bottles of iced coffee from one of the fridges.

"I want to eat everything," I joked as she handed them to me. "Everything in Japan."

"Huh?" she said.

Regret twisted my insides. "Never mind."

We sat at a stone picnic table in Kitanomaru-koen, which,

it seemed, was where everyone in Tokyo had decided to go. Families and joggers and cyclists and couples holding hands. It was so lively, almost like being at an outdoor festival—a *matsuri* full of food stalls and game stalls and people dressed in yukata. I put on my sunglasses—Jamie's sunglasses, actually—and started unwrapping my onigiri.

"Happy birthday, by the way," I said. "I didn't tell you that yesterday."

"Yeah, thanks," Mika said. "I am officially adult-ish."

"High school senior–ish."

"A legitimate high school senior in two days."

"Oh, yeah. You're right."

Mika beat an impatient tattoo against the tabletop. "Sophia, I'm going to ask you a question."

I managed to wrangle the onigiri from its packaging without separating the seaweed from the triangle-shaped mound of rice. "Okay."

"Were you just going to move to New Jersey and never tell me about you and Jamie?"

I held the onigiri halfway to my mouth. "That's—an interesting question."

"Damn straight it is."

I put down the onigiri, weighing how to respond. "Technically, though, I could ask you the same thing. I mean, if everything hadn't been inadvertently revealed in the most dramatic way possible, would you have told me about you and David?"

Mika chewed. She seemed pretty run-down, dressed

273

in the same clothes as last night with heavy black makeup tracks around her eyes. "That's different," she said. "We were dumb and pointless. And I would have definitely told you if I was *in love* with him."

My eyes widened. "I'm not in love with anyone."

Mika brooded over something for a minute. She was acting so neutral, I couldn't tell what she actually thought about all this. "Whatever. I'm not going to argue with you. But if you can't see that Jamie's in love with you, you are pretty freaking dumb."

"Did he say that?" I whispered.

"No!" she said. "No one tells me shit. But the two of you are so pathetically transparent. Every time he called me for the last three years, he asked about you. Every time I mentioned him in front of you, you got all awkward and blushy. Yes! See! Just like that!"

I picked a loose piece of rice off my onigiri. Everything that had happened with Jamie had felt so secret. "How much do you know?" I asked.

She sighed. "I tried to ask him about it the other day, but he was all doofy and vague. I know he likes you. And I know you two have been, like, making out on street corners all week. And I know you had a big blowout yesterday."

My stomach jolted. "How do you know all that?"

Her expression turned solemn. "I seriously hope you don't envision a lucrative career with the CIA."

Mika opened her bottle of iced coffee. The plastic bag sitting on the table between us rustled in the wind. Even though I knew it was my last day here, I still couldn't believe it. The air was lighter than it had been all week. I could have sat outside for hours, the day going on and on with no end in sight.

But of course, it was going to end. Just like Jamie and I had. My brain must have been on some kind of demented autopilot because it kept steering me straight back to him. To the heartbreak and the certainty and his *don't talk to me*. My stomach jolted again. "Do you want to walk? I feel like walking."

We gathered the food and coffee and went down almost the exact same paths Jamie and I had run down on Tuesday. Except they were more crowded now. People knocked into my shoulders or hustled me forward in their vigor to get through the park. Two little girls sprinted past us, their laughter floating back on the breeze. I watched them, and it made the pounding in my head grow stronger. The sun was uncomfortably hot, and the symptoms of my post-alcohol consumption came back in full force. I took Mika by the forearm and led her toward the shade of a tree.

"You okay?" she asked.

"I should tell you something," I said. "But you already know. But, whatever. This is the kind of stuff I need to say out loud."

"Uh-huh."

"I really like Jamie," I said in one breath. "I have for, like, a long time. And the only reason I didn't want him to come back to Tokyo was because, right before he left, he told me I was always throwing myself at David, and then I yelled at him and—"

"Hold up," Mika said. "He *said* that?"

"Actually, he texted it. And he meant to text it to you. I always figured that's how you guys talked about me when I wasn't around."

"Sophia. Of course we didn't. He was probably being a shit because he was jealous."

I nudged a patch of grass with my foot. "Whatever. It doesn't matter anymore. Not now that I'm leaving and I kissed David and—I know I hurt him. I hurt Jamie. Which means that he hates me and you hate me and that's why I can't e-mail him."

Mika's eyes swept over me, evaluating me. "Trust me, it would make a difference."

"How do you know?"

"Because I do. Jamie likes you, more than he likes most people. Just cut the self-pity act and be nice. God, if you knew how weird things were with his family right now..."

"Yeah," I said, feeling even more sick. "He told me."

Mika scowled. She twisted the cap of her bottle off and then on again. "Well, I'm glad he talks to *someone* about it. He doesn't to me, but I know things have been screwed up all year. I overheard his parents fighting in the lobby the other day, about keeping his birth mom away from him."

"What?" I asked. *Why hadn't he mentioned that?*

Mika scratched her ear. "He was miserable every time we Skyped. The only thing that cheered him the fuck up was moving here. And don't kill me for saying it, but he seemed seriously relieved when he found out he was coming back before you left."

Thinking about that made everything hurt even worse. Jamie had cared about me. He'd *kept* caring about me—until I'd shoved him aside as violently as I possibly could. "God," I said. "I am actually a horrible person."

"You are not." She pointed at me with her plastic bottle. "But you should see him. Today."

My head was swimming with too much information. I sat down, my back pressed against the tree trunk. She slid down next to me so we were shoulder to shoulder.

"Why do you want me to see him?" I asked, closing my eyes. "I was so pissed at you for lying about David. You're allowed to be pissed about this."

"Dude, I'm not. I totally knew the you-and-Jamie thing would happen. You realize I've had three years to get used to your long-distance mooning, right?"

"But you're mad at me about something," I said. "Aren't you?"

There was a silence. A tentative one. I opened my eyes, and Mika was staring at her shoes, blushing.

"The thing is," she said, "it really sucks that you're moving, okay? But you know what else sucks? Staying. Like, I've been meeting new people and saying good-bye to them since freaking kindergarten. They always go somewhere new and get new lives and forget about me, and it's the goddamned worst."

Mika sounded vulnerable. The opposite of how she'd been all week, surly and defensive toward me. I'd assumed that had been about Jamie and David. But maybe it wasn't. Maybe she was trying to protect herself from losing something as well.

"And you know what else?" she said, sitting up taller. "I don't even know if I'd be friends with dweeby Jamie if we hadn't lived in the same place for so long. But you're— you're really important. So I don't care about you and Jamie. I don't care if you get married and have weird curly-haired babies and live in a castle in France or whatever. Just—don't forget about me, okay?"

"Of course not," I said and grabbed her wrist. Because maybe our friendship wasn't perfect, and maybe we were both a little damaged for it, but she'd always been there for me. And I wasn't about to let that go. "I'm really going to miss you."

She was attempting to be nonchalant, but her eyes wavered. Mika didn't have the same emotional face as Jamie, but I could read it now. "Whatever. But forget about me, bitch, and I will haunt your dreams."

I pushed her shoulder teasingly. She fell over, sat up, and pushed mine back.

"Hey," I said. "If I ever live in a castle in France, you can totally have your own tower or something."

She paused, and then smiled. The most beautiful, genuine Mika smile I'd ever seen. "Deal," she said, sticking her hand out to shake mine. "But only if it has a fucking moat."

———

We walked back to the hotel and stood in the lobby, swaying in the air-conditioning. Mika had to go home. She was meeting some cross-country kids for a pre-season run, and then she was busy all afternoon. "My parents are making me write sample college essays," she said. "Because this is adulthood, apparently."

As soon as she was through the sliding glass door of the hotel, she turned around, came back, and hugged me. She buried her head in my neck, and I felt her take a long, unsteady breath. When she pulled away, there were tears in her eyes. And I was crying, too.

"Okay, okay." She lifted the collar of her shirt to wipe her face. "People can see this. We're in broad daylight."

I took the elevator up to my room, threw open the curtains, and collapsed onto the unmade bed.

CHAPTER 31
SATURDAY

---

00 : **15** : **16** : **02**
DAYS   HOURS   MINS   SECS

ALISON WAS SITTING ON THE OTHER BED. She had her legs crossed and was bouncing them up and down. There was a pair of sunglasses tangled in her hair, and she was wearing my favorite pair of her shoes—red lace-ups with crosshatch stitching on both sides.

How long had she been there? Had I been asleep?

"I hope you've been drinking water," she said. "And I hope you haven't been sleeping this whole time."

I pulled the sheet around my shoulders like a cape. Dorothea Brooke was on the floor, drinking from her travel bowl. I reached over to scratch her back. "I'm not sleeping," I said. "I'm hungover."

"This is unhealthy," she said. "You need sunlight, and you need open spaces."

"I'm not a plant."

"Get up," she said, still bouncing her leg. "This is important."

"Why?" I asked. "Why are you doing this all of a sudden? Why are you trying to expose me to life? Expose yourself to life, you big hypocrite."

"I found somewhere you need to go." She was standing now and pacing the aisle between our beds. Something was wrong. There was sweat around her hairline and on her shirt.

I hoisted myself onto my elbows. "Have you been *exercising?*"

She dumped my flip-flops in front of me. "Sophia."

I sighed. "Come on. I'm exhausted and sad. Can't you just let me feel sorry for myself?"

Alison kicked the bed frame lightly. "This is important."

———

"Sleeping during the day is bad for you," Alison said as the glass door of the hotel swept open. She put on her trusty pair of sunglasses.

"Ha!" I said. "You're such a—"

In the almost blinding sunlight outside the hotel, I saw a boy. A boy wearing a slouchy knitted cap, bending over to get something from a backpack.

It was him.

It was him, and I was going to run the hell away.

It was him, and I was going to eat a mint because my breath was probably terrible.

It was him, and I was going to tell him I was sorry, and then I was going to fade into the mists of time forever.

But it wasn't him.

I exhaled and fell against Alison's side. She shouldered me off. "For God's sake. Don't swoon all over me."

"Sorry," I mumbled, glancing in the direction of the slouchy-hatted boy. He wasn't really a boy. He was probably in his twenties, older than Jamie. Taller, too, and he had an unlit cigarette hanging from his mouth. In my semi-dazed state, I might have stayed there longer, forcing myself to accept the definitive proof that this person—a backpacker probably, a tourist—wasn't Jamie. But Alison was already clipping down the street away from me. I had to jog to catch up with her.

We headed through the Imperial Palace grounds and kept right on going toward Iidabashi. The air was crisp, and it didn't really seem like summer anymore. The sun was sitting lower in the sky, and the light had turned almost golden.

"Where are we going?" I asked, hopping a little to keep up with Alison.

"So far," she said, "we're just walking."

"The last time you and I walked somewhere together, it did not end well."

The light at a pedestrian crossing turned red, giving Alison no choice but to break her stride. "That's because you refused to tell me what's been happening with you and your gang of miscreants."

She had a point. "Do you want to me to tell you about my gang of miscreants now?" I asked.

The light turned green.

"Well, we're still walking," she said.

I told Alison about Jamie. And about Mika and David. I told her about staying in Shibuya all night and about getting drunk and letting David kiss me. I told her how awful it was knowing you would miss someone but knowing that all your missing would get sucked into a vacuum because, once you left, the person you cared about wouldn't be a complete, genuine person anymore. Just a blurred, inconsistent memory.

Saying it out loud made me feel crazy. It also made me feel like I was standing on the glass floor in Tokyo Tower, mentally rehearsing what would happen if the transparent platform dissolved away. And it also made me feel okay. A little less alone.

We turned onto a narrow street lined with trees and apartment buildings. Alison stopped and I stopped, too.

"What's wrong?" I asked.

"Nothing," Alison said. "Except. This is it." She lifted one hand and made a halfhearted flourishing gesture. A deadpan ta-da.

"What is it?" I asked.

"The place," she said. "The apartment."

"The apartment?"

Alison took me by the shoulders and pointed me at a squat brick building behind us. It had black metal balconies on every floor and a parking lot tucked to the side.

"Third story," she said, tilting my chin up. "The apartment we lived in with Dad."

It didn't seem like much. The innocuous black balcony was crowded with plants and a couple of red plastic chairs. There was a sliding glass door behind the chairs, but the glass was reflective. I couldn't see inside.

"Are you joking?" I asked.

Alison shook her head.

The apartment we'd lived in with Dad, the first time we lived in Tokyo. I'd figured it still existed, of course, but I'd never been back. Because it was too distant and awkward and way too weird. Plus, I'd had no idea where it was.

I turned on Alison, suddenly and inexplicably furious with her. "How long did you know this was here?"

Alison shifted her weight from one foot to the other. "I made Mom take me this morning. I didn't think she'd want to, but she was oddly at peace with the whole thing."

I scrambled for something to say, but everything I thought of was wrong. Maybe I could try to make myself feel the way I'd felt the last time I was here. But that was impossible; I'd been five then. And this building could have been any random apartment building in any random part of the world.

"This is not what I expected," I said.

Alison sighed. "I know. I remember it being taller."

"That's not what I meant."

A woman came out of the parking lot. She had bobbed hair and was talking on a cell phone in French. The French school was near here, I realized. This was the neighborhood where all the French expats lived.

"I figured you should see it," Alison said. "You know, before we leave forever."

"Well." I folded my arms over my stomach. "There it is."

"Come on," she said. "We're here. We might as well check out the front door."

Together, we walked into the parking lot. And that was when I remembered the day it snowed and Dad took us down here. I'd pulled the snow off car windows with my hands while Mom took pictures from the balcony. I remembered unbuckling my seat belt and running out of the car and Dad catching up to me, yelling. I cried so hard that Alison yelled back at him, in French.

That same parking lot was so much smaller than I remembered. Only six or so spaces with a few trees clustered at the edges. The building itself was five stories tall and made of orange-red brick. The front door had a cast-iron handle attached to it that used to be too heavy for me to pull by myself. Dad would open the door with me, all four of our hands holding on tight.

I pressed my palms against my temples. "How have I never been here?"

Alison sat down on the curb. "Because it's depressing."

"It's surreal," I said. "And it's nothing at all like I remember. Where's the Thai restaurant across the street?"

Alison dipped her head and gave me a confused look

over the top of her sunglasses. "The Thai restaurant? You mean the one with the lanterns?"

I nodded.

She pushed her sunglasses back up. "That was in New Jersey. Across from the first rental house."

"Really?" I sat next to her and traced a small scab on my knee with my thumb. This all felt so strange. And wrong, like trying to pull on a jacket I hadn't worn since preschool. "So I should probably mention that you were right," I blurted.

"About the restaurant?"

"No." I tucked my hair behind my ears. "About Dad. I called him yesterday to ask if I should come to Paris and he reacted—exactly the way you said he would."

A check-mark-shaped crease appeared on Alison's forehead. I waited to see what she'd do. Gloat, maybe. Or give me a lecture. About betrayal and lost childhood and Sylvia Plath or something. I braced myself for it.

"You know the girl who broke up with me last year?" she asked.

"No," I said, surprised. "Of course I don't. You never talk about her."

"Well, shut up, then. Because I'm talking about her now." She tilted her head back and sighed. Her hair was so long, it brushed the sidewalk. "The girl in question was named Cate. She broke up with me because she had another girlfriend. An *ex*-girlfriend at some bumblefuck university in Indiana."

I took off my sunglasses and played with the earpieces. Music was blasting out of an open window above us, something yelly and French. "So they weren't really broken up?"

"Nominally," she said. "*Nominally*, they were broken up. But they spent the whole year talking to each other and thinking about each other, and they were in love. That's how Cate explained it—they were so *in love*."

I wanted to hug my sister, but I knew she would kill me. So I just put my hand on the slab of sidewalk between us. "Do you want me to beat her up for you?"

Alison guffawed. "Yeah. Be my guest." She picked up a pebble from the ground and started rolling it between her palms. "You know what, though? I knew she would dump me. I didn't know when, exactly, but it was inevitable. Letting people get close to you, it sucks. That's why I've been MIA all year. Because it hurts a hell of a lot less than trying to stay in touch."

"I understand," I said carefully. "I feel that way all the time."

The corner of my sister's mouth lifted slightly. "Nice try, baby sister, but you're not like that. You give people a shot." She nudged my side. It was almost like it was when we'd only had each other. She was the shoulder I'd slept on during countless international flights. She was the person I'd hid with during Dad's wedding reception, eating cheese smuggled in napkins and griping about how everyone kept calling us *les petites Américaines*.

"Here's the truth," she said abruptly. "It wasn't dumb that you wanted to go to Paris."

"Don't mess with me," I said. "I still feel like my head might explode."

"This isn't a joke. I can't stand what he said to you, and I still think he's a self-centered bastard, but I get why you'd want to be there. I get why you'd want that life."

I stretched out my feet, sliding them down a dip in the cement. After everything else that had happened last night, the stuff with Dad seemed better somehow. Manageable. "Maybe it's supposed to be this way," I said. "I don't want to leave Mom yet. I'm not sure I can lose her, too."

"I don't *hate* him," she said. "But I hate how this feels. I hate that we're not good enough for him." She still sounded angry, but less angry. Like she was conceding something. She glanced up at the building. "And I mean, it's not like our lives would have been perfect if he'd stuck around."

"You were right about that, too," I said, following her gaze. "It was kind of a crappy apartment."

"Good," she said. "I'm glad we agree. Because if everything gets shot straight to hell, you're the one person that I... You're my person. You know?"

She was wearing sunglasses so I couldn't see her eyes. But I could see her.

Alison was almost seven when Dad left. He used to pick her up and hold her upside down by the ankles. He used to call her Christopher Robin. After he left, Alison crawled into my bed every night for two years.

"God, Alison," I said, "you're my person, too. You always have been."

She snorted. I couldn't see her eyes, but I knew she was rolling them. "Obviously."

CHAPTER 32
SATURDAY

———

00 : 12 : 40 : 51
DAYS   HOURS   MINS   SECS

MOM WAS IN OUR ROOM when we got back.

It took approximately twenty seconds before I broke down and told her the whole disreputable tale of my alcohol abuse. I hated doing it. Disillusioning her. Making her realize that I was just like all the other Bad Teenagers out there. Not that she hadn't figured it out already.

"You look like you have food poisoning and the plague," she said, rubbing her forehead. "Is this my fault? Is this about Paris?"

That made me cry. No, I told her, this wasn't about Paris. But also, I didn't want to go. Even if Dad had told me to move there, it wouldn't be home. Not the way I'd always imagined it would be. And I couldn't leave her behind—I just couldn't.

She was upset. Mostly because I was hungover. Mostly because she thought moving me away from my friends at the start of my senior year was a cruel and unusual punishment. She said she couldn't even ground me, because the move itself was basically an extreme form of grounding.

I sat on the bed and cried and said she could ground me until I was forty because I deserved to be locked away from humanity. She hugged me, and Alison sat next to us and leaned her head against Mom's back. We were messy and emotional, and it was wonderful. It was home.

"This week has been crazy," Mom said, tucking my hair behind my ears.

"Yeah." I sniffled. "No shit."

———

On the last night of the last day of my last week in Tokyo, Mom took me and Alison out for sushi. We went to a restaurant with a crowded countertop and ate thick scallops and glossy fish eggs on rice and bowls of warm miso soup chock-full of tofu and seaweed.

Back at the hotel, Alison and I watched the annual Tokyo Bay fireworks on TV. There were *hanabi* happening all over Japan that week. Across the country, spectators dressed in yukata stood huddled together, watching the sky. "Can't see them from the goddamned window," Alison said. "Too many goddamned buildings."

Then I took a shower. I put on pajama bottoms and a Regina Spektor concert T-shirt and crawled into my hotel bed. The curtains were open enough to show me a wedge of glittering night. The city was painfully beautiful, a firework that never faded. I rolled onto my side and pushed the wet hair away from my neck.

It occurred to me that I hadn't heard from David since last night, but I didn't really care. Not because I thought he was evil or anything. It was more that I had nothing to say to him. He wasn't the person I'd always hoped he'd be, and, in all fairness, neither was I.

I hadn't heard from Jamie, either—but that, I did care about. Even though thinking about him made pain wind its way through my body. We'd both been angry and we'd both said horrible things, but I was the one who'd pushed away first. I'd lit the match that destroyed this week.

Still, a part of me wished I could see him. I wished I could tell him I was sorry and that it really sucked, but we weren't supposed to last beyond tomorrow, anyway. We'd always been facing good-bye.

What other choice did we have? A long-distance relationship? That implied dating, and Jamie and I definitely weren't dating. I wasn't exactly an expert on romance, but I didn't think kissing someone, refusing to respond to their messages, and then kissing someone else in front of them constituted a "relationship."

Or we could be friends. Exchange e-mails and texts until the day we grew apart, until he started dating someone else. I didn't want that to happen. I didn't want to experience the unavoidable breakdown of our connection, so I was going to be happy with this week. This week that I'd spent holding on to Tokyo as tightly as I could. This week that had been made up of counting seconds and waiting for everything around me to finally disappear.

But. Maybe it didn't have to end that way. Because maybe Mika was right—maybe I did love Jamie. Even if he didn't love me. Even if he never had. I must have loved him, because being with him was like waking up at the end of a long plane flight. Like looking at the star-shaped twinkly lights spun across my ceiling. I thought about stars and how their light lasts long after the star itself has faded. I thought about how home is still home even when it's thousands of miles away.

That was this week. That was Jamie.

I heard Alison shut her laptop. "Are you going to sleep?" she whispered.

"Sort of," I whispered back.

"And it's not yet the melodramatic hour of two in the morning. How grown-up of you."

"You're one to talk."

She made an amused sound that wasn't quite a laugh. "Did you set an alarm?"

My watch was lying on the nightstand. "Mom called the front desk," I said. "We've got a seven a.m. wake-up call."

"Great." Alison sighed. "Bon voyage to us."

She turned off the lamp at the side of her bed, and the darkness in the room made the city glow brighter. A flash of lightning, frozen.

———

It's my birthday. And the morning of my last day of middle school, the last day of my first year at the Tokyo International Academy....

And Jamie is waiting near the gate, scanning the crowd for me. I push past a group of kids signing yearbooks. "Happy last day of school," I say.

"Happy birthday, Sophia!" he says, bouncing on his heels.

"Blah," I say. And even though it makes me nervous, I glance at the entrance to the high school. Older kids swish through the door. Boys with their arms around girls, everyone looking exactly like adults.

"I can't believe we'll be there next year," I whisper.

"I won't," Jamie says, his features pinched and anxious. "Hey, this is my last day. We have to say good-bye in approximately a few hours." He reaches into the front of his backpack, pulls something out, and shoves it into my hand.

I hold up the Totoro pin. "What! This is the MOST awesome."

"It was cool hanging out with you this year," he says, like it's all one word. "I'll, um, miss you."

I roll my eyes. "Jamie, it's no big deal. We'll still be friends. We'll talk every day."

"Really? Because I have no idea if my parents are going to let me visit, and you'll be busy, and this could really be good-bye. You know, for permanent."

I close my hand around the pin. "Only if you let it be."

CHAPTER 33

SUNDAY

———

00 : 00 : 00 : 00
DAYS HOURS MINS SECS

THE FIRE ALARM WAS GOING OFF.

I sat up, gulping for air, unsure where the nearest fire exit was, unsure where I was. Tokyo? New Jersey? Paris? I didn't remember going to the airport or saying good-bye to anyone. But what I did remember seemed flimsy and dreamlike. The T-Cad at night, a slurred neon boulevard, Jamie's reflection overlaying the whole city.

It took me a second, but then I noticed the partially open curtains. The sun was starting to rise, and the sky was purple and blue with orange stripes across it like plane tracks.

Right! Of course. The hotel. And—the fire alarm was going off?

"Tell me what that sound is!" Alison shouted. "I will burn it to the ground!"

"It's . . ."

My watch.

"It's my watch," I said.

"Are you deranged?" she snarled. "You set your watch for five o'clock in the morning?!"

No. My watch was still on the nightstand, where I'd seen it before I went to sleep. It was beeping like crazy, and the screen was flashing:

$$00 : 00 : 00 : 00$$

I picked it up and jammed the button on the side. The beeping stopped. "Everything is okay," I announced. "The sound is not happening anymore."

"Oh my God!" Alison was sitting up as well now. She jutted her bottom jaw at me. "What the hell? Our flight doesn't leave till almost noon. I do not want to be experiencing consciousness right now!"

"Sorry," I said, pressing a few more buttons, hunting for an explanation. "This wasn't supposed to happen. I set it for when we get on the plane."

"You and your metaphysical countdowns! Always with the goddamned metaphysical countdowns!"

"They're not metaphysical." I tapped the watch's screen. "They're just countdowns."

The only possible explanation was that I'd miscalculated the time. But that had never happened to me before. Like, actually never. I knew how to schedule a countdown. I could have been a professional timekeeper, if I so desired. The watch was still in my hands. I ran my fingers over the embroidered flowers. They were raised and nubby, especially where the pink thread was starting to unravel. I half expected it to tell me what was going on. I half expected it to beep again.

I half wanted it to.

Alison lay back down and jerked the comforter all the way over her head. Dorothea Brooke rested her cheek on my forearm and seemed as awake as I felt.

I tried to think this through. The last time I'd checked the countdown was in Shibuya, in the ramen shop with Jamie. I'd taken it off the next morning and hadn't even touched it again until that night, when Jamie and I were packing. After we'd finished, Jamie had handed me my watch. He'd told me not to forget it. And before that, I'd left the room to take the tea mugs downstairs. Which meant he could have picked up my watch and . . .

Oh.

Oh my God.

I grabbed the clothes I'd laid out the night before. Green sweatpants, yellow tank top, underwear, socks. I rushed to the bathroom to assess the remaining clutter. There were toiletries strewn around the sink, and my clothes from yesterday balled up on the floor. I brushed my teeth and shoved hair ties and face wash into my sushi-printed makeup bag. As I was doing all this, I repeated to myself: *Don't get your hopes up, don't get your hopes up, don't get your hopes up.*

I gathered up the final scraps of my existence and zipped them into my suitcase. My laptop, my passport, and the last of my money were crammed into my backpack.

"Explain yourself," Alison said. She was sitting up again, and she seemed pretty unimpressed with everything I was doing.

"I can't explain," I said, slinging my backpack onto my shoulders. "Not now. Tell Mom I'll meet you at Tokyo Station, on the platform for the Narita Express at nine."

"Nuh-uh," Alison said. "There is no way on earth I'm letting you leave."

My flip-flops were by the closet. I felt an irrepressible surge of optimism. The early countdown wasn't an accident. It had happened for a reason. I slid my flip-flops on and hoisted my suitcase onto its back wheels. It was heavy, but I could handle it.

I could handle this.

"Please," I begged my sister. "After this, I swear I will never do anything fun or crazy ever again. Nothing. I'll just go to school and study and, even if I get a driver's license and a car, I will use those powers for good, not for evil. Like, I'll grocery shop for Mom or visit our grandparents every afternoon. I'm going to be the most boring, well-behaved teenager in the whole world, starting at nine this morning, if you just let me go *now*."

She was going to knock me out, I could tell. Or call Mom. She was going to lock me in the bathroom and tell me I could leave this room over her dead body.

But she didn't do any of those things.

She got up, grabbed her shoulder bag, and pulled out a wad of thousand-yen bills. "The last of my yen," she said, stuffing it into my hand. "Take a taxi if you're running late."

I closed my fist over the money. She was the best person in the universe, and I was about to tell her so when she held a hand up to stop me. "Seriously. Go now. Because I'm still half-asleep, and when I wake up, I'm going to begin the long process of regretting this for the rest of my life."

I opened the hotel door.

———

Everyone in Shibuya had an umbrella.

Everyone except me, of course.

I propped my suitcase upright, swung my backpack around, and took out the T-Cad sweatshirt I'd packed in case it got cold on the flight.

It was six thirty on a Sunday morning, but there were still people in the plaza around the station. Clubbers staggering home arm in arm, women in matching pink tracksuits power walking in circles. Some young Australian tourists hovered near one of the station entrances. They were wearing ripped jeans and bandannas tied around their heads. One of them leaned back to take pictures of the tops of buildings.

Across the plaza was Hachiko. Loyal Hachiko with his

nose held high, still waiting for someone. I'd wheeled my suitcase past him once, but I decided to do it again. Even before I reached him, I knew, for a fact, no one would be there. Hachiko was a place people went to meet, and no one had anyone to meet at six thirty on a Sunday morning. Regardless, I walked toward him, and I thought, *Don't get your hopes up, don't get your hopes up, don't get your hopes up.* But with every step, I got my hopes up a little bit more, defying my logical brain.

No one was there.

Except me, of course. Because I was an idiot. An idiot who came here for a set of carefully deduced reasons.

They were:

If Jamie had reset my watch, it was because he wanted to see me before I left. If he reset my watch, it was because he wanted me to wake up early and go somewhere to meet him. And the only place I could think of was Shibuya. It was where I'd first seen him one whole week ago. Where I'd spent all night with him, every second unspooling and holding us in its amber. Before that awful night in Roppongi, I was supposed to meet Jamie in Shibuya, at Hachiko.

And so that's where I went now. Me and my suitcase and my big, pathetic hopes.

I laid my suitcase on the ground and sat on top of it, pulling my hood over my head. There were raindrops on the backs of my hands and my bare feet. I wiggled my toes. The adrenaline high from racing to Shibuya was starting to wear off. And I was left with the knowledge that this was over. That soon I would be on a plane, moving away from this week and this place and this life.

But strangely, I wasn't panicking. It was like I'd passed the event horizon and I was being absorbed into a black hole, but I was done fighting it. I looked up. The buildings reached toward the sky like outstretched fingers, and the sound of traffic swelled and crashed over me.

When my thoughts settled, I was surprised to find they settled on this poem Alison used to have scrawled on her bedroom door. It was called "Parting," by Emily Dickinson, and it was all about loss. About how, when certain things are gone, it can feel almost like death. Something sudden, violent, and final.

The end.

Once the dust of that ending clears, though, there's possibility. I saw that now. Countdowns can be reset. In the wake of the end, beginnings can be made. I had no idea what my beginning would look like, but I thought it might be out there. Waiting for me.

But first, I needed to say good-bye to Tokyo. Hachiko sat stoically in the rain, so I reached up to pat his side before dragging my suitcase toward the crossing. It was comforting to be part of the morning crowd. People surrounded me, all of them facing forward, going somewhere. The sky was gray, but somehow that made the city even more brilliant. All these colors pulsing on the billboards and TV screens above me.

The light at the crossing turned green, and hordes of bobbing umbrellas started moving across the street at the same time, like they were part of a choreographed dance.

But I didn't follow them.

I closed my eyes and listened to the rumble of footsteps and the echo of voices from giant screens and the whir of trains, coming and going. The rain continued to wash down on me, and it reminded me that this was real and I was real, and for one whole second, that was the only thing in the world that mattered.

When I opened my eyes, the light was still green. And Jamie was crossing the street toward me.

CHAPTER 34
SUNDAY

———

AS SOON AS JAMIE SAW ME, he started to jog. He didn't stop until he was standing right in front of me.

I held back a surprised laugh. I gripped the handle of my suitcase like I was worried it would fly away.

"How?" he asked. "How are you even here?"

He looked wonderful. Like, so wonderful it hurt. Bright green shirt, messy morning hair, freckled skin. His smile was perfect. I stared at his overlapping front teeth and his lips, which were the color of pale pink strawberries.

"You reset my watch," I said.

Even though I was doing my best, I couldn't maintain eye contact. My gaze stumbled down to his feet. He was wearing red sneakers with white stripes.

"You didn't respond to my e-mails," he said. "I figured you debunked the stupid watch thing and changed it back."

"Please let me say I'm sorry." My voice cracked. "Please."

"Okay," he said softly. "You can say it. But just so you know, I'm sorry, too."

I refused to concentrate on anything except his graying shoelaces. My vision blurred with tears. "Don't be stupid, okay?" I rubbed my eyes with the sleeve of my sweatshirt. "I'm the screwup in this scenario. Don't try to take that from me, because I've earned it."

He wrapped his finger around one of the ties of my sweatshirt and tugged. "Hey," he whispered.

I didn't look up. He tugged it again. "Hey. Sophia."

My eyes met his.

He was so awake. He reminded me of the morning. Not this gray morning specifically, but morning in general. Something clear and hopeful. I could really see his green eyes now. They were as green as his shirt, as green as the stretches of land I'd seen from the windows of airplanes. Bright green. Neon green.

The light changed to red. People huddled on the cement banks of the crossing as cars filled the wide road. Someone's umbrella partially covered our heads, but they weren't paying attention to us. Everyone was looking ahead. And we were looking at each other.

"Ask me again," I whispered.

He bit his lip and scrunched his eyebrows together. "Ask you what?"

"Ask me what I'll miss about Tokyo."

He looped the fingers of his other hand around my other sweatshirt tie. "Sophia Wachowski," he whispered slowly, taking his time with my name. "What will you miss about Tokyo?"

I gripped the front of his T-shirt. "You, Jamie. Every time you asked me, I wanted to say, 'you.'"

He pulled me toward him by my sweatshirt ties and kissed me just as the light turned green. The crowd moved forward and around us the way an ocean wave breaks around a rock and rushes to the shore.

———

Jamie rolled my suitcase for me. We went to Starbucks. He held my hand as we waited in line and as he ordered a green tea latte and as we walked out the door again. There wasn't anywhere to go, no stores open or anything. The streets were small and twisty and deserted. We weren't talking, so all I could hear was rain hitting the pavement.

We turned into the mouth of an alley that was even narrower and more deserted than the streets before it. Still not talking, still gripping hands. We walked and walked until we reached a brick alcove with a vending machine in it. There was no one else on the street.

I tossed the empty latte cup into a trash can and dropped my backpack on the sidewalk. Jamie let go of the suitcase and then he was pressing me into the alcove, between a brick wall and the vending machine. The machine made a droning noise, and I heard cars on the major avenues nearby. There were all these reminders that we were on a street, *in public,* but it felt like we were secluded.

I was pulling him toward me, bodies lining up, hip points connecting. And we were kissing each other like we had to, like it was the last time. And of course it was. Maybe that's why I didn't question my hands when they glided under the back of his shirt. Or my leg when it wrapped around both of his and tugged him closer and closer still. He broke away for a second, and I took that opportunity to yank my sweatshirt over my head and toss it on the ground.

Oh. Dear. God. I was out of control! I was doing exactly what you're not supposed to do. You're not supposed to *throw* yourself at someone. This, I had learned from movies and TV shows: If you throw yourself at someone, they will think you are sad and desperate. But I guess I didn't care about these movie-made social conventions, because I was literally *throwing* myself at him.

No—not at him. Into him. Into his arms and chest and shoulders. When he shifted, my tank top lifted up and my stomach touched his T-shirt and it was perfect, this was perfect.

"Sophia," he said, pulling away a little, his voice lower than usual. Hoarse. I rubbed my cheek against his, focusing on the heat of his skin.

And this was it, wasn't it? Whatever happened now was all that would ever happen, and even though I cannot stress enough how much I don't care about poetry, I started thinking about this other poem we'd read for English class called "To His Coy Mistress." It's about how we're all going to get old and die so we might as well *have sex*, or something approximating it, while we still can. Which is terrible logic, and what if this wasn't the last time?

But what if it was?

And why was I thinking about poetry?!

My elbow banged into the side of the machine. "Ow! Shit!"

"Shit." Jamie pulled away from me. There was a beautiful red blush down his neck. "Shit. Are you okay?"

"Yeah." I rubbed my elbow. "I'm fine."

He took a step back. He was staring at me, every emotion from the last week etched in his expression.

"Maybe we should stop?" I said, like it was a question.

"Yes," he said. "I don't know. Yes?"

"I think I'm making a fool of myself."

"What?" He shook out his hair with his hand. "Are you crazy? I can't think of anything that's more of a not-fool than you are."

I laughed a little because I couldn't help it. "Those were nonsense words."

"Seriously," he said, sounding less flustered. "There's nothing you've said or done today I won't be thinking about for a long, long time. Not foolish. All perfect."

He lifted my hand, and I trailed my lips over the backs of his knuckles. Hidden together like that, the morning became something calm. Something secure. And I was glad just to be standing there, pretending we had more time.

"Can we walk?" I asked.

His eyes locked with mine and his smile was so self-assured and sexy, I could have died. "You read my mind."

He helped me put my backpack on, and I saw what was across the street. "Jamie," I said. "Oh God. Jamie, do you even realize where we are?"

We were facing the entrance of a love hotel, standing right across from its unlit doorway and the blinking red heart hanging on the side of the building. There was a placard out front listing the price per hour for each room and a yellow sign over the door with an arrow on it and one ominous word—IN.

I covered my mouth with my hand and laughed. Jamie started laughing, too. "Shit. Oh, holy shit."

We were both laughing now. No, giggling. Hysterically giggling. Jamie took my suitcase and we broke into a run, still laughing, still holding on to each other's hands.

CHAPTER 35
SUNDAY

———

WE WERE WALKING. AND KISSING. Less desperately, but still desperately. Every once in a while, he stopped to kiss my cheeks and nose and lips. I put my sweatshirt back on and tugged the hood over my head. He slipped his hand inside my hood and ran his fingers through my ponytail.

"Can we go somewhere to talk?" he asked. His cheeks were red and I was kissing them, one after the other. We were standing by a bakery and a clothing store with the shutters pulled down.

"This is somewhere," I said.

"Right," he said, smiling.

It had stopped raining, and his wet hair was pushed back again. I pulled a few strands of it down by his ears, momentarily straightening the curls. Then I smoothed my hands down his chest. I had this crazy thought that if I stopped touching him, he'd disappear completely.

"Are you never going to wear a hat again?" I asked. "Because of me?"

"I wore a hat to Roppongi," he said.

"Yeah. Because you were pissed at me. You did it for hat revenge."

He puffed out his chest, insulted. "It wasn't hat revenge."

I pinched one of his cheeks. "You're such a liar."

His chest deflated. "Okay, fine, it was hat revenge. But hey, speaking of *that night*..."

"AGH! NO!" I covered my ears. "Do we have to? Can't we make a blood oath to never speak of *that night* again? Upon pain of death?"

He bit his bottom lip. "Why were you so mad at me?"

He sounded careful, like he was afraid of what I might say. Like, at any moment, we might fall back into that place we couldn't come back from.

"I wasn't mad at you," I said. "I was just—"

"*Really* mad at me?"

"No." I tugged one of his curls. "I was mad—about Paris. Alison said my dad doesn't want me to move there. She said he'd never wanted me there, actually. So I called him and, big surprise, he really doesn't."

"He told you that?"

"No," I sighed. "But he might as well have. I don't think he thinks of me as family. Not his *real* family." My voice weakened. I was trying to picture myself in Paris now, but the picture was even more confusing than ever. I saw a scared little kid gripping her big sister's hand as their dad ushered them into a cab to the airport. I saw all those years of resetting a countdown, of resetting myself for another fall.

310

Jamie put both his hands in my sweatshirt pocket and touched his forehead to mine. His eyelashes caught the morning light. "You could have talked to me about that."

"But I didn't want to talk. I know it sounds stupid, but I didn't want to care about anything when all of this has to end." As soon as I said it, I realized it was true—I'd hurt him because I couldn't face being let down. Not again. Not by someone else I trusted. I pressed my foot against his. "I couldn't," I whispered.

"Because you were leaving?"

"Yes. And because I'd probably never see you again and because I loved you..."

He pulled his head back, but his hands dug deeper into my pocket. "I love you."

I tucked my face into his neck. Honestly, it freaked me out a little—saying it, hearing him say it back. Maybe we were being rash. Maybe it would be better if we'd just kept it to ourselves.

Why make this any harder than it already is?

"Well, I shouldn't have blown up at you," he said. "I shouldn't have just walked away."

"But I shouldn't have gotten drunk," I said. "Or kissed David."

"Yes. I will concede that point to you."

I laughed into his neck. A bicycle bell rang behind us, and Jamie led us closer to the storefronts. My suitcase clunked along behind.

"We should talk about something else," I said. "Something *not* me. How's everything with your parents?"

Jamie frowned. "My parents?"

"Yeah," I said tentatively. "Mika mentioned that they'd been fighting the other day. About—your birth mom?"

He drew back. "She said that?"

I started to panic. Oh God, I had no idea why I'd picked that topic. It was clearly a mistake. "Sort of. Not really. She said she'd overheard them in the lobby, but she didn't go into detail or anything."

"Right," he said, but his eyes were distant. Lost in a haze.

"Right," I said, floundering now. "But it's fine. Let's change the subject."

Across the street, an advertisement for a new superhero movie was painted across a huge white wall. I stared at the bright splashes of red and played with the ties of my hood.

"Everything is so screwed up right now," he said. "My parents keep fighting because they don't want my birth mom to see me after she bailed last Thanksgiving, and they can't decide what to do if she tries. And that's the thing. If they say she can't, she can't. Until I'm eighteen, I don't have a choice."

"Jamie," I said. "All of that sucks."

He shrugged. "It's not like there's some obvious answer. It's not like I feel at home with any of them."

I took a small step back. And I thought about the first

time I'd left Tokyo. How that moment had always seemed like the one where I'd lost my home—my family.

And then I thought about what Jamie had said when we sat above Shibuya Crossing. About belonging. About how you can still choose where you belong.

I gripped the straps of my backpack. "I don't think it works that way."

"What do you mean?"

"I mean, just because you don't have this perfect place to always go to, it doesn't mean you don't have a *home*. That can be everywhere—wherever you want." I pressed my hands to his chest. "This can be home."

The distance fell from his eyes, and he wrapped his hands around mine. "You know what the weirdest thing about this week is? That most of the time, it's like I'm not really back. You're the one person who makes me feel like myself. You make me feel like I'm *actually here*."

"Is that why you love me?" I whispered.

"No." He placed one hand inside my sweatshirt hood and touched his thumb to my cheek. "I think that is me loving you. I think all of those feelings are the love ones."

"In that case"—I took a deep breath—"I love you, too."

CHAPTER 36
SUNDAY

———

I HAVE TWO HOURS LEFT WITH JAMIE.

I have one.

I don't have any.

CHAPTER 37
SUNDAY

———

THE NARITA EXPRESS IS THE TRAIN that will take me to Narita Airport, where I will get on the plane that will take me to Newark, New Jersey.

"Okay," I say.

Jamie and I are standing in Tokyo Station, outside the Narita Express ticket barriers. I'm holding my ticket with one hand and his hand with the other. "Okay," I say again. "My train leaves in fifteen minutes, but let's not stand here. If my mom and sister aren't on the platform yet, they'll be here soon, and I actually can't say good-bye to you in front of them."

"Don't be upset," Jamie says. "There's nothing to be upset about. Let's just say good-bye in an easy and casual manner."

"That was such a stupid statement, I have no words for it. I'm not going to punch your arm and say, 'Later, bro.' "

He grins. "That wasn't my point. My point was, it's not a big deal, because we'll see each other soon."

Someone's suitcase bumps mine. This is the most crowded place we've been all morning. Full of people with heavy bags and heavy, determined looks on their faces. "Come on," I say. "Let's just... Come on."

We walk away, but there's no place private enough for us to stand. This is one of the largest, busiest train stations in Tokyo. We flatten ourselves against the wall of a fluorescent hallway teeming with passersby and hold each other by the elbows. I know my hands are shaking, but I'm not mortified or anything because his are, too.

"What did you mean, soon?" I ask. "How will we see each other again soon?"

"I mean next year," he says.

Although I should find the sentiment sweet, I don't. It's too illogical. "Um, no. There's no next year, Jamie."

"You can come back for graduation."

"No," I say, sterner than I mean to. "It's just, my parents already spend a lot of money on plane flights to Paris for me and Alison. They can't send me to Tokyo for graduation. And anyway, that's just graduation. It's one day."

"That's twenty-four whole hours!" he says. "That's approximately a million seconds! Right?"

"Don't even joke."

He seems worried now. The crease between his eyebrows is back. "I'll get a part-time job. I'll save money to pay for a flight for you. That way you can save your own money for MIT."

I'm trying to memorize what he looks like up close. All

his freckles, and the green and gold in his eyes. And even though I'm trying not to think about time, there's still this countdown ticking in my head. Ten minutes from now, I'll be gone. Ten minutes from now, he won't be with me anymore. Something inside me threatens to break—I rub my thumb against his arm to remind myself he's still here.

"Let's not pretend this is going to work," I say. "You've got two years at the T-Cad, and I'm going to college next year, and it's not like we can date, because that would be crazy. The semi-adult thing to do is to let each other go. If we meet again someday, then fine."

He grimaces. "I really hate the sound of that semi-adult thing."

I remember how upset I was to see him in Shibuya Station at the beginning of the week, all those thousands of years ago. Too much has changed. There's no going back now.

"You want to know something about black holes?" I say hurriedly.

"Um." He crinkles his eyes in amusement. "Okay?"

"I know, I know. Just shut up for a second. So the thing is that time moves slower around them. Or anyway, it seems to. So if you were standing at a distance, watching a clock hovering next to a black hole, the clock would tick slower."

"Right," he says. "That was a good science fact. Will there be a quiz later?"

"What I mean is..." I hold his elbows tighter. "This is a black hole. Or this week has been, anyway. Every second was longer than just a second, you know? And I mean that in a really good way because I love the idea of black holes. The idea that all of this space and time isn't really fixed, that we can change it."

He touches his nose to my cheek, and his voice is a murmur in my ear. "Maybe we're stuck here. Floating in space. That wouldn't be so bad."

"This has mattered so much to me, Jamie," I whisper, "and I love you, and you are everything I like best about Tokyo, and you *are* Tokyo, and I will miss you so much."

He lets go of my elbows and tugs me into him. Now I'm trying to memorize his smell. I wish I could take it with me.

"This sucks," he whispers. "This is the worst thing that has ever happened to any human ever."

I roll my eyes, which stops me from crying. "You're really levelheaded and not at all dramatic about this."

He keeps hold of me but pulls his face back a little. "I'm going to be an optimist here and I'm going to say 'See you next year' because I'm gonna go to North Carolina next summer, and I'll get my driver's license, and then I'll drive to you."

"This is it, Jamie. Even if I never see you again, what matters is now."

"Oh fuck." He laughs. "You really aren't an optimist, are you?"

"Oh, I totally am." I kiss him one last time and try to taste every bit of him. Green tea, mint, Jamie. I press my nose to the place where his neck meets his collarbone and wrench myself away before it gets to the point where I physically can't bear to do it.

On my way to the ticket barriers, I tell myself this isn't so bad. That I'm glad he's not running after me. In the station, life goes on. The morning goes on. And he doesn't seem that far away yet, even though I might never see him again.

Which makes me think it might not be distance or time that takes you away from people. Maybe you decide when you let them go.

But I can't let go yet.

I get to the ticket barrier and turn around—to find him standing right behind me.

"I'm sorry!" He holds up his hands. "I totally followed you! Again!"

I kiss him with my arms all the way around his neck. I kiss him and ignore the sign above my head that says five minutes until my train leaves. (Mom and Alison probably have seats already. They're probably freaking out.)

I let go of Jamie, put my ticket through the barrier, and push through. There are people waiting behind him. They think he's going through as well.

"You're so much better at this than I am," he says, anxiety filling his face as the small plastic gate closes between us.

"That is the most wrong thing you've ever said." I feel the tremble in my voice. He touches my wrist, right above my watch. It's only a watch, but for years, it's had so much control over my life, over all my endings. But that control was a lie—my endings belong to me. I rip my watch off and shove it into his hand. He grips it, surprised. "See you next year," I say.

He takes off his leather wristband and crushes it into my palm and then he's kissing me and I'm kissing him and I'm crying now. Really crying.

There's a train conductor in the nearby ticket booth gesturing for us to move. I grab my suitcase and take a few steps back, and Jamie does the same. Other people start going through the barrier. They're shoving me away and away and away from him.

I'm holding the handle of my suitcase with one hand and the leather band against my chest with the other, and I'm holding completely still. Until there are too many people between us. Until I can't see him anymore.

I fall back, everything inside me snapping. It was only a moment, but now he's gone.

The end came and I'm still standing.

Mom and Alison are waiting for me on the train station platform. "Oh good," Alison says as I haul my bags toward them. "You're alive."

Mom cups her hand around the back of my neck. "Jesus. Where were you? We couldn't even call."

"I made it," I say. "I'm here."

I look around. Other travelers move toward the yellow line on the platform, watching as the train's snub nose glides toward us. Seconds spin out and around us like spiderwebs.

Alison takes out her ponytail, shakes out her hair, and points at my hand. "What *is* that thing?"

I open my palm, where it's lying. Crushed and fragile, like a fallen leaf.

"Nothing," I say, but when she frowns, I add, "I'm just borrowing it."

The train stops and the doors exhale open. Mom starts bringing our stuff onto the train, and, for the few seconds before I follow her, I slide on the leather wristband. It's too big and too light, only glancing against my skin. It feels nothing like a watch and everything like good-bye. But I can feel it nonetheless, almost beating, almost breathing against me. The warm, living ember of a star.

ACKNOWLEDGMENTS

If this book is a love letter to Tokyo, this part is a love letter to all the people who cheered me on, picked me up, coaxed me to my computer, and fed me cake as I wrote it. Without you all, I'd still be eating cookies and avoiding my Word doc.

Thank you, Molly Ker Hawn, for being a thousand times more wonderful than I dreamed an agent could be. You are a publishing force to be reckoned with, a fount of apple cake knowledge, and the dose of strength and laughter I usually (*always*) need. I am lucky my work found its way to you.

I am constantly floored by my wise, whimsical, and sharp editors: Bethany Strout, my jaw hung open the first time I read your editorial letter. You *got* this book, and you pushed me—consistently, patiently—to improve it. I am singing Tori Amos songs in your honor. Karen Ball, thank you for tirelessly guiding my language and for helping me unearth hidden gems in Sophia and Jamie's journey. Their story could not have been in better hands. An enormous, heartfelt thanks to Farrin Jacobs, Pam Gruber, and Leslie Shumate for your warmth and unceasing support.

I could fill page after page with a list of people at Little, Brown in the United States and the United Kingdom who changed my life (and this book) for the better. Thank you for being my first publishing home in so many ways. Unending gratitude, glitter stickers, and strawberry mochi to *all* of you—and extra strawberry mochi to those who are my fearless advocates and dear friends. You know who you are.

To my parents: You are the most brilliant people I know. Thank you for being my home no matter where you are in the world and for giving me years of travel and adventures to pull inspiration from. I complained (a lot) at the time; I have been grateful every day since.

Lesley Glaister, this book would never have been written without you. Thank you for getting me through the first fifteen thousand words and for saying, "You're on the right track. Keep going." Thank you to John Burnside for believing this idea had promise, and to my fellow St. Andrews creative writers for letting me bombard you with the same story for a whole year.

Susan Manly and Angus Stewart, *arigatou gozaimashita* for reading this manuscript with such forgiving eyes. Extra thanks for the vegetarian dinners and glasses of champagne. They helped a lot.

I'm grateful that the staff at the University of St. Andrews Special Collections didn't say anything when I was so lost in a book fog I showed up to work in pajamas and bright purple lipstick.

Thank you, Jessica, for being the Sophia to my Alison.

Thank you, Julie Haack, for being my New York City.

Thank you, Jennifer, Laura, and Lindsay, for making my own YA story bearable.

To my ASIJ and Sapporo crew, I never wanted to leave you behind. Thank you for all the karaoke nights and konbini picnics. They mattered so much to me—they *still* matter.

And finally, thank you, Rachel Holmes. For fortifying me with maple syrup lattes and lemon bars. For saying, without reservation, "You will," when I told you I wanted to write a novel. For always reading, always listening, always thinking, always rolling your eyes, always laughing, always gently prying the manuscript away when I needed a break but didn't realize it. You breathed life into each and every word that ended up in this book. With my whole sparkly neon heart, thank you.